Praise for the Midnight Breed series by LARA ADRIAN

BOUND TO DARKNESS

"While most series would have ended or run out of steam, the Midnight Breed series seems to have picked up steam. Lara Adrian has managed to keep the series fresh by adding new characters . . . without having to say goodbye to the original ones that made the series so popular to begin with. Bound to Darkness has all the passion, danger and unique appeal of the original ten books but also stands on its own as a turning point in the entire series with new pieces to a larger puzzle, new friends and old enemies."

—*Adria's Romance Reviews*

"Lara Adrian always manages to write great love stories, not only emotional but action packed. I love every aspect of (Bound to Darkness). I also enjoyed how we get a glimpse into the life of the other characters we have come to love. There is always something sexy and erotic in all of Adrian's books, making her one of my top 5 paranormal authors."

—*Reading Diva*

CRAVE THE NIGHT

"Nothing beats good writing and that is what ultimately makes Lara Adrian stand out amongst her peers.... Crave the Night is stunning in its flawless execution. Lara Adrian has the rare ability to lure readers right into her books, taking them on a ride they will never forget."

—*Under the Covers*

"...Steamy and intense. This installment is sure to delight established fans and will also be accessible to new readers."

—*Publishers Weekly*

EDGE OF DAWN

"Adrian's strikingly original Midnight Breed series delivers an abundance of nail-biting suspenseful chills, red-hot sexy thrills, an intricately built world, and realistically complicated and conflicted protagonists, whose happily-ever-after ending proves to be all the sweeter after what they endure to get there."

—*Booklist (starred review)*

DARKER AFTER MIDNIGHT

"A riveting novel that will keep readers mesmerized... If you like romance combined with heart-stopping paranormal suspense, you're going to love this book."

—*Bookpage*

DEEPER THAN MIDNIGHT

"One of the consistently best paranormal series out there.... Adrian writes compelling individual stories (with wonderful happily ever afters) within a larger story arc that is unfolding with a refreshing lack of predictability."

–*Romance Novel News*

Praise for Lara Adrian

"With an Adrian novel, readers are assured of plenty of dangerous thrills and passionate chills."

–*RT Book Reviews*

"Ms. Adrian has a gift for drawing her readers deeper and deeper into the amazing world she creates."

–*Fresh Fiction*

Praise for the 100 Series
contemporary erotic romance
from
LARA ADRIAN

"There are twists that I want to say that I expect from a Lara Adrian book, and I say that because with any Adrian book you read, you know there's going to be a complex storyline. Adrian simply does billionaires better."

—Under the Covers

"I have been searching and searching for the next book boyfriend to leave a lasting impression. You know the ones: where you own the paperbacks, eBooks and the audible versions...This is that book. For those of you who are looking for your next Fifty Fix, look no further. I know, I know—you have heard the phrase before! Except this time, it's the truth and I will bet the penthouse on it."

—Mile High Kink Book Club

"I wish I could give this more than 5 stars! Lara Adrian not only dips her toe into this genre with flare, she will take it over . . . I have found my new addiction, this series."

—The Sub Club Books

"If you're looking for a hot new contemporary romance along the lines of Sylvia Day's Crossfire series then you're not going to want to miss this series!"

—Feeling Fictional

Look for these titles in the *New York Times* and #1 international bestselling

Midnight Breed series

. . . and more to come!

Other books by Lara Adrian

Contemporary Romance

100 Series
For 100 Days
For 100 Nights
For 100 Reasons

Historical Romance

Dragon Chalice Series
Heart of the Hunter
Heart of the Flame
Heart of the Dove

Warrior Trilogy
White Lion's Lady
Black Lion's Bride
Lady of Valor

Lord of Vengeance

Romantic Suspense and Paranormal Romance

Phoenix Code Series
(with Tina Folsom)
Cut and Run
Hide and Seek

Masters of Seduction Series
Merciless: House of Gravori (novella)
Priceless: House of Ebarron (novella)

CLAIMED IN SHADOWS

A Midnight Breed Novel

NEW YORK TIMES BESTSELLING AUTHOR

LARA ADRIAN

ISBN: 1984041851
ISBN-13: 978-1984041852

CLAIMED IN SHADOWS
© 2018 by Lara Adrian, LLC
Cover design © 2017 by CrocoDesigns

www.LaraAdrian.com

Available in ebook and trade paperback. Unabridged audiobook edition forthcoming.

CLAIMED IN
SHADOWS

CHAPTER 1

Impatience prickled in Aric Chase's veins as the bullet-proof black SUV sped through London's early evening traffic. Mathias Rowan was behind the wheel, the Order's team commander for this city looking as grim and on edge as Aric had ever seen the Breed warrior.

Rowan's comm unit buzzed with the third incoming call since they'd left the command center heading for Heathrow airport. "Give me the status," he demanded over the wireless receiver.

"Two dead humans, another close to it," advised one of the Breed warriors of his patrol squad, his deep voice grave on the speaker. "It's a damned bloodbath down here, Commander. We ashed the Rogue who did it, but you know as well as I do that the bastards tend to run in packs."

"Yeah, I know," Rowan muttered. "Keep me posted,

Thane. Tell Deacon and the rest of the team to do whatever it takes to contain this situation. If we need to enforce a curfew on the human civilian population to keep them safe and out of our way, don't think Lucan Thorne won't call for it."

The seasoned team leader had a right to be concerned. In the States and abroad, the Order had been fighting one disaster after another during the past twenty years since mankind learned about the Breed's existence, but nothing like the relentless hits they'd been taking in recent weeks—the worst of them courtesy of a shadowy terror group calling themselves Opus Nostrum.

Their members hid behind layers of anonymity, but their work was making headlines all over the world, starting with an attempt a couple of weeks ago to detonate an ultraviolet explosion at a peace summit between Breed and human dignitaries from the Global Nations Council. That plot had been thwarted by the Order, but Opus's failure to take out the Breed members of the GNC, including Lucan Thorne, its chairman and the Order's founder, had made the group even bolder, their attacks more brazen.

It had only been a few nights ago that they had delivered a staggering blow in this very city. Because of Opus Nostrum, London's JUSTIS building, headquarters of the powerful branch of law enforcement comprised of both Breed and human officials, was now a pile of smoldering rubble. More recently, in Washington, D.C., Opus loyalists embedded as security detail inside the GNC office had opened fire during a daytime meeting, killing every human member of the council before turning their weapons on themselves.

Now, Opus had apparently added Rogues to the mix.

The Order had good cause to suspect the recent uptick in Bloodlust among Breed civilians was narcotic-induced. It wasn't the first time someone had decided to make blood-addicted monsters out of Aric's kind, but by God it would be the last.

Opus Nostrum had to be stopped. There was nothing Aric wanted more than to be part of the team that made that happen. He only needed to earn the chance.

And that meant getting back to headquarters in D.C. where the real action was.

As if he could guess the direction of Aric's thoughts, Mathias Rowan glanced at him. "You sure this is the life you want?"

"Are you kidding? It's the life I was born for." He grinned. "Surprised you'd ask, considering how long you've known my father."

Rowan grunted. "True. Don't take this the wrong way, but there are times I worry you've got too much of my old friend Sterling Chase in you. I've never seen a new warrior so eager to get his hands dirty in the field."

Aric shrugged. "I'll take that as a compliment, sir."

A wry male chuckle sounded from the backseat. "You take everything as a compliment, daywalker."

Smirking, Aric pivoted to offer a one-fingered salute to his best friend and fellow warrior, Rafe Malebranche. "Credit where credit is due, man, that's all."

Ordinarily, he might have egged Rafe on with reminders of their various exploits and conquests, the usual dick-measuring and ball-busting that their fathers, Chase and Dante, had also built their friendship on back in the day. But tonight Aric checked the impulse.

He and Rafe weren't alone in the vehicle with

Mathias Rowan. The two comrades had an unplanned companion en route with them to D.C., a meek female who'd been huddled close to Rafe since they departed for Heathrow.

"How are you holding up?" Aric asked her.

She gave him a weak nod, but glanced up at Rafe as she spoke. "I'm all right. So long as I don't think too much about what happened, I suppose I'm all right."

Her name was Siobhan O'Shea, and she had been the reason they were there in the first place—or, rather, her murdered flat mate, Iona Lynch, was the reason.

The dead woman had been a potential key witness for the Order in its pursuit of Opus Nostrum's members. Unfortunately for her, before Aric and Rafe could intercept Iona Lynch and bring her in for questioning, someone else had made certain she could never tell her secrets. Now that promising lead on Opus was severed and the Order had an unwanted ward to look after.

Not that Rafe seemed displeased with the idea.

Siobhan leaned against him as the vehicle rounded a corner, contact he didn't appear to mind at all. The soft-spoken, pretty Breedmate had been brutally assaulted along with her friend, but thanks to Rafe's ability to heal with his hands, she didn't carry so much as a scratch on her. In the time since she'd been in the Order's keeping, Rafe had somehow slid into the role of her personal protector.

"You're safe now," he assured her. "I gave you my word, remember?"

Her answering smile was soft, but uncertain. "I can't thank you enough for all you've done for me. I only wish you could've saved Iona too."

So did everyone else in the Order, considering all of the information they might have been able to squeeze from her. But the woman had been too far gone even for Rafe's incredible gift.

The weight of that fact seemed to settle heavily on Siobhan now. As she struggled to hold back tears, Rafe stroked her pale hair and murmured quiet words of comfort.

Aric wondered what other comforts his friend had been tempted to provide her.

Not my problem, he thought as he turned around in his seat. *And better him than me.*

As much as Aric enjoyed female company, he didn't have the time for romantic entanglements, nor the interest. He had his eye on another prize—a warrior team of his own to command one day—and nothing was going to stand in his way of earning it.

Not even the lethal brotherhood of Opus Nostrum.

Least of all, them.

Commander Rowan's comm unit buzzed with yet another call as they arrived at the airport and made their way to a private hangar where one of the Order's fleet jets waited, fueled and readied for the eight-and-a-half hour flight back to headquarters.

"Lucan Thorne's calling," Mathias said as he put the SUV in park. Instead of talking on speaker, he disengaged it and brought his comm unit to his ear. "Rowan here."

He glanced at Aric while the Order's leader spoke on the other end of the line. "We're at the hangar now. They were just about to board for D.C." Mathias listened for another moment before holding the phone out to Aric. "He wants to talk to you."

Aric took the device from him with a mix of unease and curiosity. "Yes, sir?"

"Change of plans," Lucan said. "I need you to make a stop in Montreal before continuing on to headquarters. I've already informed the pilot."

"Montreal," Aric considered aloud. "That's Nikolai and Renata's turf."

The Russian-born warrior was one of the Order's elder members. Niko and his Breedmate had met in that city years ago and since settled there to head up the command center in Montreal. The formidable couple was expecting the birth of their first child any day now, although based on the all-business tone from Lucan, Aric doubted this abrupt redirect had anything to do with a social call.

"Niko knows you're coming," Lucan said. "You'll be briefed on the details of your mission once you arrive. Say nothing to anyone else until then."

His mission.

Holy shit. How long had he been waiting for this moment?

Finally, the chance to prove himself the warrior he knew down to his marrow he already was.

Would Lucan test him with a seasoned Order member like Niko? Or would they send him on patrol with one of the Montreal warrior teams first, make him work his way up from the bottom?

He could hardly wait to find out.

"Yes, sir." A smile tugged at the corners of Aric's mouth as he answered Lucan's command. "Hell yes, sir."

CHAPTER 2

The vampire lurked behind her in the darkness, concealed by the dense forest parkland. With the moon obscured by heavy clouds, the only light was the distant twinkle of Montreal, which sprawled in the valley far below Summit Woods.

Kaya Laurent couldn't see the threat that stalked her as she made her trek through the trees, but she felt it with every urgent beat of her pulse. The Breed male had her in his sights, just waiting for the opportunity to attack.

And he wasn't alone.

Two others were with him somewhere in the woods, closing in on her like a pack of wolves.

Kaya hurried along the bramble-strewn path, adrenaline fueling every step. She had no hope of outrunning her pursuers, but she had to try. Behind her in the shadows, a twig snapped under a heavy foot. She ran faster, her heart climbing into her throat.

Dammit.

Her goal was in right in front of her, less than a quarter-mile ahead. If she could reach the large oak at the perimeter of the woods, she'd be home free.

If she pushed herself, she might actually make it before—

"Shit!"

Nearly three-hundred pounds of fast-moving Breed male hit her from behind like a freight train. Even though she was mentally braced for the attack, the sudden collision jolted a cry out of her and sent her to the ground in a punishing crash.

Kaya grunted, forcing her body into action even as her head filled with an explosion of stars. Rolling away a mere instant before her attacker would have pinned her beneath him, she scrambled to her feet. At that same moment, the second vampire materialized out of the night woods. Then the third, moving in to block her path on the other side.

Not that she actually intended to run.

All she could do now was fight—and pray like hell she survived the next few minutes.

Her pistol was already in her hand. Without warning, she opened fire, three rapid shots that would have been bullseye hits if her assailants had been anything but Breed. Two of the males dodged, but the third let out a roar as her bullet struck him dead-center on the chest.

A burst of red blooming over his sternum, he dropped to the ground.

"Yes!"

One down, two to go.

The largest of the trio grinned at her through the

darkness. He was a monster of a male, massive shoulders and dark, menacing features that looked far too amused as he loomed closer.

Kaya started to squeeze the trigger again, but in a blink of motion too fast for her to follow, the big male knocked her gun out of her fingers. It sailed off into the trees. "Now, what are you gonna do?"

Her fingers went to one of the knives sheathed on her belt. He lunged. She threw the blade, but had no chance to see if she made her mark. While her attention was focused wholly on the big male in front of her, she'd lost track of the third one.

"Too bad for you." Large hands clamped around her neck from behind. "You're dead, sweetheart."

"Fuck!" Kaya snarled in frustration, her body sagging as the certain death-grip loosened from her throat and her would-be killer chuckled. She pushed some of her long brown hair out of her face, her breath racing. "Let's go another round. I can do better."

The Breed warrior she'd shot with a paint bullet got up from the ground, peeling out of his red-splattered shirt with a curse. He shook his head. "Count me out. You'd go at us like this all night if we let you."

Kaya arched a brow. "What's the matter, Webb? Afraid I'll drop you again?"

He laughed, giving her one of his grins that made the tall male go from basic handsome to pure Adonis. "Lucky shot tonight, that's all. But you'd better watch your back. I'll get you when you least expect it."

"She's getting better all the time," his comrade added. One of the large hands that had been poised to twist her head off a moment ago now cuffed her shoulder in praise. "Good job, Kaya."

"Thanks, Torin." She smiled at the exotic-looking warrior with the shoulder-length mane of burnished blond hair. Although he was as deadly as anyone in the Order, the laid-back warrior had been nothing less than welcoming the past couple of weeks she'd been training with their team.

The biggest member of the squad, the olive-skinned, dark-haired behemoth named Balthazar, walked over and returned Kaya's lost weapons. "Next time, keep your eyes open to your full surroundings."

"All right, Bal." With a nod, she took the paint gun and blade from him, holstering both on her belt.

Applause sounded from the sidelines as Kaya's friend, Mira—the sole female of the Order team Kaya desperately wanted to be part of—strolled over to meet the group. Accompanied by her mate, Kellan Archer, Mira was garbed in all-black like the rest of the warriors, her combat boots crunching softly in the bramble as she approached from her observation post.

"Dammit, I screwed up," Kaya admitted. "I'll keep practicing. I can do this."

"I have no doubt, or you wouldn't have gotten this far." Mira smiled. "You're an excellent combat fighter, Kaya. No one expects you to be able to take out three of the best Breed warriors in the field to prove yourself to the Order."

Kellan gave Mira a proud look. "Besides, there are other skills that are just as valuable to a team."

The couple spoke from experience. As capable as Mira was with her daggers and physical agility, she wasn't Breed. She didn't have the sheer brute strength and power of their kind. That hadn't stopped the ambitious female from getting promoted through the Order's ranks, however. Mira had made it all the way to captain, a feat Kaya couldn't help but admire, even envy.

All her life, Kaya had dreamed of having somewhere to belong. A child of the streets from the time she was a little girl, she'd longed to find a place where she felt needed and respected. A place where she mattered. Where she could feel safe.

During the more than year since she'd met Mira, she'd seen a glimpse of what that life could be like. After training under her friend for the past two weeks, Kaya couldn't think of anything she wanted more than to be a full-fledged member of the Order.

Mira gestured to her team. "Let's wrap up and head back to base."

They'd been running her through the paces since sundown, so despite Kaya's eagerness to prove herself and hone her skills, the thought of a hot shower and clothes that weren't caked in dirt and forest debris sounded like heaven.

As a group, they trudged up the wooded incline. The Montreal command center sat at the top of the city's eponymous hill, land given to the Order in exchange for its protection in the years following First Dawn and the violence that became epidemic afterward. Kaya had never seen anything as impressive as the enormous mansion and the labyrinthine nerve center beneath it. She'd spent half a month there and she doubted she'd covered even a fraction of the massive compound.

Mostly by design.

Until she was a full member of the team, her clearance restricted her to the residence and patrol squad areas unless she was accompanied by Mira or another warrior. Kaya didn't mind the lack of trust. It only made sense. They had a right to be cautious when it came to Order business. After all, the warriors had been under siege from one enemy or another for decades. Far longer than that, if you counted all the centuries that the Breed had been trying to keep the peace between their kind and man before the secret of their existence had been revealed twenty years ago.

"Patrols roll out within the hour," Mira advised the men as the team reached the command center. When Torin, Bal, and Webb walked away, she turned a considering glance on Kaya. "You looked good out there tonight. Don't think Niko hasn't noticed how hard you're working too."

"Nikolai?" Kaya stood a little straighter at the mention of the formidable commander who also happened to be Mira's adoptive father. Although Mira would decide when Kaya's training period was over, it was the Montreal commander who would be the one to assign her to the team. "Did he say he's noticed me, Mira? I swear, he's hardly said two words to me since I arrived."

Kellan chuckled. "Niko's hardly got time to say two words to anyone now that Renata is so close to having that baby."

"It's true," Mira agreed, smiling affectionately. "He's an absolute basket case—although he would never admit it."

"Never," Kellan said, then reached out and stroked his mate's cheek as if he couldn't control the impulse. "I probably will be too. When the time comes."

The couple exchanged a look that Kaya pretended not to see. It felt too intimate, a wordless conversation that made the air feel suddenly thick and heavy with meaning.

Kaya cleared her throat. "I'm ah . . . I'm going to drop my gear, then head to my quarters and take a nice long shower. I'll probably be finding leaves and pine needles in my hair for days."

Mira laughed from under the curve of Kellan's arm. "Get some rest. You've earned it."

Kaya left them to their whispered talk and private glances, glad to escape the heated emotion that always seemed to crackle between the recently mated pair. Their bond had been a long time coming—a miracle that had managed to defy both fate and death. Kaya couldn't begrudge them their happiness, but it made the emptiness in her life feel all the deeper.

She entered the weapons room and unstrapped the paint pistol and her blades. Elsewhere along the corridor, she heard the warriors' low voices rumbling with conversation and laughter. The sounds of the command center had become a familiar part of her daily routine in the short time she'd been there. Bal's deep baritone. Torin's velvet drawl. Webb's low purr.

Kaya let her mind wander as she took apart the gun and cleaned all the parts. A thousand thoughts and memories crowded her mind as she worked, some of them pleasant, some . . . not.

She didn't know how far she'd gone adrift in her own head until she felt a vague shift in the air around her. The hair at her nape prickled, at the same time Webb's warning flashed through her subconscious.

Watch your back. I'll get you when you least expect it.

Kaya's lips curved in the beginnings of a smile. *We'll see about that.*

Her grip tightened around the hilt of one of her

blades. Behind her, she sensed his approach even though he moved in utter silence.

Kaya sprang into motion. In a fraction of a second, she pivoted, bringing the edge of her dagger right below the Breed male's squared jaw, poised to kill.

Except it wasn't Webb's face she stared into now.

It wasn't any of the Order warriors from the Montreal command center.

Eyes the color of a spring leaf held her gaze from beneath thick golden-brown brows and dark lashes that any female would envy. There was no fear in those unblinking eyes, only surprise and a trace of wry amusement. "Now, this is a hell of a welcome."

Kaya scowled at the tall, muscular Breed male dressed in civilian clothes. She didn't move her blade. "Who the fuck are you?"

He smirked, too arrogant by far. "I was just about to ask you the same thing."

"This area is restricted. Who let you in?"

One beefy shoulder lifted in a shrug. "Nikolai and Renata told me I'd find Mira down here. Knowing my friend, I expected to find her working out with her blades."

"Your friend?"

Oh, shit.

Kaya backed off, pulling her dagger away from him just as Mira rushed into the room on a delighted squeal and threw her arms around the handsome male. "Aric!"

His gaze lit up as he caught Mira in a hug, lifting her up and spinning her around in his arms. "You look great, Mouse," he said, setting her down on her feet again. "Where's the lucky bastard you took for a mate?"

"Right here." Kellan entered the weapons room and

clasped Aric's hand in greeting. "Good to see you, man. We didn't know you were coming."

He gave a cryptic smile. "Well, here I am."

"Is Rafe here too?" Mira asked. "I haven't seen him since . . . well, since everything that happened a couple of weeks ago." She glanced at Kellan, heavy emotion ripe in her lavender-tinted eyes. "Where is he, Aric? I'm so excited to see you both."

"Rafe's looking forward to seeing everyone too. I'm sure he'll be down soon to find you."

Kellan cocked his head. "Last we heard, you two were leaving London with the Breedmate you rescued in Ireland a couple of nights ago. Chiffon-something."

"Siobhan O'Shea," Mira corrected impatiently. "Does that mean you brought her with you?"

"She's with Rafe. He and Renata are getting her situated in the residence."

Aric's gaze kept straying to Kaya as he spoke. She didn't miss the spark of interest in his light green eyes, nor the trace of humor that tugged at the corner of his lush mouth.

"I'm sorry," Mira blurted. "Aric, have you met my friend Kaya Laurent?"

"We were just getting acquainted," he said, that arrogant smile deepening as he extended his hand to her. "I'm Aric Chase."

His fingers wrapped around hers, warm and firm. She didn't want to acknowledge the current of awareness that sped through her veins as their palms pressed together. Ordinarily, Kaya avoided touching people she didn't know, a caution she'd developed early in life to shield herself from the power of her extrasensory talent. But her ability to read someone's mind with a touch didn't work on the Breed.

So the jolt of electricity she felt while Aric's strong hand engulfed hers had nothing to do with that. The look he gave her said he felt it too.

Kaya withdrew from his grasp and folded her arms over her chest. "Chase?" she repeated, once the name he gave her finally penetrated the unsettling drift of her thoughts.

"Aric's father commands the Order's team in Boston," Mira offered helpfully.

Kaya worked to stifle her groan. Bad enough she'd just put a knife under the chin of a visiting warrior; she'd nearly assaulted Sterling Chase's son. Aric's mother was something of a legend too. The first female Breed ever known to exist, Tavia Chase was a daywalker besides— a gift she'd passed down to her offspring, Aric and his twin sister Carys.

As far as hierarchy went within the Order, Aric Chase was practically royalty.

"Nice to meet you," Kaya murmured lamely.

"Likewise." His eyes travelled her up and down in a slow appraisal. His dimpled grin spread into an amused smile, then he chuckled.

"Something wrong?" Visiting royalty or not, she bristled at the idea that he would mock her in front of her team leader and friends.

She flinched as he reached out to her without warning. His hand skimmed past her right cheek, to the side of her head. Smiling, he pulled a gnarled twig from the tangle of her hair.

Kaya snatched it away from him, her lips pressed flat over the curse that leapt to her tongue.

"You're welcome," he told her quietly, just as a hard

rap sounded on the doorjamb.

Nikolai filled the space of the open door, the commander's glacial blue eyes intense as he met the gazes of everyone in the room, finally settling on Aric and Kaya. "Good. You're all here."

Mira tilted her head at her father. "What's going on?"

"Lucan's called a meeting. He'll be linked in to the war room from D.C. in two minutes."

She nodded. "I'll go tell the team."

"Actually, it's not the team he wants to meet with tonight." Niko's grim gaze left Mira's. "Aric, Kaya. I need you both to come with me."

CHAPTER 3

A ric left his bewildered friends in the weapons room and fell in line behind Nikolai and the lithe, brunette beauty who looked like she'd just returned from days of intense wilderness training. Either that, or a vigorous roll in the hay—assuming the hay was full of pine needles and moss and several seasons' worth of fallen leaves and bramble.

Both possibilities intrigued him.

Especially the latter.

He couldn't help but admire the view as he followed Kaya Laurent's swift, long-legged stride up the corridor. She wore black fatigues that hugged every curve, her emptied weapon belt cinched around a slender waist. Sleek, silken tendrils of coffee-brown hair had escaped the ponytail that rode at her back, bouncing with each clipped step she took at Niko's side.

They walked into an open meeting room and the

commander closed the door behind them. "Take a seat."

Aric walked to the round table and sat down in one of the empty chairs that surrounded it. He waited for Kaya to take her place beside him, but instead she circled to the opposite side and sat about as far from him as she could get.

He smirked, watching her do everything she could to ignore him. Evidently, he hadn't won any points with the lethal beauty.

"So, I guess we can skip the introductions," Niko said as he strode over and seated himself between them. "Looks like you two have already had a chance to meet."

"Yes, sir." Kaya didn't spare Aric as much as a glance while she spoke. "We've been introduced."

"Kaya was kind enough to explain some of the command center policies to me when I bumped into her in the weapons room."

Now her gaze swung to him, a flicker of shock in her deep brown eyes. She was outraged, but kept her reaction on a short leash. Despite her silence, a flush of furious color splashed across her high cheekbones.

God, she was beautiful. He'd noticed that the instant he laid eyes on her. Even if he wasn't gifted with a flawless memory, it would be impossible not to notice every feature and nuance of the female who'd gotten his attention so thoroughly by pressing the razor edge of her dagger under his chin.

Nikolai's head swiveled from Kaya to him in question. "Care to explain?"

Aric cleared his throat. "We've met, sir."

"Good. Then let's get started."

He no sooner said it than the wall-length flat-panel screen lit up with an incoming video call. Lucan

Thorne's dark-haired, grim-faced image filled the display. The Order's founder wasn't calling from his private office at the D.C. headquarters, but from the technology center. Banks of touch screens and wafer-thin displays illuminated Lucan from all sides.

As the two commanders exchanged perfunctory greetings, Kaya had gone utterly silent, her gaze locked on the screen while she surreptitiously brushed at the dirt smudges and small debris that clung to her clothing from whatever she'd been doing in the moments before this meeting had been called.

Aric wanted to tell her not to worry. Even disheveled she was a sight. Not only because she was gorgeous, but for the way she carried herself. Confident. Competent. Determination shining in her dark eyes.

Nikolai gestured to her now. "Lucan, this is Kaya Laurent, the trainee I told you about."

Trainee?

The way she handled herself with a weapon, Aric had assumed Mira's friend was already a member of her team or well on her way to becoming one.

The Order's leader gave Kaya an acknowledging look. "I've heard good things. Not only from Niko but from Mira as well."

"Thank you, sir. I'm doing my best."

"Keep it up." Now, Lucan's shrewd gray gaze swung to Aric. "Ready to get to work?"

Aric grinned. "Always."

"I've asked you both to be here tonight because we have a task that requires a certain combination of skills," the warrior elder explained. "Opus Nostrum has been coming at us hard since the Order killed their leader, Reginald Crowe, a few weeks ago. Between bombings and assassinations and the recent uptick in Rogue activity around the world, Opus is doing its damnedest to keep us busy. Apparently, they believe if they make sure the Order has one fire after another to put out, we won't have the time or resources to come after their members."

"They thought wrong," Nikolai interjected. "We're not going to stop until we've torn the mask off every one of the bastards who make up their cabal."

Lucan nodded. "Which brings me to the reason for this meeting. Gideon's run across some intel that suggests a high-value target with possible Opus ties will be attending a big social gathering in Montreal tomorrow. We need to have eyes and ears on the inside, but it's imperative that we don't tip our hand that we're closing in on this new lead. Not to Opus, and not to the bastard we're all but certain is allied with them."

"What kind of event are we talking about?" Aric asked.

"A wedding reception," Lucan replied. "For Anastasia Rousseau and Stephan Mercier."

"You're talking about the former Prime Minister's granddaughter," Kaya pointed out. "Her wedding has been the most anticipated social event of the year. From everything I've heard, there are likely to be close to a thousand people in attendance."

Lucan's expression said he already knew all the particulars and had accounted for every one of them. "We need someone present to verify our intel firsthand. The best way to do that is to get inside the target's head."

Nikolai turned to look at Kaya. "That's where you come in."

"You want me to read the mind of someone at the

reception? No problem." Tenacity glittered in her gaze. "Just tell me who I'm looking for, and I'll handle it. I only need to get close enough to touch him."

"Unfortunately, that's not going to be easy," Niko said. "Our target is high profile. He'll be guarded on all sides."

"And we can't afford to let him know that he's been made," Lucan added. "Which means we need to take extra precautions to ensure he's got no memory of any interaction with you, assuming you're successful at getting close enough to read him—"

"I'll be successful, sir."

At that confident blurt, Niko slanted her a wry smile. "No one here doubts you, Kaya. Or you, Aric. You've both exceeded expectations in your training. That's why you've been tapped for this operation."

"Combined with the fact that neither of you has been active on patrol," Lucan said. "The risk of being outed as members of the Order won't be a factor."

Aric chuckled. "Never thought my lack of experience in the field would be considered an asset."

"This time, it's exactly what we need," Lucan replied. "And since the wedding reception is being held at noon in the Rousseau estate's garden, the fact that you won't go up in smoke before you have the chance to mind-scrub the target makes you uniquely qualified for this assignment."

"Point to the daywalker," he quipped. "I won't let the Order down."

"See that you don't." Lucan glanced to Kaya too. "We're counting on both of you to make this happen. We can't afford to let this new lead slip through our fingers. It's going to take teamwork to get it done, and get it done right."

Kaya nodded, but the look she gave Aric was less than enthused. "I'll do whatever it takes, sir."

"That's what I want to hear," Lucan replied. "Let's run through some scenarios for rolling out this op. Meanwhile, Gideon's working on new IDs for both of you. They'll be waiting for you in the morning, along with your invitation to the reception."

"And we're certain our target is going to be there?" Aric asked.

Lucan grunted. "He'll be there. Your target is the groom."

CHAPTER 4

Kaya smoothed her palms over the skirt of her dusty-rose silk dress, trying not to notice the slight tremble in her fingers. Damn her nerves. It took a lot to rattle her, but as she waited in the car beside Aric at the tall iron gate outside the Rousseau estate, her heart seemed determined to climb into her throat.

They had been held up for several minutes and counting while a guard posted at the entrance went back into his shack to verify the invitation and IDs Aric had given him. Behind the brand-new Mercedes sedan the Order had procured especially for this mission, a line of waiting vehicles had grown to nearly a dozen deep.

"What's taking so long?" Kaya dipped her head down as she spoke, barely moving her lips in case either of the armed security attendants flanking their car might be watching for signs of suspicion.

"Relax," Aric murmured. "Everything's fine. We're

going to a wedding reception, not a funeral."

She hoped he was right. How the Breed male could grin and make jokes when her stomach was twisting into a knot over the importance of their assignment, she had no idea. For Kaya, everything she attempted was undertaken with a sense of gravity and an intense need to get the job done right. To get it perfect.

Today she felt that need more than ever.

All her hopes hinged on this mission. Years of dreaming for a better life, for some sense of purpose. Weeks of hard training and determination. It all boiled down to this one final test. There was no room for nerves or doubts. Failure was simply not an option.

It didn't help her unease at all that she was draped in yards of silk and chiffon instead of the combat gear she preferred. The sumptuous fabric felt as alien against her skin as it could be to a woman who'd spent a good part of her young life in thrift store rags and ill-fitting hand-me-downs. Instead of a weapons belt bristling with the blades and guns she'd learned to wield, today she wore only diamond bracelets and jeweled rings.

As for Aric, he was maddeningly cool in the driver's seat. With his wrist draped casually over the steering wheel, the other arm resting on his muscled thigh, he looked as if he could sit there all day waiting for one guard to run their fake credentials while another searched their open trunk. A third man prowled the perimeter of the car with a leashed Rottweiler actively sniffing for explosives or other security risks, and still another pair of guards watched the gate armed with automatic rifles clutched in their hands.

Unfazed by any of it, Aric glanced over at her. "You look incredible, by the way."

The compliment took her aback. They hadn't talked about anything besides strategy and mission objectives since they left the command center, so she wasn't quite sure what to do with his praise.

"I'm not used to wearing this kind of thing," she whispered, self-consciousness deepening as he stared at her. "The bodice is so tight it's cutting off the air to my lungs and this flowy silk skirt keeps snagging on my finger calluses."

He gave her a slow appraisal. "Well, if the idea was to make you blend in with the other women attending this party, we're off to a bad start. You're a knockout."

He looked more than passingly good himself, despite Kaya's unwillingness to admit she'd noticed.

In his graphite-gray suit and tie, Aric could have just stepped out of a men's fashion photo shoot. Broad, straight shoulders and thick biceps filled the jacket, hinting at the immense strength that no amount of fine tailored clothing could hide. He was the kind of male who would draw gazes no matter what he was wearing, and not even Kaya was immune.

As hard as she tried to act otherwise.

The sudden knock on Aric's window didn't even make him blink. He pushed the button and as the glass slid down, the guard who'd returned with their IDs bent to peer into the car. Kaya fixed a bland smile on her lips when his gaze flicked to her.

"Mr. and Mrs. Bouchard." He glanced at their IDs and invitation once more, then gave a curt nod and handed Aric the documents. "You're all set. Enjoy the event."

"Thanks. I'm sure we will."

Kaya didn't let out her breath until they had rolled

away from the gate. "Thank God, we got in."

Aric chuckled. "I had no doubt. Gideon's a magician when it comes to hacking and covert ops tech. William and Elizabeth Bouchard may not have existed before last night, but anyone digging into our identities today is going to find them fully sourced and ironclad. The last thing we need to worry about is our cover. Getting inside was the easy part." He swiveled a wry look at her. "The rest is going to be up to you."

She exhaled a humorless laugh. "No pressure at all, right?"

They had gone over their strategy for the operation several times on the drive from base command to the Rousseau estate. There were multiple paths they could take in order to get Kaya close to Stephan Mercier, ideally without raising anyone's suspicion. Once she had the groom in reach, all she needed to do was lay her hands on him.

For at least sixty-six seconds' time.

That was how long it would take for her extrasensory ability to establish connection and begin siphoning a person's thoughts.

Once she had the floodgates open, his mind would give up any secret she asked it to betray.

Up ahead of them now, a security guard was directing traffic to a large lot already filled with luxury vehicles and insanely expensive sports cars. Aric followed the hand signal that sent them toward an available parking space toward the back of the crowded area.

Kaya frowned as they took their spot amid row upon row of tightly packed automobiles. "I hope we won't have to get out of here fast when this is over."

Aric killed the engine, then pivoted to face her. "You nervous?"

She scoffed at his concerned look. As if she would admit anything of the sort, especially to him. Her partner in this mission didn't need to know that beneath her forced calm she was wound as tightly as a spring. The Breed male causing a deeper sense of unsettlement in her didn't need to know it, either.

She shrugged. "Of course I'm not nervous."

"Good."

His hand shot out, cupping the back of her neck and pulling her close. Before she had any idea what he was doing, Aric's mouth crushed against hers. The kiss was shocking, searing. Intensely sensual. As his lips moved over hers, a lick of fire spread quickly through her body.

Kaya moaned before she could stop the sound from forming. As soon as she realized the pleasured noise came from herself, she jolted. Her eyes flew open and she let out a startled cry.

Aric's lush mouth muffled the feeble protest. His kiss was full of confidence, as if he already knew her lips and understood just how to seduce her. The fact that her body seemed eager to allow him to only made her outrage more explosive.

Kaya brought her hands up to his chest in flustered reflex, ready to shove him away.

But Aric was already backing off. He released her just as abruptly as he'd taken hold of her, a knowing gleam in his eyes.

"What the fuck?" Kaya sputtered the indignant curse, even while heat ignited inside her, powerful and uninvited. "What the hell do you think you're doing, asshole?"

"Getting that out of the way in case we need to do it once we're inside. We can't have you reacting like that in front of our target." He smoothed the pad of his thumb over his lower lip, wiping away the trace of her pink gloss that lingered there. "Ready, Mrs. Bouchard?"

He didn't wait for her reply. While Kaya struggled to find her breath again, Aric pivoted away and climbed out of the vehicle. She reached for the door handle on her side, but before she could take hold of it he was already there. Smoothly, he opened her door and reached in to offer his hand.

"My lady," he said, those mesmerizing green eyes lit with an arrogant gleam.

Rather than answer with the reply burning the tip of her tongue, Kaya clamped her molars together and pasted a pleasant smile on her lips as she accepted his assistance. What she wanted to do was slap his hand aside and drop him on his smug ass in the parking area. But she'd need an arsenal of weapons and more than a couple weeks of training to pose much of a threat to a Breed male, particularly one built as solidly as Aric Chase.

She might have been tempted to try anyway, had it not been for the possible notice of more arriving guests in the parking area nearby.

Instead she returned the smiles of the other attendees alighting from their vehicles, then linked her arm through Aric's as he walked her across the brick-paved drive toward the entrance of the grand estate.

CHAPTER 5

A nother round of security checks waited for them inside, although the guards posted in the opulent foyer were garbed more discreetly than their counterparts manning the main gate. Aric nodded to the men in black suits and wireless earpieces, noting without reaction that each carried a sidearm holstered beneath the smoothly pressed fall of his jacket.

Kaya's steps slowed as they entered, her gaze drawn to the urns overflowing with fragrant ivory flowers and lush greenery. Garlands festooned with champagne-colored ribbons and delicate lace dripped like gilded froth from the curving bannisters of the foyer's twin stairwells.

"Look at this place," she murmured. "It's incredible."

"This way, if you would, please, ma'am," one of the guards said to Kaya. The muscular, red-haired man gestured toward the metal detectors and full body scanners temporarily erected in the elegant entry of the Rousseau mansion.

Aric lingered behind her as she placed her small handbag on the conveyor then glided through the gauntlet of cold machinery, a vision in shimmering, diaphanous blush-colored silk. His veins throbbed as he watched her graceful, unrushed gait, his blood still pounding from the aftershocks of that impulsive kiss.

To say nothing of the rest of his anatomy.

Kissing her had not been in the playbook for this mission, but once the idea took root in his mind, there had been no ignoring it. Yes, he'd done it for the good of their cover, as a means of breaking the ice between him and the fake Mrs. Bouchard. But now she had regrouped flawlessly and he was the one knocked off his game.

Damn.

So not what he'd intended.

It took concentrated control to keep his body's reaction in check. His fangs ached to punch out of his gums. All over him, his *dermaglyphs* prickled to life in response to watching Kaya while the memory of their kiss still scorched his lips.

Desire tinged his vision with the first hints of amber as she raised her arms and waited for the scanner to clear her for passage. The stretch lifted her already buoyant breasts and thinned her slender waist to an hourglass curve that made his hands itch to be wrapped around it.

He groaned low under his breath. It wouldn't take more than a backward glance from her now to transform his irises from gold-flecked green to an unearthly molten glow.

He'd better check himself fast, or he was going to blow this operation before it even began. Nothing like turning full-on Breed to put the brakes on a gathering of perfumed and powdered humans.

"Sir?" The guard standing beside him in the foyer gave him an expectant look. "Please, step forward and proceed to the scanner."

"Oh." Aric cleared his throat and nodded. "Yeah, sure."

He followed the path Kaya had taken before him, then joined her where she waited on the other side of the machines. With the stern discipline of his warrior training, he somehow managed to tamp down the Breed side of his nature by the time he and Kaya approached the short line of attendees being greeted personally by the bride's parents.

Anastasia Rousseau's father took hold of Aric's hand and gave it a couple of perfunctory pumps as soon as he released the previous guest. "Good afternoon and welcome."

"Thank you, sir." Aric nodded to the gray-haired billionaire and smiled at his immaculately preserved wife. "Congratulations on a beautiful day. Elizabeth and I couldn't be happier for Stasi."

"How kind. Thank you." Mrs. Rousseau's fine brows rose on her unlined face. "Are you a friend of our daughter's?"

"Stasi and I went to university together for a while," Aric said, putting Gideon's cover dossier to good use as he shook the elder woman's hand. "I'm William Bouchard. Er, Will. And this is my bride, Elizabeth."

Mrs. Rousseau smiled warmly. "How do you do, dear?"

"Fine, thank you. Everything looks so beautiful in here, Mrs. Rousseau," Kaya said, not missing a beat as she shook the woman's hand. "I can't wait to see what you've done outside for the reception."

"Why, thank you, my dear. I do enjoy dabbling."

"You do a bit more than dabble," Kaya pointed out. "Congratulations on your interior design award last month. The magazine couldn't have chosen a more deserving recipient."

"What a lovely thing to say." The bride's mother beamed. "How wonderful that you both could make it today. I'm sure Anastasia will be delighted."

The old man smiled, too, but he studied Aric longer than he had the other guests ahead of him. "Was it McGill you said you attended with her, son?"

"No, sir. UBC. It was my grandfather's alma mater as well." He tilted a wry look at Phillipe Rousseau. "I probably shouldn't tell you this, but your father the Prime Minister and my grandfather were rivals on the soccer field in their day."

"Is that so?"

"Yes, sir, I'm afraid it is." Aric grinned through the lie, thankful for the depth of Gideon's research. "I hope you won't hold that against me now."

"Not at all." The bride's father chuckled and clapped him on the shoulder. "Go on and enjoy the reception, both of you."

"With pleasure, sir."

Grinning, he took Kaya's hand and led her away from the Rousseaus. Now that the seeds of their social groundwork had been laid, they had some time to scope out the terrain they'd be working once the reception was under way.

"Go easy on the flattery," he murmured as they walked toward the French doors opened to the estate's gardens. No one else was in hearing distance of him, but he was careful to keep his voice low enough for Kaya's ears only. "It was a nice touch to mention the award, but you don't want to be too memorable. Not that you can do much to avoid that."

She let his backhanded compliment pass without acknowledgment. "It wasn't flattery. Margaret Rousseau really is a talented interior designer. Her work has been on a dozen magazine covers and this most recent award was for a project she contributed to a children's charity organization."

Aric grunted. "Someone did their homework last night."

She slanted him a haughty look. "I stayed up most of the night poring over Gideon's notes. I must've read everything twenty times, just to make sure I wouldn't forget even the smallest detail."

He shrugged. "I only read the files once."

"You can't be serious." Kaya stopped short and frowned at him, lowering her voice to a harsh whisper. "That's either incredibly arrogant or dangerously stupid."

He shook his head. "Genetically gifted. I've got an eidetic and photographic memory. If I read something or see it once, I can recall it perfectly anytime."

She gaped mutely for a moment, then expelled a sharp breath. "Have you ever struggled over a single thing in all your life?"

"Not really."

She rolled her eyes at his unrepentant grin. "How nice for you."

He chuckled. "So I hit the gene pool lottery. Do you want me to apologize for that fact?"

"I don't want you to do anything—other than not screw this up for me today."

She started walking again and he fell in beside her. "You don't have to worry about me, sweetheart. You and I share the same goal. I want it too badly to let it slip through my fingers."

"So do I."

"Good," he said. "Then I guess we're agreed."

"On one thing, at least."

They stepped through the open French doors and into the full heat of the brilliant noontime sun. Broad marble steps spilled down onto the back lawn of the mansion's grounds like a carpet made of gleaming stone. Tables and chairs dressed up in white cloth and floral garlands peppered the thick green grass and surrounding gardens, each arranged for optimal view of the immense limestone pavilion that was the pearly jewel at the heart of the magnificent grounds.

Under the soaring dome roof, a tuxedoed twelve-piece orchestra played Mozart's "Eine Kleine Nachtsmusik" for an empty dance floor and what was easily hundreds of arriving reception guests. Aric and Kaya descended the steps together and were immediately greeted by one of many circulating waitstaff carrying trays of champagne and hors d'oeuvres. Being Breed, Aric could consume neither beyond a taste or two, but Kaya eagerly accepted one of the slender flutes.

With her glass in hand, they strolled over the soft lawn. They found a quiet spot of their own to observe the gathering and wait for the moment their target arrived. Aric scanned the hundreds of guests, silently taking stock of the faces. He was intent on his task, but he couldn't dismiss the weight of Kaya's brown eyes studying him over the rim of her glass.

He frowned. "What's the matter?"

She took a sip, a smile tugging at the corners of her mouth. "Just making sure you're not going to start sizzling out here in the sun."

His brows shot up. "Was that a joke? Why, Mrs. Bouchard, I had no idea you cared."

She laughed, then raised the flute to her lips once more. "You're an ass."

"So you've mentioned," Aric replied, watching with far too much thirst of his own as her delicate throat worked to swallow another sip of champagne.

She caught him staring and a flush of pink swept across her cheeks. She pressed the back of her free hand against the rising color in her face. "It does seem awfully warm out here. Maybe we should find you some shade while we wait for the happy couple to arrive."

"Trust me, I can take the heat if you can." He smirked when her chin lifted in defiance. "Besides," he added, "I never squander the chance to enjoy a gorgeous day. I know too many others who can't ever experience this gift for me to take it for granted."

Kaya tilted her head at him, a skeptical look on her pretty face. "Empathy? That's an unexpected twist."

He grunted. "Hey, I may be an arrogant asshole with more blessings than I'll ever deserve, but that doesn't mean I don't have enough self-awareness to recognize something extraordinary. Especially when I'm looking right at it."

Whatever sharp retort she'd been meaning to deliver faded into silence as she blinked up at him, her gaze softening on him for the first time since they'd met.

Aric realized only now how close they stood to each other on the grass. No one to hear them, no one to intrude on them despite the sea of people milling about in all directions.

He took a breath and his senses filled with Kaya's enticing scent, a mixture of cinnamon and roses and something more elusive. Sunshine warmed her skin and dark hair, which only intensified the fragrance that was uniquely hers. Every Breedmate had her own blood scent, and Kaya's was wreaking havoc on Aric's focus and control.

It wasn't as if he was hungered for female company. He was far from a saint, but he made it a practice to avoid intimate entanglements with women bearing the teardrop-and-crescent-moon birthmark of a Breedmate. If he needed a reminder of why he kept his appetites confined to human women only, Kaya Laurent was it.

Even so, the urge to touch her was nearly overwhelming.

More tempting was the desire to kiss her again, though if he did that now, it would have nothing to do with their mission or the effort to fortify their covers.

No, if he touched her, it would be for purely selfish reasons.

And because the silent invitation in her eyes told him that she was feeling the same crackle of arousal too.

Aric swallowed on a dry throat as he fought to keep his hands fisted and still at his sides.

He couldn't think of a worse idea than letting his attraction to Kaya overshadow his attention to their assignment. Regardless, he was on the verge of losing that argument with himself when a cheer suddenly went up from the gathered crowd.

Kaya sucked in a shallow gasp, though whether in reaction to the abrupt clamor of excitement from all around them or from relief over the timeliness of the interruption, Aric couldn't be sure.

He swiveled away from her, adding his wooden applause to the enthusiastic greeting the newlyweds were receiving as they emerged at the top of the marble steps. Their golden-haired target, Stephan Mercier, kissed his bride to the delighted shouts of the onlookers. The groom earned an even greater cheer when he bent his beautiful bride over his arm and swept her into a smooth, swoon-worthy dip.

Aric groaned, hardly able to stifle his disdain for the suspected Opus sympathizer. Kaya, too, wore an expression of cold business as she watched the happy couple descend the stairs hand-in-hand while the orchestra segued from garden music to a jaunty rendition of the "Wedding March".

Aric slid a glance at his partner. "Game on. You ready?"

She nodded, her smile as dazzling as it was determined. "Let's do this."

CHAPTER 6

Unfortunately, Lucan's advice that it wasn't going to be easy getting close to their target had been correct. A security detail of ten grim-faced men in dark suits and sunglasses kept a close eye on both the bride and groom as they greeted some of their guests on the way to the wedding party's table inside the pavilion.

The guards remained posted nearby through all of the endless toasts and the lavish luncheon that followed. There was no quick path for getting Mercier alone for even a few seconds, never mind the minute-plus that Kaya needed.

Which left Aric and her with one good chance to make their move.

As the orchestra conductor announced the formal introduction of Mr. and Mrs. Stephan Mercier with their first dance as husband and wife, Aric's hand closed around Kaya's under the table. She was sure the chaste kiss he pressed to her temple was only part of his act—just as his unexpected claiming of her mouth back in the car had been—yet that didn't stop her pulse from skittering in her veins at the brief contact.

He smiled at their tablemates as he began to rise from his seat. "Will you all excuse us, please? The first dance is always Elizabeth's favorite part of a wedding."

"Yes, it is," Kaya agreed, allowing him to assist her out of her chair while the other couples seated with them nodded absently or offered indulgent smiles.

Kaya kept her expression schooled as she and Aric crossed the garden at a deliberately casual pace. They weren't alone. Other guests had a similar idea, no less than twenty couples converging on the covered structure where the bride and groom were slowly swaying and twirling to a romantic ballad.

Aric still held on to her hand as they approached the pavilion with its fairy tale decorations. For one disorienting moment, Kaya found it difficult to separate herself from the comfort of his touch in such a beautiful setting and the sobering gravity of what they had come here to do. She'd never dreamed of rainbows and roses, so why the sight of so much romance and fantasy made her heart flutter now, she had no idea. Nor did she want to know. Not when the rest of her was focused on her mission.

Aric led her to a spot as close as they could get to the dance floor. Then they waited and watched. Applauding and smiling as the mother of the groom and the father of the bride took their turns dancing with their children.

Finally, it was time for the guests to join the celebration on the dance floor. Smoothly, with as much stealth as a skilled assassin, Aric took her in his arms and glided with her into the crowd. Although he managed to make their pursuit look accidental, in no time at all Kaya found herself dancing directly behind Stephan Mercier and his bride.

Aric lowered his head in a nearly imperceptible nod, the only warning she had before he backed her right into the groom.

"Oh, my goodness!" Kaya exclaimed. She staggered awkwardly, pivoting around to apologize. "I'm so sorry. Pardon us, please."

Mercier merely grinned, still swaying with his arms around his bride. "No problem at all. I'm sure it was my fault."

"Not so fast," Aric interjected with a chuckle when it appeared Mercier would have carried on without further conversation. "We've been watching the two of you dance. From what I've seen, the only one here with two left feet is me. Stasi, you've never looked more beautiful."

Her brow pinched as she tilted a quizzical look on him. "Thank you . . . ah . . ."

"Will." Aric gave her a charming smile. "Will Bouchard. From UBC. It's all right if you don't remember. We only had a few classes together."

"Oh, yes," she replied, politely taking his bait even though her warm eyes held no recognition whatsoever. "Of course, I remember you, Will. How nice that you came."

"Wouldn't miss it for anything." He grinned, flicking a warm glance at Kaya. "This is my wife, Elizabeth."

Mercier's new bride nodded. "Very nice to meet you."

"Likewise," Kaya said. "Congratulations on your

wedding."

"Thank you. I hope you and Will are enjoying yourselves so far?"

Kaya glanced adoringly at Aric, resting her palm lightly against his cheek for added effect. "We certainly are."

He went still as her touch lingered, his face taking on a dangerous edge. Faint embers crackled to life in the green depths of his eyes as he stared at her, but then he blinked once and they were gone. He tore his gaze away from Kaya to look at Mercier.

When he spoke, his voice sounded thick and rusty. "Would you mind terribly if I cut in for the rest of this song? I was telling Stasi's father as we came in that I hoped we'd have a quick chance to catch up."

Kaya saw their target's hesitation and she hurried to set the hook. "Oh, Will. They just got married. Let them enjoy their time together."

"No, no. It's okay," Anastasia said. "I'd love to dance with you, Will. And I'm sure Stephan will enjoy dancing with Elizabeth too."

"Of course." Mercier's lips stretched in a tight semblance of a smile, but his eyes remained shrewd and untrusting as his wife stepped into the arms of another man.

Little did he know, at the moment it was Kaya who posed the bigger threat to his happiness. If the Order's suspicions proved true about Mercier's support for Opus Nostrum, his glittering world would soon come crashing down around him.

With Aric whisking Anastasia into the growing crowd on the floor, Kaya slipped her hand into Mercier's and placed her other on his shoulder. He steered her into a mechanical series of steps as the orchestra played and the pavilion swelled with even more people.

Where Aric had been strong and assured as he'd held her, Mercier's palm was moist against her fingers, his lean body stiff and distracted as he pushed her around the dance floor. Kaya didn't need the psychic confirmation of her Breedmate ability to tell her that Stephan Mercier was a nervous, agitated man.

Although he'd appeared poised and confident with his bride at a distance, up close it was clear that his mind was a thousand miles away. Kaya only needed to touch him for a few more seconds before she could follow his thoughts to wherever they led. Until then, her main goal was to put him at ease with her long enough for the connection to take root.

She smiled up at him as they waltzed past the small orchestra. "Thank you for indulging my husband's request to dance with your wife. I promise I'm trying very hard not to embarrass myself by stepping on your toes again."

Mercier's rigid face relaxed just a bit at her self-deprecation. "You have nothing to worry about. You're doing just fine. Would you like me to tell you a secret, Elizabeth?"

"Yes." Kaya hoped her reply didn't sound too eager. She intended to know all of the man's secrets before she was finished with him.

"Dancing's not really my thing," he confided. "Anastasia put me through eight weeks of lessons in the hopes I'd come to enjoy it, but I can still think of a hundred other things I'd rather be doing."

Did that explain some of his distraction? Kaya couldn't say for sure. Not until she managed to get inside his head, that is.

She laughed in response to his harmless little admission. "Well, have no fear. Your secret is safe with me."

At least, that one was.

"Hopefully there won't be any formal dancing required on your honeymoon in Seychelles," she added, then immediately wondered if she'd gone a step too far when Mercier's blond brows lowered over questioning eyes.

"You know where Stasi and I planned to honeymoon?"

Shit. Maybe she'd studied the operation intel a bit too closely.

"I'm sorry, I hope you don't think I'm being rude." Kaya used her momentary awkwardness to full advantage while she formulated her answer. "It's just that many of the big social sites and magazines have been talking about this wedding in detail for weeks. It was kind of hard to miss all of the gossip."

"Ah." He grunted in acceptance. Thank God.

"Actually, the honeymoon has been postponed," he volunteered. "Some business has come up that requires my attention here at home. Seychelles will have to wait, much to my bride's dismay."

And so what if Anastasia is barely speaking to me since she found out? Does she really think I'm going to walk away from a deal worth a hundred million dollars? The privileged little bitch will certainly be eager to help me spend it.

Kaya swallowed. She had anticipated the moment her mind would infiltrate his, but it still came as a shock to feel the jolt of Stephan Mercier's thoughts speaking in her head as clearly as his voice.

It took some effort to pretend otherwise while she was trapped in his gaze.

"Oh. What a shame," she murmured casually. "But I'm sure whatever you have to do is quite important."

He gave her a mild nod. "Yes, it is."

Important? You have no idea. No one does, not even Stasi. She wouldn't understand. Probably not even a hundred million dollars would be enough to make her understand.

In time, she will. I'll make sure of that.

In time, the whole world will understand.

Then they'll all recognize me as a hero. But better than that, I'll be as rich as a goddamned king.

Kaya kept her expression mild, even as a chill swept over her. Although he hadn't yet incriminated himself in anything other than the prospect a lucrative, if ill-timed, business deal, Stephan Mercier was obviously not the golden, charming man he appeared to be on the outside. That alone didn't mean he was linked with Opus Nostrum.

The prickling in her marrow nearly had Kaya convinced, but that wouldn't be enough for Lucan Thorne or the Order. She needed to dig deeper for solid confirmation, and that meant she was going to have to push Mercier harder.

And fast.

Their dance would be ending soon. When it did, there would be no second chance to get this close to him again. Not without his new bride or any one of dozens of the estate's security personnel standing in her way. Even now, she was well aware of the team of men in dark suits lurking in various points of the pavilion, keeping a careful watch on the Rousseaus' cherished daughter and the man who'd just married into their politically powerful family.

Kaya regarded him with what she hoped was an admiring gaze. "One thing the wife of a powerful man must learn to accept early on is that she not only wed the man, but his work."

Mercier nodded approvingly. "How right you are, Elizabeth. And how rare it is to find a woman who recognizes that truth. Perhaps I could persuade you to impart some of your wisdom and advice to Anastasia."

He gave her a sly wink that made Kaya's skin crawl. Nevertheless, she laughed as if she were charmed. "I'm sure she'll come around to seeing things for how they really are. If anyone knows what it means to sacrifice personal wants for the greater good, it's someone like your wife. After all, she comes from a long line of successful people who've devoted themselves to duty and country."

"That she does." A mercenary smile stretched his lips. *Precisely why I courted her in the first place. That, and the many doors that her family's name could open for me.*

Kaya felt a pang of regret for Anastasia Rousseau. It was obvious the happy, unsuspecting woman thought she'd found her prince, when in reality she'd just bound herself to a snake.

Worse than a snake, if the sick feeling in Kaya's stomach could be trusted.

Time to poke Mercier's soft underbelly and see if she could get him to bite.

Kaya shrugged, exhaling a wistful sigh. "Still, it is a shame that the reality of work and obligations has to intrude on a beautiful event for you and your wife. Days like this are such a welcome escape from the fear and terror that's become our daily routine lately."

"Yes, they are." Mercier's lips thinned in a chilling smile. "But we will never know true peace so long as we're living among blood-drinking monsters."

Her stomach clenched. She hadn't been expecting him to openly express his hatred for the Breed so freely, but he was hardly the first human unafraid to publicly condemn the entire vampire race as monsters. Protesters and militant groups vocally opposed to the tentative truce that had been in place for the past twenty years were epidemic in recent months.

And at the heart of all the strife was Opus Nostrum, gleefully pulling strings and sowing seeds of mistrust on both sides of the problem.

It took immense control to simply continue dancing and smiling blandly instead of defending her friends and the rest of their kind. Kaya's struggle must have shown in her face. Or in the furious shudder she was unable to contain.

"Have I upset you?" Mercier asked, leaning closer than was necessary. "Forgive me. Weddings are no place for politics or talk of war."

Kaya froze. "Is that what you think is going to happen—war with the Breed?"

"My dear, it is inevitable."

Especially if I have anything to say about it.

Very soon, I'll have a hundred million reasons to make it an absolute certainty that we push the bloodsucking animals into war with mankind.

And then the whole world will beg Opus to eradicate the scourge from the Earth.

Shit. There it was. All the confirmation the Order needed to drop a net on Stephan Mercier.

Kaya didn't need anything more from the bastard.

But it was difficult to walk away without giving him a dose of truth.

And besides, Aric would still be coming in behind her for the clean-up. After a quick mind scrub, Mercier would have no recollection of anything he and Kaya spoke about.

"You consider the Breed monsters?" She kept a firm grip on him, her blood simmering even as she spoke in a sweetly conversational tone. "They're not the ones who tried to set off an ultraviolet detonation at a peace summit last month. It wasn't the Breed who razed JUSTIS headquarters in London a few nights ago, either. Nor did they assassinate half of the Global Nations Council, then boast about it to anyone who would listen. Opus Nostrum did all of that and more. If anyone is ripe for eradication, it's the cowards hiding behind that organization."

Mercier's feet stilled. His eyes took on a wary sheen, but he only chuckled as if she were a dull child in need of schooling. "You have a lot of interesting opinions, Mrs. Bouchard. You might do well to keep some of them to yourself. You never know whom you might offend if a careless statement reaches the wrong ears."

Her tongue wouldn't be so loose if she had any idea how many people from all walks of life have quietly pledged their support to Opus. Time to ditch the bitch. Before anyone overhears her and assumes I could be anything but loyal to the cause.

Especially someone like the man who'll be dropping a cool hundred million from the organization into my bank account in a couple of days.

Mercier's gaze left hers and flicked out over the crowd. It was a purely reflexive glance that on its own would mean nothing. But having come on the heels of his last thought, the casual search of the reception guests in that moment was more telling than anything else he'd said or thought all day.

Holy shit. Had he just let it slip that one of Opus's members was here at the estate?

Kaya followed Mercier's gaze into the crowd that was spread out over the lawn and gardens. At first, she wasn't sure what she was looking for. But then, she found him.

A portly dark-haired man casually making his way out of the reception.

Without looking back, he walked up the marble stairs and through the open French doors of the mansion.

Whoever he was, he was determined to get out of there without drawing attention to himself.

Which only made Kaya's curiosity deepen.

"Thanks for the dance," Mercier muttered. He released her as if he'd been burned, their connection instantly severed.

She no further use of it, anyway. Right now, she had her sights locked on bigger game.

There wasn't a second to waste.

Not even to signal to Aric somewhere on the dance floor that their mission objective had suddenly taken a sharp left turn. Her conversation with Mercier was a problem they would have to clean up later. Right now, there was only one thing Kaya had to do and that was ID the man currently attempting to leave the reception unnoticed.

Kaya stepped away from the pavilion to cut an arrow's path across the grass then up the stairs to the mansion. A smattering of wedding guests congregated inside, their conversation and laughter punctuated by the rapid tick of her high-heeled sandals as she hurried through, her gaze searching for Mercier's Opus contact.

Holy hell, there he was. Several yards ahead of her, weaving around Phillipe Rousseau and a circle of well-dressed gentlemen chatting and smoking cigars just off the foyer. Kaya picked up her pace. She'd chase the bastard down in the parking area if she had to. Anything to get a glimpse of his face. Better yet, a glimpse into his mind.

Although how she would manage that with a small army of guards posted all over the estate and the surrounding grounds, she wasn't certain. She only knew she had to try.

One of those uniformed men watched her intently as she strode toward the foyer. She recognized him from their arrival. Beneath his cap of close-shorn red hair, his gaze held on her with pointed interest, even suspicion.

"Can I help you with anything, ma'am?"

Kaya smiled and shook her head, her feet still moving in the direction of her target. "I just . . . forgot something in the car. But thank you."

He didn't return her smile.

She kept walking, alarm seeping into her when she sensed him behind her now, following at her heels. When his strong hand clamped around her arm and forced her steps to halt, every nerve ending in her body jangled with sudden dread.

Dammit. Had Mercier sicced security on her? But then, if he had, she would likely be facing a team of armed guards on orders to escort her off the property, not just one man who seemed to have a more than passing interest in her.

"What are you doing?" she demanded, trying to

wrench out of his grasp without success.

"A better question is, what are *you* doing?" He kept his voice down as if to avoid upsetting the other guests, but his hold on her left no room for negotiation. "I'm going to need you to come with me now."

Given little choice unless she wanted to create a very public scene, Kaya walked with him. He brought her into a vacant room down one of the main floor's hallways, pushing her inside. He shut the door behind him, then turned around to face her.

Kaya crossed her arms, her heart racing. "Have I done something wrong?"

He didn't answer, but his eyes scrutinized her with a familiarity that unnerved her. "You and I both know you're not who you say you are."

Oh. God. Kaya swallowed. "I have no idea what you're talking about."

He chuckled. "Damn, you're good. But then, you always were." He reached behind him and turned the lock. Then he started to advance toward her. "It's been a long time. Two years, is it? Three, maybe?"

She shook her head. "I swear, I've never seen you before today."

Another chuckle, but this one had a menacing edge. "You can drop the act now. Just what kind of game are you running here, Raven?"

CHAPTER 7

Where the hell had she gone?

Aric saw Kaya abruptly leave the pavilion. Her pace had been purposeful, even verging on urgent. If there had been any graceful way to extricate himself from his dance with Mercier's bride, Aric would have gone after her immediately.

Now, she'd been inside the mansion for several minutes and counting.

Something wasn't right.

With murmured excuses as soon as the song ended, he left the dance floor and weaved through the clusters of swaying couples, his warrior instincts growing increasingly taut with each brisk step he took.

No sign of Kaya among the other reception guests inside. He scanned each cluster of well-dressed attendees, searching for a splash of dusty rose silk or Kaya's long dark hair.

It was as if she had simply vanished.

And then he heard it.

Just the slightest bump of noise coming from one of the closed rooms along the main floor's hallway. To any of the humans in attendance the sound was too muted to register at all. But to his Breed ears, it was unmistakable.

The sound of a scuffle.

His senses on high alert, he ducked into the passageway. Behind one of the ornately carved doors, another tangle of movement sounded. Followed by the unmistakable thump of a body hitting the floor.

Fuck.

Aric freed the lock with sharp mental command. Then he threw the door open.

Holy shit.

"Kaya."

She straddled the big body of one of the estate's security detail. The guard who'd cleared them through the metal detectors when they arrived lay supine on the room's thick Oriental rug, his face splotched red as he struggled and sputtered under Kaya—no easy feat when her bent knee was jammed against his throat.

Her pretty dress was torn in several places, her glossy dark hair drooping into her face in wrecked disarray. Her breath gusted through her parted lips, one of which was split open and bleeding.

A growl exploded out of Aric. There was no stopping the battle rage that flooded him as he flicked his furious gaze back to the man who'd hurt her. His vision burned instantly, hotly, amber. His fangs ripped out of his gums, not only in anger, but in reaction to the sudden olfactory blast of Kaya's blood.

The guard's eyes flew wide when he realized what Aric was. There was horror in those human eyes, but there was hatred too. "Fucking bloodsucker!"

In a panicked scramble beneath Kaya's hold on him, the man somehow managed to free his service pistol as Aric stalked forward.

The shot he squeezed off was wild, aimless. But it was lucky. Aric felt the bullet's sting as it grazed his shoulder. He glanced down in reflex, and when he looked back at Kaya it was just in time to watch her crush the guard's throat under her knee.

Her fury was swift and cold. Lethally so.

"I had no choice," she murmured softly, while outside the room the sound of gunfire had ignited panic among the reception. She looked up at Aric, her eyes stark, but without apology. "The son of a bitch was on to us."

He frowned. "How?"

She shook her head as she climbed off the body. "I don't know. He seemed to believe he knew me."

"Did he?"

Her gaze strayed to the dead man on the floor. "I never saw him before in my life."

Aric had questions for his partner, dozens of them. But they would have to sort everything out later. Right now, they had a bigger problem to deal with.

Screams of frightened wedding guests and the cattle stomp of rapidly moving feet filled the air. But not everyone was fleeing the mansion. Guards swarmed. Their heavy boot falls and low shouts sounded in the hallway just outside the room.

"The shot came from somewhere down here," one of them called to his comrades.

Damn it.

They were too close already. Aric might elude them by calling upon his Breed genetics to speed him past the men like a chill breeze, but Kaya didn't have that gift. And he'd be damned if he left a partner behind—even if she was the one who brought this trouble down on them.

Aric ground out a curse and grabbed Kaya by the wrist, stepping away from the body and pulling her into a corner of the room just as a trio of uniformed men burst inside.

Her eyes rounded as he held her tightly against him, with one arm keeping her close, the other bent between them, his index finger pressed over her lips to encourage her silence.

"It's Portman," one of the guards said. "Shit. He's dead."

Another let out a hissed curse. "Who the hell did he piss off? Looks like someone drove a hammer into the poor bastard's larynx."

Dread seeped into the dark brown pools of Kaya's eyes as the men spoke only a few feet away from them. Aric willed her to stay calm. Any movement could betray them now. He didn't blink, just held her uncertain gaze as steadily as he held the rest of her, unmoving, with barely an inch of space between her face and his.

He understood her worry. Kaya couldn't see the shadows that hid them from the armed men searching the room. Aric had to count on her to trust him now, to trust his ability. With Kaya melded against him, he bent the gloom of the small chamber, gathering it around them like a cloak. All while trying to ignore the erotic sensation of her soft curves fused against the front of his body.

His skin felt too hot, too tight, burning everywhere they touched.

"We got blood over here," announced the third man. "At least Portman left us something to go on. Looks like his final shot hit its mark."

"Call it in," ordered one of the others. "Alert the gate too. As of right now, this whole fucking place is on lockdown. Nobody leaves the estate until we've turned every corner inside out."

Aric kept the shadows close even after the men had gone. "Are you okay?"

Kaya nodded. "What about you? Your arm—"

"Already healing," he said with a shrug, showing her the vanishing wound.

"You just saved our lives, Aric."

He gave a grim shake of his head. "Not yet. We still have get off the property. Driving out of here is no longer an option, so that means we're leaving on foot."

"How? You heard those guards. They're putting men at every corner of the estate as we speak."

"There's three hundred acres of woods abutting the property to the north."

"Yes," Kaya agreed. "All of it surrounded by a ten-foot high electric fence."

He wasn't going to mention that technicality, but it didn't surprise him that she was already aware of it given the way she'd devoured the rest of the operation intel. And damn if he wasn't impressed, despite the gravity of their current situation.

"Let me worry about the logistics. I just need you to stick close to me and do what I say. Think you can handle that?"

She didn't even attempt to argue. That's when he knew she was truly afraid. For all of her toughness and apparent need to be in control, what happened between her and the man who assaulted her in this room had Kaya Laurent rattled.

He gently caught her chin and lifted her gaze to his. "You can trust me. Okay?"

"Okay."

As she quickly slipped out of her heels, he crept toward the open door and looked out. The hallway was empty now. The mansion was being cleared of wedding guests and all but a handful of security personnel.

"Come on," Aric said, taking her free hand. "The only way we're getting out of here is by getting lost inside the crowd."

He saw the flicker of apprehension in her eyes, but when the time came to make their dash between the clusters of people being corralled back out to the gardens, she proved herself a match for both his pace and his nerve.

It wasn't easy keeping the shadows gathered around them as they hurried out to the sunlit lawn. The pack of moving bodies all around them was the only thing he had to work with, and once he and Kaya made their break for the perimeter of the massive property, he wouldn't even have that small advantage on his side.

Aric took the first opportunity he had to veer away from the crowd, using the shade behind one of the large white catering tents for cover. "Shit," he bit off in a harsh whisper. "The closest edge of the tree line is about a hundred yards from here. I can't shield both of us that far in open daylight, so we're going to have to make a run for it."

Kaya's beautiful face was set in a look of pure determination. "I'm ready."

God help him, it was all he could do to resist touching her now. There was chaos and danger churning all around them, but all he wanted to do was bury his hands in her tangled hair and kiss her. Instead he dragged his hungry gaze from her trusting brown eyes and measured their chances of escaping without being caught.

The odds weren't good. Guards fanned out over the rolling lawn and gardens, some trying to calm anxious guests while others prowled the grounds like soldiers eager for a fight. Aric cursed under his breath. If he and Kaya didn't get out of there fast, their fucked up mission was heading straight into the catastrophe zone.

"Okay," he uttered quietly, spotting a narrow break. "Now, Kaya."

Together, they dashed for the next tent several yards away. When the coast was clear for another brief moment, they hunkered low and scrambled another few yards along the edge of the gardens, using the shadows behind elaborate topiary and fountains to hide them as they arduously worked their way toward the thick forest that rose up like a wall along the furthest edge of the estate.

"We made it," Kaya said, breathless as they ducked into the cool shade of the towering trees.

Aric didn't have the heart to tell her otherwise. He reached down and grabbed a fistful of her gauzy pink skirt, making her gasp when he tore a long piece loose.

She frowned as she watched him jog in the opposite direction of where they were headed and stuff the scrap into some of the bramble. "What's that for?"

"The dogs."

He'd been hearing them for several minutes, barking in the distance as the canine units were loosed along the perimeter of the property.

Now Kaya heard them too. He saw her dread deepen as the baying and howling grew louder.

Closer.

He took her hand. "Let's go. We can reach the fence before they're on top of us. If the guards send more dogs in from behind, your scent on that piece of silk will keep them occupied for a few minutes. Long enough to give us a chance to get on the other side."

Or so he hoped.

While bending shadows would shield them from being seen, it was useless against the scent-tracking capabilities of a pack of highly trained dogs.

"This way," he said, leading Kaya deeper into the thicket.

They raced hell for leather over the uneven ground, dodging low branches and sharp switches that lashed them as they passed. She still held her sandals in her hand, which would have been little help to her anyway on the loamy carpet and rock-strewn path they cut through the woods.

If Kaya was uncomfortable, she didn't seem to notice or care. She navigated the terrain as ably as he did, never mind that she was doing it barefoot in a dress. She'd make one hell of a warrior one day, provided this botched mission didn't get both of them bounced right out of the running.

"There it is, Aric." She pointed ahead of them to where a tall hedge of silver links topped with razor wire gleamed in the sparse light of the woods.

Not only was it electrified, but also equipped with small surveillance cameras. Aric disabled them with a focused mental command. The fence would require a bit more effort.

"Give me one of your shoes," he told her as they neared the structure. She handed over one of the delicate designer sandals and he tossed it at the fence.

At the instant of contact, a loud pop exploded, sending sparks shooting out in all directions like fireworks. Even though the ten-thousand volts was expected, Aric cursed in frustration. He could probably short it out with his mind, but only for a few seconds. Not long enough that he'd be willing to risk Kaya's life by asking her to climb it.

"Put your arms around me."

She gave him a dubious look. "What for?"

"So I can save your pretty ass. Hold on to me, Kaya. Now."

As soon as she'd looped her arms around his neck, he brought her close then leapt straight into the air and over the ten-foot top of the lethal barricade.

When they dropped softly onto the ground on the other side, Aric found it difficult to let her go. Their hearts were racing in similar tempo, a heavy throb that couldn't be blamed entirely on adrenaline. He could feel her blood rushing through her veins as he held her. Everything Breed in him responded to that steady drum of her pulse.

Everything male in him was painfully, rigidly aware of the abundance of lush curves and firm muscle now pressed deliciously against the length of him.

Kaya stared at him, the darkening of her deep brown eyes making her face look even softer, less the courageous, capable partner and more the strong, beautiful woman he was doing his damnedest to resist.

He cleared his throat around the emerging tips of his fangs. "You can thank me now," he murmured, unable to resist the sardonic jab.

If he didn't make a joke guaranteed to piss her off, he was probably going to kiss her right then and there.

She backed out of his loose hold and crossed her arms, though not quite fast enough to conceal the way her pebbled nipples pressed against the snug bodice of her dress. "Now that we're half a mile in the woods, got any brilliant plans for how we're going get back to the command center?"

"Only thing we can do. Hike another couple of miles inland. There's an old logging road that cuts into the forest up there." He fetched his phone from the pocket of his suit pants. "I'm calling in to base to send someone to meet us there for an evac. Then you and I are going to have to face Lucan Thorne and Niko to explain why we're coming back from this mission empty-handed."

"We're not."

"What do you mean?" He frowned at her, already holding the device to his ear. "We're not, what?"

"Returning empty-handed. I got what the Order wanted from Mercier. Not only that, I got a partial visual on an Opus member. He was here at the reception. I was chasing him down just before that guard confronted me."

"Holy shit." Aric raked a hand over his head. "You serious?"

She nodded. "We've got enough on Mercier to satisfy headquarters, and we have a new lead on Opus Nostrum right here in Montreal."

"Why didn't you tell me?"

"I just did." She gave him a wry look over her shoulder as she started walking ahead of him, the tilt of her mouth smug. "You can thank me now."

CHAPTER 8

Four hours later, Kaya's bravado had evaporated as she stepped out of the shower in her private quarters back at the command center and wrapped herself in a thick terry robe. The soles of her feet were a bruised, abraded mess after the narrow escape through the woods outside the Rousseau estate, but it was her pride that stung the most after enduring a long debriefing session upon her return to base with Aric.

The two of them had been interviewed separately by Nikolai in the war room and Lucan Thorne reporting in via video from D.C. Kaya had done her best to give a thorough, honest account of the operation that had started out so well, then ended in gunfire, death, and chaos.

All because of her.

She could only imagine what Aric told the Order commanders in his recount of their mission. He'd been summoned first, and had been dismissed from the meeting room before she'd been brought in to tell her side of the story. Not that she would blame him if he threw her under the bus. She couldn't have foreseen her unexpected confrontation by the guard, but she damn well could have handled it better than she had. Now, instead of a surgical mission to extract intel and cover their tracks afterward, they'd been the cause of a spectacle making headlines all over the world.

Kaya groaned. Her humiliation only deepened when she thought of the awful news coverage Niko and Lucan had played for her during her debriefing. Multiple phone cameras had captured the pandemonium. Reception guests screaming in terror. Tables and chairs toppled over as if a tornado had swept through the garden. Uniformed security officers brandishing weapons as they corralled elegantly dressed attendees like cattle while still other guards combed the grounds for an unknown killer at large.

It was only by some miracle—and Aric's shadow-bending—that they managed to avoid being detected, or worse, taken into custody.

Although the two grim Order leaders had been impossible to read during their questioning of her, Kaya had been preparing herself for the worst. Her duffel bag was already packed with her few personal belongings. On her bed was a thin sweater and pair of jeans she planned to wear for the moment when someone eventually came to escort her off the property.

She flinched when a knock sounded on her door not even five minutes after she'd slipped into her clothes. Apparently, they weren't going to waste any time cutting her loose.

"It's open," she said, walking gingerly on her bare feet to the closet to retrieve her boots.

She'd been hoping Nikolai might send Mira to deliver the bad news, but when she turned around to see who'd come in, her stomach did a little flip to find Aric standing there.

"Thought I'd come by and see how it went for you with Niko and Lucan."

He looked incredible, freshly showered and dressed in a muscle-hugging black T-shirt and workout pants that rode enticingly low on his trim hips. His golden-brown hair was still damp, the ends of the thick waves curling at his nape and over his arresting leaf-green eyes.

If he'd come out of his meeting with the same feeling of discouragement that she had, he certainly didn't show it. Cool and calm as ever, he leaned one bulky shoulder against the door jamb as he studied her.

When she didn't immediately answer his question about her debriefing, his glance moved from the boots in her hand to the packed duffel resting on the floor. "Going somewhere?"

She attempted an indifferent shrug. "Just getting ready in case it turns out I am."

He strode farther inside without waiting for her permission, bringing with him the woodsy scent of his clean skin and hair, and that more elusive masculine spice that twined around her sense like a drug.

"I didn't take you for the type to give up that easily on something you want."

"Well, life is full of little disappointments. I find it helps to be prepared." She placed her boots on the floor, then seated herself on the edge of the bed to relieve some of the pain in her abused soles. "Did they show you the news reports from this morning?"

"I saw them. I think the whole world's seen them by now."

"God." Kaya exhaled a quiet curse. "I'm sorry, Aric. I really screwed things up today. Probably for both of us."

He lifted his shoulder. "Our exit strategy could have used more finesse, but things could've been a hell of a lot worse."

"I killed that guard," she reminded him.

"Only after he fired at your partner. Our mission objective was fucked as soon as that gun went off. Nothing you did after that would've changed the way it all went to hell. Besides, we still managed to come out of there with valuable intel that not only gives the Order license to go after Mercier, but also brings us closer than ever to one of Opus Nostrum's members. And that's all credit to you, Kaya."

She slanted him a wary look. "Are you just trying to make me feel good? If so, don't bother."

"If I was trying to make you feel good, believe me, you wouldn't have to ask. You'd know it."

Her cheeks flared hot at the way his low voice caressed those words. She didn't want to acknowledge the awareness that had sparked between them from the instant they first met—awareness that had only intensified during their shared mission today.

"You don't have to be nice to me, Aric. I own my mistakes."

"So do I," he said. "And we both made some critical ones today. You may have complicated things for us by taking out that guard, but under the same circumstances I would've done the same thing. And that's what I told

Lucan and Nikolai today."

"You did?"

He nodded. "I also told them I was the one who fucked up even more by not scrubbing Stephan Mercier's memories before I left the pavilion to look for you. That was my job, and I didn't do it. He's probably already been in touch with Opus Nostrum to let them know something wasn't right about us."

Kaya had considered that unfortunate likelihood before now too. "I said it was my fault you didn't have time to scrub him. If I had paused long enough to let you know what I was doing, you wouldn't have needed to come looking for me. You could have been erasing our tracks with Mercier while I went after his Opus contact at the reception."

Aric grunted, a smile tugging at the corner of his mouth. "You saying you covered my ass, partner? Here I was, thinking you only wanted to drop me on it."

She laughed in spite of the weight of her worries. Her chances of making the Order as a teammate may have dried up today, but at this moment, she relished the feeling of camaraderie she shared with Aric Chase. She had dismissed him as an arrogant, entitled jackass when they met, but looking at him now she felt a strengthening respect that surprised her.

And the start of a caring she wasn't prepared for at all.

"You did good today," he said. "I just wanted to make sure I told you that before I clear out of here and head back to D.C."

"You're leaving?" Why the hell that idea should put a pang of disappointment in her breast, she had no idea. "When will you go?"

"As soon as tonight, probably. This trip to Montreal was just a detour. Until Lucan called me with the Mercier assignment, Rafe and I were on our way to D.C. with the woman we brought with us from London."

"Oh. Right, of course." Kaya hadn't been introduced to Siobhan O'Shea, but Mira had filled her in on the awful ordeal the shy Breedmate had endured the night that Aric and Rafe had rescued her and taken her into the protective custody of the Order. "Your friend seems to like her quite a bit."

That Rafe was attracted to the pretty strawberry-blonde was obvious to anyone who saw the pair together for even a few minutes.

Aric smirked. "My friend's got a thing for damsels in distress."

"What about you?"

He slowly shook his head. "I don't have a type."

Kaya snorted. "Of course not. You're more of a free agent, I'll bet."

His gaze stayed locked on hers. "More or less."

If she had to guess, she'd go with *more*. After all, she'd felt the heat of this Breed male's allure firsthand. Aric Chase was charismatic, magnetic. And damn if he didn't kiss like the devil too.

She should be relieved he was leaving Montreal.

Especially after what happened today.

Her encounter with that security officer had left her more rattled than it should have. She had never seen the man before, but the fact that he'd been so certain he knew her—by a name she hadn't heard in years—continued to bother Kaya even now, for reasons she preferred not to consider.

She had secrets no one knew.

Old secrets, but still powerful enough to destroy everything she'd worked for.

And if anyone at the Order uncovered them, there would be no place for her on any team. No, they would condemn her as a liar for all the time she'd kept those secrets buried.

Worse, they would have every right to consider her an enemy.

Letting herself get sidetracked by a charming player like Aric was a mistake she refused to make. It was good that he wasn't sticking around. If she were smart, she'd wish him gone from Montreal immediately.

And Kaya was smart.

It was the only way she'd survived this long.

She gave Aric a wry smile. "I'm sure the women of Washington, D.C., will be delighted to have you back."

He stared as if he wanted to say something more, then thought better of it. "Actually, I don't expect I'll stay in D.C. for long. The plan has always been for me to join one of teams in Seattle once I'm cleared for patrols."

Which would put him even farther away from Montreal. And so much the better. "What's in Seattle?"

"Rafe's father, Dante, heads up the command center out there. He and my father have been like brothers for the past twenty years. It only seemed fitting that I serve under Dante since Rafe is normally a member of one of my father's teams in Boston."

"You mean, when he's not being sent off to Ireland with you to rescue random damsels in distress?"

Aric grinned. "Something like that, yeah."

"How very chivalric," she tossed back, enjoying their back-and-forth despite her determination to keep him at arm's length for however many hours he would remain in Montreal. "I guess chivalry's to be expected when we're talking about the Order's golden prince."

He scoffed. "Prince?"

"Oh, come on. Don't pretend you don't know. The only name that carries more weight in the Order than your family's is Lucan Thorne's." Kaya studied his handsome face, all those sharp angles and broad slopes that combined to give him a classic, regal look that few women could resist. "Who else do you know who can say they're not only the son of the first daywalking Breed female in existence and the hero of the Order who killed that madman, Dragos, two decades ago?"

"My father would never take all the credit for that. He had the entire Order with him that day, including Niko and Renata." Nevertheless, Aric's eyes danced with familial pride. "And there is one other person I know who can make the same claim as me. My sister, Carys."

Kaya nodded at the mention of his fraternal twin. "Is she a lot like you?"

"Too much," he said, a loving smile tilting his sculpted lips. "My sister is a force of nature, always has been. You'd like her, I think. The two of you have a lot in common."

"Such as?"

"Intelligence. Determination. Courage. Beauty." He smirked. "Carys got all the good traits between us. I guess that makes me the bad twin."

Kaya smiled. "I don't know about that," she said, weathering a wistful sense of envy for the way he spoke so adoringly about his sibling. "I think you've got a few passable qualities too."

"Care to elaborate? I've got a couple of hours to

spare."

She laughed. "No way. You don't need anyone helping to make your head swell. Least of all me."

His grin widened. "Why not let me be the judge of that?"

It wasn't until he started to move closer to her seat on the edge of the bed that Kaya realized she was losing control of the situation. It was so easy to get swept up into banter with him. Easier still to forget that they really weren't friends, that they would never be something more either. She could not allow that. Not with anyone, but especially him.

Because after just one day Aric Chase had done something no other man had managed before him.

He'd made her feel safe with him.

And that was the most dangerous thing of all.

When he came to stand in front of her, Kaya dodged, stepping down onto the floor. The soft rug was cushiony beneath her bare feet, but that didn't keep her from wincing with discomfort.

Aric scowled. "Are you all right?"

"I'm fine."

"No, you're not." His brow rankled further. "Sit down. Let me see your feet."

He didn't give her a choice. Taking her shoulders in his strong hands, he set her back on the edge of the mattress then crouched in front of her on the floor, taking one of her feet tenderly into his hands.

He sucked in a hissed breath as he examined the contused and lacerated soles of her feet. "Jesus Christ."

"It's not that bad."

His gaze flicked up at her, sober, even angry. "You should have said something to me. I wouldn't have pushed you so hard through those woods, Kaya. For fuck's sake, I could have carried you—"

"Like hell you could have." She scowled at the suggestion. "I never would've asked you to do that for me."

"No shit. You're far too stubborn for that."

The gentleness in his voice only made her outrage spike hotter. She tried to draw out of his grasp, but he held her ankle firmly in the palm of his hand. His touch was warm, careful. His handsome face grave with concern.

She didn't want to acknowledge how good his hands felt on her, nor how even his light touch as he continued to inspect the cuts and bruises on her skin made her heart race in her breast, her blood rushing like molten liquid through her veins.

When he glanced up now, she could see some of the same tension and awareness in his taut expression. And in the faint flicker of amber that lit the depths of his bright green irises.

He swallowed as if his tongue had become thick in his mouth. When he finally spoke, there was a rasp in his deep voice that caressed her senses like velvet.

"I'll ask Rafe to come see you before we leave. He can heal this for you."

Aric's touch lingered even after he said it, his thumb idly stroking the fine bones of her ankle. God help her, she could hardly breathe under the friction of his fingers on her skin. She wanted him to touch her everywhere. To kiss her without the pretense of a covert mission.

She wanted these things even though she knew any one of them could be her undoing.

"Aric . . ." she murmured, uncertain what she meant

to say.

The sound of their comm units buzzing at the same time saved her from tumbling headlong into another disaster with him today.

Only then did Aric release her. He answered the call, rising to his feet with a grim look on his face as he listened. "Christ. When?" He glanced at Kaya. "I'm actually with her now. All right, I'll let her know. We're on the way."

Kaya stared at him in question as he ended the summons.

"That was Niko. Stephan Mercier's dead. Someone cut out his tongue about an hour ago."

CHAPTER 9

Although Mercier's death was a disturbing development, the interruption couldn't have come at a more ideal time. If Aric needed to be reminded of his duty—and it seemed damned clear that he did—Niko's summons had been just the wakeup call he needed.

Not that his body agreed with that argument.

With his veins lit up and hot with desire, he waited for Kaya to slip a pair of shoes onto her injured feet, then followed her out of her quarters.

Touching her had been a mistake. He should have known that, considering how the memory of holding her earlier today—kissing her—had been driving him to distraction for the past several hours. All he'd done now was brush his fingers over her ankle and everything male in him was awake and pulsing with the need for more.

With the need for *her*.

As he walked the long corridor beside her, he tried to tell himself the need was merely animal attraction, nothing more. She was a beautiful woman and he was a man unaccustomed to denying himself any of life's pleasures. It was only natural that the part of him that was purely male—and far from human—stirred with the need to possess her.

But what he felt looking into Kaya's eyes just now spoke to something deeper inside him.

Her physical pain made him want to soothe her.

It was the other, deeper pain that alarmed Aric the most. Because seeing that made him want to protect Kaya, slay whatever demons had put such a hauntedness in her soft brown eyes.

Chivalric, she'd called him?

Like hell. He practically snorted at the idea as he watched her hips sway with each careful step, her long limbs and the trace cinnamon-and-roses scent of her skin putting a throb in his fangs that had nothing to do with heroism or honor.

The only thing saving him from proving that to her was a flight out of Montreal tonight.

He couldn't wait for the wheels to be off the ground.

"Come in," Niko said, his ice-blue eyes grave as he greeted Aric and Kaya at the door to the war room. "I've called everyone here to go over the news that just came in."

Gathered around the large table were Kellan and Mira, her team of three Breed warriors seated across from them. Nikolai's black-haired Breedmate Renata had taken the chair at the far end of the table, her slender hands resting atop her enormous baby bump.

Rafe had been called to the war room as well. Aric

strode in and took the chair next to his friend, allowing Kaya to have the seat closest to Niko at the head of the meeting.

"As you've all been made aware, this morning's op ran into a few . . . complications," Niko said, his commanding tone conveying only cold acceptance, not censure. "Apparently, those complications got the attention of Opus. About an hour ago, we learned that Stephan Mercier's vehicle was found in a parking garage downtown. His driver and bodyguards had been shot execution-style. Mercier's death hadn't been that merciful."

Nikolai tapped a screen built into the glass surface beside him and a holographic image formed in the center of the long table. The photo was horrific. Mercier's body lay sprawled across the blood-soaked leather backseat of his chauffeured car, his head tipped back at a grotesque angle. His mouth was agape, nothing but an empty black maw stretched into a permanent scream.

At the other end of the table, Renata made a gagging sound and turned her face askance. "Jesus."

"Ah, shit." Niko cut the visual at once. "Sorry, love."

Mira reached over for the other woman's hand. "Rennie, are you all right?"

Renata gave a wobbly nod, her chin-length bob swinging. "I will be, once this baby finally decides to arrive."

"I don't think it'll be long now," Mira said, smiling tenderly at the Breedmate who'd been both a friend and an adoptive mother to her since she was eight years old. "I can't wait to hold my little brother."

On the other side of Aric, Rafe grunted. "You may have to fight my mother to get to him."

"Or mine," Aric said, chuckling now. "Hell, even Carys is making plans to be here with the rest of the Order for the birth and presentation ceremony. That kid's going to have no shortage of attention once he makes his appearance."

Renata smiled. "It'll be nice to have everyone together again." She shot a wry glance up the table to her warrior mate. "And I'm looking forward to getting back out on patrols as soon as I'm able, too."

It was no idle comment. Renata was one of the most fierce, skilled warriors in the Order. In addition to the quartet of daggers she was known to wield, or any of the other weapons she'd proven herself lethally qualified to use in combat, she was also gifted with an immense ability. Armed with just the power of her mind, Renata could immobilize and debilitate anyone who dared to cross her.

Pregnancy had muted that ability, as it did with all Breedmates, but once she had her baby that gift would resume. And it would also pass down to her child, who would be virtually unstoppable once he reached adulthood.

"I don't know if I like that plan," Nikolai said. His brow was knit with a frown, but the gaze he held his woman in was filled with adoration. "I like seeing you round in the middle with my child. Maybe we should have a dozen babies before I let you suit up for patrol again."

"Before you *let* me, vampire?" She narrowed her jade-green eyes, even as a smile stretched her lips. "Maybe instead of giving you a dozen babies, I should string you up and use my blades to—"

"All right," he said, laughing with her. "I can see this

won't be an easy negotiation. Not that anything ever was easy with you, love."

She arched a dark brow. "You get bored when things are too easy. That's why you can't live without me."

He gave her a private, intimate look. "Only one of many reasons."

Although he tried to resist, Aric's glance strayed to Kaya. She watched the exchange between her commander and his mate in silence, a small smile tilting the corners of her mouth. Aric had a feeling she would be the kind of woman to keep her mate on his toes too. And why the notion of Kaya with another Breed male should needle him with a pang of annoyance, he didn't want to know.

"Anyway," Renata said to Nikolai, gesturing for him to go on. "You were telling us about poor Stephan Mercier and his missing tongue."

"Yes." The commander cleared his throat and went back to the business at hand. "There's no need to guess who killed him. Whether Opus suspects he was compromised by us, or whether they know it for a fact, these people don't leave loose threads."

"No, they don't," Rafe agreed. He looked around Aric to pin Kaya in a shrewd stare. "You spoke with Mercier the longest. Did you give him any reason to think you were an Order operative?"

"Jesus, Rafe. Of course, she didn't." Aric's response sounded defensive, even to his own ears.

"Just trying to piece things together in my head," Rafe said.

And while his question wasn't out of bounds, Aric knew his friend too well and for too long to dismiss the probing intensity of the gaze that had yet to leave Kaya.

"Maybe you tipped your hand to Mercier without realizing it," Rafe suggested.

Aric waited to hear Kaya deny it, but when he glanced at her, he found her expression less than certain. "I don't think he knew I was with the Order. Not that he conveyed to me through his thoughts, anyway."

"But you can't be sure?" Rafe pressed.

She hesitated. "No. I can't be sure. He said some things about the Breed—he thought some things—that I couldn't let lie."

"Such as?"

"That the Breed are monsters. A scourge that deserves to be erased from existence."

Aric grunted. "Not the first time we've heard that."

"Nor will it be the last," Nikolai finished grimly.

Kaya shook her head, angry color rising in her cheeks. "Mercier meant it. He was gleeful about the idea that he could have something to do with making war happen between the humans and the Breed. I couldn't stand there and let him spew his hatred in front of me. I guess I felt the asshole needed to be set straight on a few things."

"Hey, I've been there before, too, Kaya." Mira gave her friend a gentle look from across the table. "But as a warrior, you have to check your emotion at the door."

"Or risk the entire mission," Rafe added.

"I didn't mean to put anything or anyone at risk," Kaya replied, openly contrite. "Mercier was unjustly deriding the people I care about, people I would lay down my life for. He was wrong, so I reminded him that it was Opus Nostrum who'd been behind all of the recent violence and division."

"And now we've lost the very lead you went there to

confirm," Rafe pointed out. "It was a rookie mistake. Covert op means always staying within your cover."

"Yes." Kaya held his scrutinizing gaze. "I know what it means."

"Damn, Rafe." Aric shot his comrade a hard look. "Go easy on her, man. This was her first field mission and she did great. So, we lost Mercier. He was a bottom-feeding scum. At least Kaya siphoned some useful intel off him. And she also provided us with an even stronger lead on Opus."

"That's right," Niko agreed. "That is, if we can ID the man she saw leaving the reception."

Kaya's brow pinched with regret. "I wish I'd gotten a look at his face. Even a glimpse would've been something useful."

"You would have, if it hadn't been for that security guard getting in your way," Aric pointed out.

"What do we know about him?" Renata asked from the far end of the table, her hand idly caressing the swell of her belly. "Have we been able dig anything up?"

"We have," Kellan offered from beside Mira. "His name was Jacob Portman. Real piece of shit, if you'll pardon my French. He'd been on the Rousseau security detail for about a year. Got his training as a JUSTIS officer doing port patrols on the river a few years back, but he got bounced for excessive force after killing an unarmed Breed youth down on the docks. Emptied his service pistol into the kid's back, according to the files."

Aric met Kaya's sickened look. "Sounds like you did the world a favor taking out that heap of garbage."

"That's not all," Mira added. "Tell them what else you uncovered on him, Kellan."

He nodded. "Portman used to run with an

assortment of militant groups when he was a teen. They called him 'Red' back then."

"How original," Aric drawled, picturing the human's crown of bright ginger hair.

"According to his juvie file, his fellow gangbangers called him that mainly because he liked to watch things bleed," Kellan said. "Especially things with fangs."

Nikolai cursed low under his breath. "Sounds like Portman could've been ripe for indoctrination by Opus too. Do you think he confronted you because he suspected you were part of the Order, Kaya?"

She had gone very quiet, very still. She glanced up now, almost as if she'd drifted off somewhere. "I'm sorry?"

"Portman," Niko prompted. "You said he thought he knew you from somewhere."

"That's what he said. But he was wrong." Her answer was resolute, without a second's hesitation. "I'd never seen him before today. And I swear to you he'd never seen me before, either."

"You think he was lying?" Mira asked. "Or was he just mistaken?"

Kaya shook her head. "I can't say for sure. Maybe I just have one of those faces."

Aric gave her a reassuring glance. "Not a face I'd ever mistake for another."

Her gaze lingered on his for a long moment before dropping away, color suffusing her cheeks. When she spoke, her voice was soft and sober.

"I failed everyone today, and I'm sorry. The last thing I ever wanted to do was let any of you down. Now, I've messed everything up. The reception footage has gone viral. Opus Nostrum is all but certain to know they're in the Order's crosshairs again. Mercier's dead, and the only lead we might've taken away from all of this escaped the premises before I could get close enough to ID him."

"Maybe not." Niko leaned forward in his chair. He touched the panel again and this time a display full of data and photo files appeared in the center of the table. "Gideon sent over every surveillance still and video feed captured at the Rousseau estate today. We've got the guest list from the wedding and the reception, as well as registrations for every vehicle that passed through the gates. All you have to do is comb through all of it until you find our subject unknown."

"There must be thousands of photos and records," Kaya murmured.

Niko's mouth quirked. "Consider it penance. You too, Aric."

"Sir?" He frowned. "I'm supposed to be returning to D.C."

"And you will. After you and Kaya get through that intel." Niko glanced at Rafe. "You're sticking around too. I've already cleared it with Lucan. Now that we know we've got an Opus lead here in Montreal, I could use an extra pair of boots on the ground."

"You got it," Rafe said. "Nothing I'd rather do than help put another Opus member in the ground."

"I don't know about that." Aric smirked at his friend. "Seems like there is one thing you'd rather be doing."

Rafe's intensity of a moment ago diffused at the quip—and at the reference to the female he'd been spending nearly all of his time with since they'd arrived in Montreal. He sent a light punch into Aric's shoulder, but he didn't seem able to hold back his smile.

Across the table from them, Mira lifted her brows. "So, it is true? Don't tell me the untamable Rafe Malebranche may have finally met his match."

That he didn't deny it outright or try to deflect with any one of the dozens of reasons he'd used in the past to explain why he had no interest in settling down was answer enough for Aric.

"Holy shit," Aric uttered, shocked and amazed. "Are you falling in love with Siobhan O'Shea?"

Rafe didn't get the chance to answer. At that same moment, Renata hissed, her face constricting in pain.

"Sweetheart." Niko flew out of his seat and was at her side in a flash of movement. He crouched down beside her, a look of pure terror in his eyes. "Are you okay? Is it the baby? Ah, fuck. Is he coming right now?"

"Relax," she said, her voice gusting around a sigh. "It's a contraction, that's all."

Niko scowled. "You've been getting them on and off for the past couple of days."

"Yes." She reached up and cupped his cheek. "I'm fine. Trust me, you'll know when it's time for our son to make his grand entrance."

"Either way, I'm taking you to bed," Niko growled. He glanced over his shoulder at Mira. "Will you handle the night's patrol plans for me?"

"Of course." She nodded, her smile full of love and compassion for the couple who were her parents and her friends. "I've got this. You take care of Rennie."

With the commander and his mate having exited the war room, Mira gathered Rafe and Kellan and her team to one of the conversation areas away from the conference table.

Aric glanced at Kaya, both of them left to their own

devices as the squad began talking tactics and territory assignments.

"I guess we should get started too."

She nodded. "I'm sorry you're stuck here a bit longer. I know how badly you were hoping to get back to your life in D.C."

"I can think of worse things."

He was joking, but she didn't smile. Instead she touched the panel embedded in the glass in front of her at the table and opened the first of countless data files.

"Shall we get started?" she asked when he merely watched for a long moment. Her face was utterly indifferent, impossible to read. "The sooner we get through all of this, the sooner we can both get on with our lives."

"Yeah," Aric agreed, telling himself the sting he felt was merely wounded male pride and nothing deeper. "I guess you're right. Let's get it over with."

CHAPTER 10

"How many more image files left in that folder you're working on, Kaya?"

She looked at the unopened count on her tablet display and groaned. "Twenty-four hundred and sixty-two."

"Great," Aric said. "That means we're halfway finished."

She swung a hopeful glance at him. "We are?"

"With the first batch," he said, a flash of dimples in his unfatigued face.

Kaya slumped in her chair and exhaled a long sigh.

They had been working in the war room for more than five hours with barely a break. At some point, she had resorted to strong coffee, just to keep her lids open and her eyes uncrossed as she and Aric scoured file after file of photos and video stills taken during Stephan Mercier and Anastasia Rousseau's wedding and reception.

"Why couldn't Mercier's Opus contact have done us a favor and smiled right into any one of the scores of surveillance cameras rigged all over the estate?"

Aric chuckled. "Where's the challenge in that? Can't blame the guy for hiding out in the crowds and keeping his face averted every time he was in a camera's vicinity. Opus members don't tend to live long once the Order gets wind of who they are."

Kaya pulled a frown. "Well, I find his caution annoying."

Beside her at the conference table, Aric flipped through his open file of images, barely pausing more than a moment on any one of them. She watched, fascinated by how quickly his mind worked. His flawless memory may have been inherited from his mother, but Aric's keen intellect and razor focus was all his own.

And damn if it wasn't sexy as hell.

He slid his tablet toward her and pointed to a squatty, dark-haired man in the photo on the display. "That him?"

She shook her head. "I swear, if I have to spend another minute looking at pompous, entitled rich people drinking gallons of champagne and eating plates of thousand-dollar-an-ounce caviar, I'm going to scream."

"You got something against rich people? Or just people having a good time?"

"I have nothing against people having a good time."

"That's a relief." He chuckled and she made the mistake of looking up at him. He was staring at her now, studying her with an unhurried interest that made her stomach flip. "So, it's only pompous, entitled rich people that make you want to scream?"

To mask her sudden awareness of him, she gave him an arch look. "If the shoe fits."

"Excuse me?" He swiveled in his chair to face her full-on, his brows furrowed. "Did you just call me *rich*?"

Laughing, she picked up her half-empty mug of cold coffee and held it close as she looked at him. "Well, aren't you? Rich, I mean."

"Hell, no. Not me. I'm just a grunt trying to find my own way doing something I believe in." He leaned back in his seat, looking casual and far too attractive for her peace of mind. "If you mean my family, though, they've done all right. But the Chases worked hard for everything they have. Most of the men in my family made their livings in public service. My father was the first of our line to join the Order."

"I didn't know that." Kaya shrugged. "I've heard some of the Order commanders call him 'Harvard' so I guess I just assumed . . ."

"The nickname came from Rafe's father, Dante. It wasn't meant to be a compliment, but it stuck." A grin pulled his mouth into a charming tilt. "Now only my father's closest friends call him that."

Kaya smiled, thinking about the easy friendship Aric seemed to have with Rafe. "I suppose it makes sense that you and Rafe are so close. You two act like brothers."

He nodded. "In all the ways that matter, we are."

She waited for his searching gaze to release her, but it only held firmer. That penetrating stare seemed as sharp as a razor as it studied her.

"What about you, Kaya?"

"What about me?" She glanced away when the intensity of his scrutiny became too much. Instead, she busied herself with another image from the reception taken before the party had erupted in chaos.

Aric's eyes lingered on her, as steady and certain as a caress. "You've got friends in the Order, but who were your friends before you came here? Where is your family?"

"I have all the friends I need here at the command center. They're the only family I need."

"Is that why it means so much to you to be part of the team?" he asked gently. "Because the Order is the only family you have?"

"Yes." A shaky breath leaked out of her before she could hold it back. "And because without the Order, I don't have anywhere else to go."

She surprised herself, giving him that truth. She'd been friends with Mira for longer than a year and she'd never said those words out loud to her.

But saying them to Aric felt safe somehow. Maybe because he would be leaving soon.

Maybe because he was looking at her with such care and genuine interest, she couldn't deny him if she tried.

And that was a dangerous thing.

He leaned forward, shocking her when his hand covered hers atop the table. Her heart slammed against her ribs as his thumb stroked the backs of her fingers. She knew she should pull away from his uninvited touch, but God help her, she could hardly move.

She could hardly form a logical thought when his other hand reached up to caress her face. His palm was warm and strong against her cheek, his fingers achingly tender. But there was no softness in his eyes. They glowed with predatory hunger, amber flecks of light swiftly devouring the bright green of his irises.

Kaya swallowed. The shift in the air between them

had changed so suddenly, turning into something dark and seductive. They had been on the verge of this same steep plummet earlier tonight in her quarters, before Niko's call had interrupted them. She'd been counting that narrow escape as a blessing, but now she realized the postponement had only heightened the craving she had for this man.

For this powerful Breed male who was making her yearn for something more than just duty and drive. Aric's heated, hungry gaze as it slid from her face down to the pulse that hammered frantically in the column of her throat made her long for all the things she'd never dreamed she could have.

And never would.

Not when a blood bond would lay all her secrets bare, leaving her nowhere to hide.

"Kaya." He spoke her name in a hushed growl, otherworldly and dark. He drew her toward him.

Before she realized what she was doing, her whole body arched into his coaxing touch, moving slowly, unresistingly, into his kiss.

His lips brushed over hers, the motion unraveling something deep inside her. Heat spiraled along her nerve endings and into her blood, igniting a cauldron in her core. She gasped at the swiftness of her response to him. Arousal so powerful it staggered her. He captured her wordless cry with his mouth, his tongue spearing past her parted lips on a hungered moan.

Kaya didn't fight the power he had over her senses.

She craved the feeling of surrender she felt in his arms.

She wanted him—so much so, the sound of laughter and conversation drifting down the corridor took several seconds to register in her mind.

Mira and Kellan. Along with Torin and Balthazar and Webb.

Oh, God. The whole team was back from patrol and now heading this way.

Kaya pulled out of Aric's reach, scrambling back into her seat. What the hell was wrong with her? Mortified at her lapse in judgment and control, it was all she could do to collect herself and prepare to face her comrades as the group of them converged on the war room.

Aric, however, showed no outward signs of humility. Leaning back in his chair, his eyes still glimmering with fiery sparks, he looked only at Kaya as the warriors poured inside.

"Hey, you two!" Mira strode in under the shelter of Kellan's arm, laughter dancing in her eyes. She was freshly showered and dressed in casual clothes like her mate and the rest of her squad. "See, you guys? I told you they'd still be here working."

"Or something," Torin said, earning low chuckles from Bal and Webb.

Kaya groaned inwardly, knowing it was useless trying to deny anything. Especially around Torin, whose unique Breed gift allowed him to read the emotional barometer of any space he walked into. If the tall vampire with the glorious mane of long hair decided to read the room's heated emotional state now, his face gave nothing away.

Kaya cleared her throat. "We were just about to take a break. Isn't that right, Aric?"

He merely grunted in reply, an arrogant smirk playing at the corner of his mouth. Although his friends might pretend not to notice, she could see the fullness of his fangs behind his sensual lips. Just the idea made her pulse kick with an unwanted thrill.

Mira's gaze ricocheted between them in question. "Okay," she said slowly. "Well, we're all going to hang out for a while on the back terrace. Since you were ready to take a break from . . . whatever you were in the middle of . . . come join us. That means you too, Aric."

Without waiting for further argument, the petite captain strode out of the war room with her mate and comrades flanking her.

Kaya remained seated after they'd gone. "Go on, if you'd like. I'm going to stay and try to get through some more of these files."

It took Aric a long moment before he moved. Then he got up from his chair and rolled it back into place at the table. Kaya closed her eyes, holding back the breath that was frozen in her throat as she waited to hear his booted feet cross the floor. In the unending silence, she reached for her tablet and tapped to open another of the image folders.

Aric's hands came to rest gently on her shoulders. "The work can wait a while."

She swiveled her head, prepared to make a dozen excuses as to why she preferred to stay. Aric's crooked smile made every one of those lame protests dry up before they reached her tongue. He stood behind her, a wall of heat and muscle and dangerous temptation.

And those devastating dimples were going to be her doom.

"Come out there with me," he said, his voice a low growl. "Rumor has it, you've got nothing against people having a good time."

Her pent-up breath escaped on a small laugh.

Against all better judgment and the countless warning bells that told her she'd better guard her heart as much as any other part of her anatomy around this male, she closed her files then walked with Aric out to the moonlit terrace behind the command center mansion.

It was a balmy summer night, just a trace breeze blowing over the courtyard and expansive patio where a burning fire pit and tall torches illuminated the group gathered there. Mira and Kellan and the three Breed males on her squad were seated around the pit, laughing and talking like family.

Rafe was there too. And he wasn't alone. The Irish Breedmate, Siobhan, occupied a small stone bench along with him. Huddled against his side, she was wrapped in a blanket in spite of the warm night. If the sweetly shy looks the strawberry-blonde beauty gave Rafe were anything to go on, Kaya suspected any chill she may have felt was mainly an excuse to stay close to the handsome Breed male.

Rafe sent up a nod of greeting when he noticed Aric and Kaya coming to join them. Like the rest of the team, he had taken time to shower and change out of his patrol gear and weapons. Dressed in faded jeans and a dark T-shirt, Rafe had effortless, golden good looks but the shrewd instincts of a warrior. Kaya had gotten a taste of that latter side in the war room earlier tonight.

"Come on," Aric said, encouraging her to follow him when she hesitated.

She went along, if only because the only remaining seat was the other little bench situated next to Rafe and Siobhan.

Kaya saw Mira smile then whisper something to Kellan as she watched her cross the terrace bricks with

Aric. Music flowed out of the sound system, joining the comforting lull of conversations and the occasional bark of laughter. It was one of the things Kaya loved most about nights like this, the post-patrol ritual the squad often enjoyed. Even though she had yet to accompany the team on a formal mission, Kaya relished the time she got to spend with Mira and the others upon their return to base each night.

But tonight everything was different.

Walking alongside Aric then taking a seat next to him on the bench made her feel part of a different unit too. One that she didn't belong to, nor ever could.

"How'd it go out there in the city tonight?" Aric asked his friend.

Rafe lifted his shoulder. "Uneventful. Not the kind of night we were looking for. We shook down some of the usual suspects for information, but no one seems to know anything about Mercier aside from him making headlines with his marriage into the Rousseau family. And his abrupt exit from it."

"Or else they're not talking," Kaya interjected.

Aric nodded. "Good chance of that. Especially after Opus made it crystal clear how they feel about potential leaks in their ranks. Hard to tell Opus secrets when you're missing your tongue."

Rafe's glance strayed to Siobhan, who shuddered beneath the comfort of her thin blanket at the mention of the terrorist brotherhood. She was one of very few people able to count herself lucky enough to survive Opus's wrath. An innocent bystander, she had been beaten and left for dead in her flat outside Dublin just a few nights ago after Opus loyalists broke in and murdered her roommate, Iona Lynch.

Kaya smiled at the Breedmate. "Hi. We haven't met yet."

"Ah, shit," Rafe said, raking a hand over his head. "Sorry about that. Kaya, this is Siobhan."

The young woman tipped her chin down in acknowledgment. "Hello," she murmured. "Nice to meet you."

"Same," Kaya said as she and Aric sat on the neighboring bench.

Rafe leaned forward, his forearms braced on his knees. "Listen, Kaya, I'm sorry if I came off overly interrogative during the meeting earlier tonight."

She shrugged and shook her head. "It's okay."

"No, it's not," Aric said. "My friend was being a dick, so let him apologize."

"What happened?" Siobhan asked, pivoting to face Kaya.

Rafe draped his arm around his companion's petite shoulders. "We were talking about a mission that didn't go as smoothly as it should have. I just wanted to be clear on some of the facts, but I think I was pushing Kaya too hard at times."

"Nothing I couldn't handle."

"So, I noticed. Opus Nostrum is serious shit," he added. "I guess it's hard to turn off my training when it comes to those bastards and the worthless scum who are loyal to them."

Kaya nodded. "I feel the same way. And if I could've changed anything that happened today, believe me, I would have."

Rafe grinned. "I'd have rather heard this pompous daywalker took a bullet in his ass instead of his arm, but no one asked me."

Aric snorted. "No one's asking you now, either, nightcrawler."

"Ignore him," Rafe said. "I generally do." He held out his hand to her. "Apology accepted?"

"Don't let him off too easy, Kaya. Remember, you bled for that mission today too."

Rafe frowned. "You did?"

"Not really. It was no big deal."

Aric gave her a sober look. "I made her run barefoot for a couple of miles through wooded terrain."

Rafe's blond brows arched. "And you called me a dick?"

"Show him, Kaya."

"What? No." She shook her head, mortified that Aric was making a big deal out of a few scrapes and bruises. She'd endured worse injuries just trying to live day-by-day on the streets when she was a kid. "Really, I'm fine."

Rafe was already off his bench and standing in front of her. "Let me see."

"You should," Siobhan chimed in. "Rafe can help you. He helped me too."

Kaya sighed. Only because they were all giving her little choice, she removed her shoes and waited while Aric's friend checked out her wounds. "Does this hurt?"

His palm pressed flat against her abused sole. "No, it doesn't hurt."

In fact, it felt pretty good. Warmth suffused her tender skin, soothing her.

Healing her.

"You feel that?" Aric asked, watching her face intently as his comrade took away her pain and her injuries.

She nodded. Rafe's ability was amazing, but she was even more captivated by the tender, intimate look in Aric's eyes.

"I feel it," she murmured, unsure if she was talking about the heat and light restoring her body, or the greater sensation she felt every time she was close to this Breed male.

"Good as new," Rafe announced a moment later, his deep voice slicing through the haze of her tangled emotions. "And just in time for a little dancing."

Someone had turned up the volume on a slow song—Kellan, by the look of it. He held Mira's hand and guided her into the center of the expansive terrace, spinning her and then drawing her up against him. The mated couple swayed in a close embrace, eyes locked on each other.

Rafe murmured something to Siobhan, then the two of them got up and joined Mira and Kellan. Kaya watched them all for a while, desperately, achingly aware of Aric's thigh pressed against hers on the bench they shared. His body heat seeping into her skin and bones, into the rush of blood racing through her veins.

She was relieved to see Torin and Bal get up from their places around the fire pit and saunter over to her and Aric. Webb had already disappeared into the night, going wherever it was he preferred to spend his time after hours.

The two warriors nodded to Aric as they approached. "We're going to head back into the city to look for blood Hosts before the feeding curfew," Bal said. "Care to join us?"

"No, thanks." Aric's reply was immediate. "I fed before I left London. I'll be back in D.C. before I need to find a vein again."

The two vampires glanced at Kaya. Torin had the audacity to wink at her. It was all she could do not to leap up and pummel the amused look off his face.

"You should go," she told Aric as her comrades strode away. "You don't have to keep me company. I was just about to turn in for the night."

Aric smiled. "Always trying to get rid of me." He rose, then held his hand out to her. "Come on, Mrs. Bouchard. As I recall, we never finished our dance."

CHAPTER 11

For the second time in less than twenty-four hours, Aric found himself holding Kaya close in his arms while a crooner waxed on about true love and happy-ever-after. Sappy, fairy tale sentiments that should have made his molars ache with their impossible sweetness. But it wasn't his molars that ached while Kaya swayed against him.

Everywhere their bodies brushed, currents of electric heat crackled beneath his skin. Instead of making jokes or searching for other ways to demonstrate that he wasn't susceptible to the kind of hearts-and-flowers weaknesses that seemed to have overtaken the other two couples dancing nearby, Aric found himself riveted to Kaya's lovely face in the half-light on the terrace.

His veins pounded, a possessive need surging inside him as he moved to the tempo of the music and tried not to imagine how soft she felt, how the scent of her was making his mouth throb with the presence of his fangs.

Damn.

Maybe he should have gone with Mira's teammates to look for a blood Host. It was true he wouldn't need the nourishment for days, but that had little to do with the hunger he'd been battling since his first taste of Kaya. Kissing her that first time had been an impulsive mistake, though one he couldn't seem to regret.

Kissing her again in the war room tonight had been worse than impulse or a mistake. It had been possessive, a compulsion he couldn't have fought even if he tried. That need still raked him. Now, try as he could not to imagine the two of them naked and in a sweaty tangle, his mind refused to obey.

The fact that she seemed to meet him with equal passion each time they'd kissed only made his desire for her burn all the hotter. And now that she was in his arms again, it took everything he had just to keep that desire on a short leash. Especially when she gazed up at him, a note of pleasure in her dark brown eyes.

"Are you going to tell me what that cryptic smile is about or leave me guessing?"

She shrugged, still watching him with an avid interest that made his pulse kick into a higher gear. "I was just thinking that if things don't work out for you with the Order, maybe you should take up ballroom dancing."

He choked on a laugh. "Oh, thanks. Remind me never to come to you for career advice."

Her smile flashed brilliant white, the joy on her face utterly captivating. "I'm serious. You've got some impressive moves."

He grunted, arching a brow. "You haven't even seen

my best ones yet."

With her face still lit with amusement, he spun her into a low dip. Her surprised squeal and burst of easy laughter drew the attention of their friends. Someone applauded, but Aric hardly noticed and didn't care. Nor did Kaya, from the delighted look on her face as he brought her back up and held her close.

Her cheeks were bright pink, her dark eyes glittering along with her broad smile.

"Careful, now, or I might think you're actually starting to have a good time."

"I am." She did a little jig in his arms, nodding toward her shoes. "I feel like I could dance all night. Thank you for asking Rafe to heal me. And thanks for standing up for me during the meeting with everyone too."

Aric shrugged. "No thanks necessary for either one. Partners stick together."

"Is that what we are now?"

He nodded, brushing a stray tendril of dark hair off her cheek. "For better or worse, Mrs. Bouchard."

"Right," she murmured. "Until D.C. do we part."

He nodded, uncertain why the comment felt like a jab. Once his work for Nikolai was finished, he was leaving Montreal. Kaya had been making it fairly clear that she was as eager for him to go as he was. Perhaps more so.

They continued to dance in silence now, one slow song after another. Eventually, Rafe and Siobhan drifted quietly back into the mansion. Aric didn't have to guess anymore if his friend was falling hard for the female. The truth of it had been written all over his face tonight.

Christ, what had gotten into Rafe?

He'd had no shortage of women throwing themselves in his path from the time they were teens, yet Aric had never seen his best friend pay more than passing attention to any single one. Now, after a handful of days, he only had eyes for this soft-spoken Irish beauty.

Aric practically snorted at how ridiculous it seemed.

Until he considered the woman he currently held in his arms.

But whatever was going on between Kaya and him was different. She was no meek flower in need of rescuing. She was a tough, ambitious woman. Fiercely independent, formidable.

He liked that about her. Hell, he respected her as much as any other warrior he knew.

And yes, he wanted her.

Of all the complications his detour to this city might have posed for him, Kaya Laurent had been the one he'd least expected.

She seemed determined to avoid his gaze now, keeping her attention rooted on Mira and Kellan who swayed on the makeshift dance floor only a few yards away. "They make it look easy, don't they?"

Aric didn't suppose she was talking about dancing. Not the way her eyes followed the mated pair, a tender awe in her expression.

"It wasn't easy getting here, though. First they had to come through fire together," he reminded her. "But yeah, their bond is stronger than anything that could ever come between them again. Even death."

She gave a small nod. "If I didn't know them—if I didn't see Mira and Kellan together the way they are after all they've been through—I wouldn't think that kind of love was possible. Not in real life, anyway."

"My parents have it," Aric pointed out. "My sister and her mate too."

"But not you." Slowly, Kaya's gaze swung back to him. "Why haven't you found someone yet?"

"I haven't been looking." As he spoke, her deep brown eyes held him with a vulnerability that devoured every cynical remark or feeling that he might have reached for in the past to explain why he preferred casual encounters over anything that might last. He lifted his hand and stroked the silken side of her face. "Maybe I haven't been looking in the right places."

She went still in his arms, silent for the longest moment. "What are you doing?" There was wariness in her voice, even a note of anger. Although she'd stopped dancing with him, she didn't draw out of his embrace. "What are *we* doing, Aric?"

"I thought we were trying to decide whether to finish this dance or end it and say goodnight."

He wasn't merely talking about moving together on a dance floor, and she knew it. Her guarded gaze said it all. "Don't you mean good-bye? You're leaving Montreal as soon as you can."

"Yes. I am," he admitted. "I've been getting the feeling you might be happy to see me go."

The fact that she didn't answer right away took him aback. When she finally did speak, her voice was barely a whisper. "I can't do this with you, Aric. I want to go back inside now."

Her eyes said just the opposite. So did the small, jagged sigh that escaped her parted lips.

"No, you don't. That's not what you want." He shook his head, refusing to believe her lie. "You're still in my arms. You don't want to run away from me any more than I want you to."

He knew he was right when he gently cupped her face and instead of protesting, she murmured his name like a plea.

Like a softly uttered prayer.

He bent his head and she met him more than halfway, their mouths coming together in a kiss that was both tender and explosive. The connection blazed through his senses like a wildfire. He didn't want to release her, but he couldn't ignore the fact that they weren't alone on the terrace.

He broke away on a low curse, his amber-lit eyes bathing her face in an unearthly glow. There was no denying his desire for her. It was there in his transformed, heated gaze, and in the fullness of his fangs, which throbbed with the same intensity of the arousal now straining behind the zipper of his dark jeans.

"I'm afraid," she whispered, so quietly it almost wasn't a sound at all.

Aric knew what it cost her to say that. Kaya Laurent was a warrior at heart. She didn't need the Order to tell her as much. Aric didn't need anyone to confirm that about her, either. He saw her bravery and resilience in everything she did. But especially in this moment, in the wake of that soft confession.

She was tough and indomitable, yet he held her like glass in his arms now, certain that beneath the strong exterior was a woman who'd been broken in more ways than she would ever admit.

He kissed her again, then ran the pad of his thumb over the glistening softness of her lips. "Come with me, Kaya."

It was more question than demand. He had to allow her that, because if she stepped away from this terrace with him, they both knew where the night was going to lead.

She stared into his eyes in silence.

Then she slipped her hand into his.

CHAPTER 12

Kaya didn't look to see if Mira and Kellan were watching as she and Aric stopped dancing and slipped away from the terrace together. The moment felt too personal, no room for anyone else's eyes or judgment.

Right now, it was only Aric and her.

No room for the reality of the fact that his life waited in another city, while her future with the Order teetered precariously here in Montreal.

He picked up the blanket Siobhan had left behind on the terrace, then walked Kaya out onto the lawn. The mansion was built on a large, woodland hill. The forest of tall pines and enormous maple and oak trees provided seclusion for the command center, as well as acres of privacy for training exercises and other Order business.

Aric led her into the dense woods, walking what seemed to be a deliberate path.

"Where are we going?"

A smile curved his sensual mouth. "You'll see."

In a few minutes, they reached the summit and a steep ledge of granite that overlooked the city below. The tree line stopped only a couple of yards short of the edge, which provided an unparalleled view of Montreal's lights and the wide river that cut through it in the distance.

Kaya turned a surprised look on him. "You know this place?"

"When I was a kid my family used to visit Niko and Renata and Mira here in the city. Every chance I got to explore these woods, I'd end up here. There's no view like this anywhere else."

She laughed softly and shook her head.

"What's so funny?"

"This is my favorite place in all the world. Whenever I need time and space to think, I come up here." She gave his hand a little tug. "Come on. The best spot to sit is right near the edge."

He followed her out of the woods and into the open air on the ledge. They spread the blanket on the last few feet of smooth stone before the granite shelf ended in a sheer drop several hundred feet down.

Kaya sat down in the center of the small patch of wool, her legs stretched out in front of her. Aric joined her, leaving barely an inch between them and resting one arm over his updrawn knee. With the moon and stars above them and Montreal's glittering lights scattered in the distance below, neither of them spoke for a while.

Maybe it should have been awkward, coming out here with the knowledge that she would soon be undressed beneath this Breed male with him inside her, but she felt only calm when she looked over and saw Aric seated next to her.

It felt safe, perched at the edge of a lethal drop next to a man she barely knew and dared not trust.

Not beyond tonight, anyway.

Nothing could touch her up here. This hill had been a beacon for so much of her life, the only steady thing she had. Tonight it didn't only belong to her, but to Aric too.

Tonight, it belonged to both of them.

And maybe that's why she felt comfortable giving him a small piece of her truth.

"When I was little, my mom used to tell me that terrible monsters lived on this hill. She said they had hideous, sharp teeth and liked to eat children."

Aric glanced at her, his brows raised. "Not a fan of my people, I take it?"

"Not really," she replied, more understatement than he could possibly know. "I was so terrified from the stories she told me, I used to look up at this hill and wonder if anyone was sitting up here, looking at me too. Monsters waiting to swoop down into the city and chew me up. She made sure I believed every awful thing she said. She thought it was funny that I was so afraid. I don't think she was ever satisfied until I was crying or hiding in a corner somewhere begging her to leave me alone."

"Sounds like some great parenting skills."

"She was an awful, hateful person," Kaya admitted, no varnish on that truth. "From all I know of her, she was making bad choices from the time she was a teen. Apparently, things didn't get any better after she became a mother. Some of my first memories of her were watching her either passed out or sticking a needle in her arm. We were homeless more often than not. That is, when she wasn't shacking up with some gangbanger or john she'd just met."

Aric's eyes were solemn, but not pitying. Thank God for that. "I'm sorry. No kid deserves that kind of childhood."

She shrugged. "I survived. More than I can say for her. She was dead by the time I was sixteen."

"Overdose?"

Kaya shook her head. "One of her boyfriends beat her to death over twenty dollars she stole from his wallet. Even though I hated her, she was still my mother. I tried to defend her. I'm only lucky he didn't decide to kill me too. But he did . . . other things."

"Ah, Kaya. Christ." Anger blazed in Aric's eyes. "Who is this son of a bitch? Tell me and you know I'll deal with him."

"There's no need," she admitted tonelessly.

Still, his rise to her defense melted a lot of the cold that lingered inside her whenever she reflected on her past. But she wasn't looking for a hero. She'd learned a long time ago that she was the only person she could ever count on.

"Mom's boyfriend had a fetish for weapons. And because I lived in fear of monsters attacking in the middle of the night, I made sure I knew where he kept the key to the gun cabinets." She glanced at Aric. "He'll never hurt anyone ever again."

He stared at her, a look of grim understanding in his eyes. "Do you have any idea how much courage that took, doing what you did?"

"Courage?" She scoffed lightly. "I was scared to

death."

"Yes. And you acted anyway." He reached out, cradling her cheek in his palm. "What about now? Are you still afraid of the monsters that live on this hill?"

"No." She turned her face into the warmth of his hand. "After that day, I wasn't afraid of anything. I lived on the street for a while, bounced around with people I knew . . . people I thought I knew. Eventually, I ended up on this hill. I slept up here for two nights, waiting for the monsters inside the mansion down below to come out and kill me while I slept. Maybe I was daring them to. They never did."

Aric cocked his head, silently considering. "Nothing gets past Niko, so I'm sure he knew you were up here."

Kaya nodded. "When I woke up that first morning, someone had covered me with a blanket and left a backpack with food in it. The second day, I found a business card for a private youth shelter in town, run by an old man named Jack."

"Anna's Place?"

"That's right." Kaya stared at him, astonished. "How did you know?"

"I've heard Renata mention it once or twice. She spent some time at Anna's Place when she was a kid too. Jack means a lot to her."

"I didn't know that," Kaya murmured. "And, yeah, Jack was a good man. One of the kindest I've ever known. I heard he passed a few years ago, but the shelter is still up and running."

Aric grunted. "Got a feeling I know who might have a hand in that."

Kaya looked at him in question. "You don't think Renata and Niko—"

"Wouldn't surprise me at all. I don't know the details, but to hear them talk, they credit Jack for saving both their lives back when they first met." Aric stroked her cheek as he spoke. "What about you? How long did you stay with Jack at the shelter?"

"Not long." Kaya shrugged and drew out of his touch, uncomfortable with the return to her own past. "I had to leave after a couple of months."

"Had to leave?"

"Decided to leave," she amended, trying her best not to squirm beneath the careful weight of his stare. "I didn't belong there. I didn't want to bring any trouble to Jack's doorstep."

"Trouble from the people your mom had been involved with?"

"I guess so." She'd already said too much about her past and the people who inhabited it. If she kept talking, eventually she would have to start lying to him and that was a line she refused to cross. "I'd rather not think about that time in my life. It's behind me now. That's where I want it to stay."

"All right." His deep voice was quiet, but his eyes hadn't yet released her. "I'm sure it wasn't easy being alone at such a young age. I'm glad you had someone like Jack to look out for you, even for a couple of months. And I'm glad you had Nikolai and Renata looking out for you here on this hill too."

"So am I." Kaya stared out at the endless night sky and the glowing city lights in the valley below. "That first night I sat up here by myself, terrified of what I'd done, I realized it didn't matter whether you were born human or Breed. The only real monsters were the ones who live to hate and hurt other people. I decided then and there if I was going to die for something, it was going to be fighting against those things. I suppose it's ironic that the best role models I ever had for that were the warriors of the Order. About a year ago, I ran into Mira and her team on patrol in the city. She and I became friends right away. I admired her so much—envied her, really. I couldn't have been more excited when she and Nikolai finally agreed to give me a chance to join the team."

Aric leaned over and pressed a kiss to her forehead. It was a chaste brush of his lips, but it touched her as deeply as the hottest meeting of their mouths. "You're an amazing woman, Kaya Laurent. You're also going to make one hell of a warrior. No, scratch that. You already are. The Order is lucky to have you."

She smiled. "Is this the part where you try to make me feel good?"

His low, answering chuckle stroked her senses like velvet. "Yeah. This is that part."

When she glanced at him, she found his eyes ablaze with amber sparks. Silently, he caught her around the nape and dragged her into a slow-burning, doubt-melting kiss.

Kaya reached for him, too far gone to pretend she had even the slightest trace of fear or reservation. They had made no promises to each other. No expectations that this desire that had erupted so swiftly between them stood any chance of becoming something more than just this one night.

She couldn't give him anything more than that.

And he hadn't asked her to.

He hadn't demanded anything at all. His kiss right now was a study in control, too, despite that she could feel the power in his strong hands as he held her. She felt the sharp points of his fangs graze her tongue. Getting this close to the side of him that was pure predator and otherworldly should have given her some pause, but it only inflamed her more.

His fingers drifted along the side of her neck now, trails of heat radiating from his broad palm and long fingers. Her pulse throbbed as his thumb slowly caressed the sensitive skin below her ear. The unhurried melding of his lips against hers sent pleasure spiraling through her veins. It felt so good, heat pooled in her center, blooming into a deep, fierce yearning.

A growl rumbled in his chest before he tore his mouth away from hers. "Tell me if you don't want this, Kaya. If you're not sure—"

"I am." She held his gaze, reaching up to stroke her fingers over his rigid jaw. "Right now, this is the only thing I'm sure of . . . that I want to be here with you. Just tonight."

His eyes turned molten as she spoke, his pupils narrowed to thin black slits in the center of pure fire. His strong hands drifted to her shoulders, then down onto her breasts. Through the thin fabric of her shirt, her nipples peaked, the buds hard and aching as he kneaded each small mound.

Kaya moaned, wanting to feel more of his touch. She caught his hand in hers and guided him to the hem of her top. Aric understood what she needed, even without the use of the words she couldn't find. His touch was sure yet tender as he unfastened the clasp of her bra and caressed her bare flesh with his heated palm.

Everywhere he touched her, she was in flames. He kissed a slow path up the length of her throat, then along her jaw line, until his lips found hers once more. Kaya welcomed his passion, opening to him as his tongue swept the seam of her mouth. He groaned as she sucked him in deeper, growled with pure male approval as she wrapped her fingers around the back of his head and held him more firmly against her mouth.

He caressed her naked breasts, then his hand slid down her belly and into the loose waistband of her jeans. His thick groan when he found her wet cleft vibrated all the way into her marrow. She shuddered, lost to the wicked pleasure of his fingers.

"You're trembling," he murmured, drawing away just far enough to study her face. "Am I going too fast?"

"No." She shook her head, eyes riveted to all of the changes that were playing over his handsome, unearthly face and powerful body just from giving her pleasure. "You're doing everything just right."

Above the collar of his dark T-shirt and beneath the short sleeves that clung to the smooth power of his muscled biceps, Aric's *dermaglyphs* pulsed with color. The Breed skin markings deepened from their normal golden hue to shades of burgundy, gold, and violet. Kaya ran her fingers along the swirling curves and tapered arches of his *glyphs*, awed by their inhuman beauty.

"I've never been this close to a Breed male before," she admitted quietly. "I mean, not like this."

"Never?" He grunted, a smile bowing his full lips. "In that case, I guess I'd better make this memorable."

"It already is."

On a dark purr, he claimed her mouth in another searing kiss. He kept touching her, kept kissing her and stroking her as he slowly removed her clothing, unveiling her body to him from the waist up.

His fevered gaze rooted on the tiny scarlet birthmark

that rode her belly, just above her navel. Kaya moaned as his tongue traced the teardrop-and-crescent-moon symbol that had declared her a Breedmate from the moment of her birth. That mark had earned her only scorn and abuse from the people who called themselves her family. Now, Aric lavished it with worshipful kisses, his eyes crackling with care and respect and unfathomable desire.

"You'll be my first too," he said, his voice rough like gravel. "I've never touched a woman with the Breedmate mark before."

"Why not?" She was almost afraid to ask, dreading that she'd misread him somehow. If he uttered a cold word now, it would crush her.

"Because, beautiful Kaya . . . I've never met someone I wanted as much as you."

On a dark purr, he eased her down onto her back on the blanket. His mouth tasted every inch of her exposed skin, his roving tongue and teeth making her arch and shiver with arousal. Slowly, he made his way down to the buttoned waistband of her jeans. His hands moved swiftly, deftly, removing the rest of her clothing and shoes in moments.

Then his kiss continued, starting at her ankle this time and making a maddeningly unrushed trek up the length of her bare calf and knee, to the tender flesh of her inner thigh. When his mouth found her naked sex, she arched into him, her hands fisted in the blanket. Aric's kiss here was as reverent as the one he lavished on her Breedmate mark.

"Fuck, Kaya . . . you taste so sweet."

She sucked in a shaky breath, tipping her head back as the spiral of pleasure coiled tighter in her core. He parted her legs wide, his golden head moving shamelessly between them. She clamped down on her bottom lip when his tongue circled the tight bundle of nerves between her slick folds. He suckled her clit ruthlessly, his mouth and fingers stroking her into a frenzy.

She couldn't hold back her release even if her life depended on it. Pleasure crashed over her, wave after glorious, unstoppable wave. She cried out, surrendering the raw, broken sound to the woods and sky around her.

Aric was watching her when she dragged her heavy eyelids open, her breath and body heaving. His fangs flashed in the moonlight, razor-sharp points filling his mouth. The burning coals of his gaze stayed locked on her as he stripped off his clothes, then settled himself on his bent knees in the open V of her legs.

His *glyphs* were alive and seething with rich colors now, but she only needed to glance farther down to see the even more impressive evidence of his arousal. His cock jutted thick and proud between his muscled thighs.

She reached for him, filling her hands with the length and girth of him. He closed his eyes as she stroked him, his face going taut and intense with what seemed to be barely leashed control. Finally, he let out a rough snarl and rose over her.

Kaya moaned as he settled into the wetness of her cleft then pushed inside on a slow, unending thrust. She gasped as he filled her, stretching her nearly to the point of pain. His hips bucked and rocked against her, the steady tempo he started with soon gaining in power.

"Christ, you feel incredible," he uttered in that deep gravel growl that made her melt. "I don't want to stop moving inside you. Fuck, Kaya. I can't stop."

"So, don't." She smiled up at him, craving everything he gave her. "Don't stop, Aric."

He roared his approval, a wordless, animal sound. All she could do was hold on as he crashed against her, his big body dominating her, stirring something dark and fevered to life within her too.

As pleasurable as he felt inside her, it was Aric's wildness that sped her orgasm this time. He held her like he couldn't get close enough, kissing her as if he wanted to drown in her. Driving so deep she could no longer tell where his body ended and hers began. When he came, it was on a long, guttural shout, his eyes blazing, locked in an unbreakable hold with hers.

Kaya felt boneless, adrift in a sea of intense sensation and unexpected, confusing emotions. She looped her arms around his neck, as stunned and unprepared as he seemed to be for the power of what they had just shared.

He stared at her as his body slowed above her. There was tenderness in his fiery gaze . . . and torment. A low curse escaped him, muttered quietly under his breath as he reached up to sweep some of her dark hair from her face.

When he started to withdraw, Kaya held on tighter.

She gave a small shake of her head. "Don't. Not yet. I'm not ready to end this dance and say goodnight."

His mouth quirked. "You mean, good-bye?"

She couldn't pretend to see the humor in that now. Even though she knew her own survival depended on keeping her distance from this male and the tumult of feelings he was awakening in her. She didn't know what ached more, the need she felt for Aric or the futility of that desire.

He bent his head down and nipped her lower lip.

"Tell me, lovely Kaya. Has anyone ever made you come while you watched the sun rise?"

She shook her head, incapable of words.

His playful grin broke her heart. "Good. That means we've got another first to share before real life calls us home."

He rolled over onto his back, bringing her atop him. Their legs entangled, bodies still intimately joined, he drew her head down to his and claimed her mouth in a possessive kiss as he thrust his hips and began all over again.

CHAPTER 13

There were few things Nikolai relished more in life than the sight of his Breedmate nestled peacefully in the safe haven of their bed. For a warrior who'd known little else but combat and bloodshed for most of his long life, it stunned him how helpless—how infinitely humbled—he felt each time he looked at his beautiful Renata and realized that she was his.

That she lay in their bed heavy with his child—their son, who would be arriving anytime now—only made Niko's love for Renata deepen all the more.

And his desire.

Slowly, so as not to disturb the ebony-haired siren as she slept, he lifted the coverlet and slipped back into bed with the same stealth he'd used to leave it a short while ago. It didn't surprise him that Renata stirred now despite his care. Their blood bond connected them on a level that went beyond basic senses. She would feel the depth of his arousal for her thrumming in his veins even before she felt the physical evidence of it tucked against the rounded curve of her naked backside.

Her soft little moan made his cock twitch with unabashed interest.

"Your feet are cold," she murmured, sleep roughening her already sultry voice.

Niko dropped a kiss on her bare shoulder as he wrapped his arms around her. "Nothing else on me is cold, I promise."

He pulled her closer, until they were spooned together with no space between them. Renata laughed quietly as she settled against his hard body. "Is that a Magnum in your pocket, or are you just happy to see me?"

His answering chuckle sounded as hungry as he felt. "Baby, I'm always happy to see you."

He moved against her, unable to resist the heat of her soft curves. He would never tire of holding her, whether they were simply lying under the covers in each other's arms or enjoying more vigorous activity. Both of which he intended to indulge in this morning.

He had never known what true contentment felt like until fate blessed him with Renata.

"Where've you been?" she asked, sighing as she nestled into his embrace. "I woke up a few minutes ago and you weren't here."

"I heard a noise downstairs. Someone was just coming in after spending the night outside. A couple of someones, that is." He grunted, still bemused by what he saw. "Evidently, Aric and Kaya decided to catch the sunrise together."

"What?" Renata shifted in his arms, turning to face

him. Disbelief shone in her jade green eyes. "Are you saying you think they had sex last night?"

"Judging from the way they were looking at each other as they came inside, hell, they might be going at it again somewhere right now."

It was a joke, but Renata didn't laugh. "Niko, they only just met."

"Since when has that ever made any difference?" He grinned. "It didn't make much of a difference to us."

"I don't know if I like this." Renata frowned, concern bracketing her mouth. "She only acts like she's tough, Niko. Inside, Kaya's still that scared kid we found camped out on our hill a few years ago."

He couldn't argue that, nor would he try. Renata knew a thing or two about acting tough to cover deep wounds. As formidable and strong as his amazing Breedmate was, even when Nikolai first laid eyes on her, she'd been scared too. She'd been scarred in ways that staggered him even now.

"What if Aric breaks her heart, Niko?"

"What if she breaks his?" He shook his head, reaching out to sweep aside a tendril of dark hair that fell over her pinched brow. "Just about the most dangerous thing a man can do is let a beautiful, broken female into his heart. And into his bed. He's a goner before he realizes it."

Some of the worry in her eyes faded as he cupped her face in his palm and kissed her. When she finally surrendered all of her troubled thoughts on a slow sigh, Niko gathered her close and deepened the gentle meeting of their lips into a kiss that made them both moan with need.

With their legs tangled and Renata's body pressed

against the front of his, Nikolai couldn't think of any better way to greet the day. His son, however, seemed to disagree. A hard kick rippled beneath the stretched skin of Renata's rounded belly.

"Oh!" Her eyes flew wide and she drew back with a laugh. "Did you feel that?"

He nodded, unsure if he felt more wonder or annoyance at the baby's interruption. "Our boy is going to have to work on his timing."

"First, he has to get here." Renata's smile was filled with love as she placed her hand tenderly atop the swollen rise and made idle circles with her fingers. "I can't wait to hold him in my arms, Niko."

"Maybe there's something we can do about that." He smirked, letting his hand trail off her hip and into the heated juncture of her thighs. Her gaze was skeptical, but she didn't deny him when he stroked her sex. God help him, she was already hot and wet, silky against his fingertips. "They say making love during late term can bring on labor."

"Is that right?" She laughed softly, her voice breathy as he found her clit and toyed with the hard bud. "Since when do you know so much about pregnancy?"

"I know I love the way it looks on you. And I love making it happen."

He kissed her again, devouring the low moan that escaped her when his finger slid between her folds and into the entrance of her body. Despite the depth of his hunger—or his teasing about hastening her labor—Nikolai rolled her onto her back with tender, reverent hands.

On his knees between her spread legs, he gazed down at her, entranced. Worshipful. Renata had always

121

been gorgeous, but right now his mate was a goddess. He had never loved her more.

"How did a son of a bitch like me ever get so lucky?" he murmured, bending to kiss her belly. "I love you, Renata. Christ, I love you both so damned much."

"We know. And we both love you too." Her mouth curved beneath shining eyes that danced with devotion. "Now, let's talk some more about this interesting theory of yours."

"Talk about it?" He smirked, both his fangs and his arousal throbbing with enthusiasm. "Maybe we should test it instead."

Her sultry smile was all the permission he needed. She reached for his erection and her touch nearly undid him on the spot.

It might have, if not for the abrupt buzzing of his comm unit lying on the nightstand next to the bed. The incoming call showed on the display was restricted, but there were few people who knew how to reach him this way. Given the early morning hour, it couldn't be good news.

Niko bit off a curse. "Evidently, our son's not the only one with lousy timing." He grabbed the device and put it to his ear. "Talk to me. What's going on?"

One of his contacts in the local JUSTIS office, a fellow Breed, was on the other end of the line. "There's been an attack down here in Pointe-Claire today. We've got a report of multiple fatalities."

"Shit." Niko's veins went tight. The affluent neighborhood of the city was home to a large population of Breed civilians who not only lived in the area, but fed there as well. The last thing the Order needed to hear about was more bloodshed between mankind and their blood-drinking neighbors. "Tell me what happened."

"We don't know much yet. A groundskeeper called in the report less than a minute ago. Says when he showed up for work this morning, he found the residence broken into via the front door. As soon as he entered and realized something was wrong inside, the witness contacted JUSTIS. We're dispatching a crime unit now to process the scene at the Darkhaven, estimated arrival about fifteen minutes. Given the nature of the attack on a civilian residence, I thought the Order might want to go in first and—"

"Wait a second. Hold up. The attack was on a Darkhaven?" Nikolai gripped his comm unit in an iron grasp. "Are you saying the fatalities are Breed?"

"That's right. At least, that's our understanding from what little we know right now."

"Holy shit." Niko felt Renata's hand come down gently on his shoulder. He glanced at her, knowing his expression must be stark if her anxious gaze was anything to go by. "All right. Thanks for the call, man. I'll have one of my teams on site in less than ten."

CHAPTER 14

The quiet residential street was studded with fine homes and gated driveways, most of the addresses housing Breed families who had settled in the Pointe-Claire neighborhood not long after First Dawn twenty years ago. With the wide expanse of the Saint Lawrence River rolling picturesquely behind the large Darkhaven residences and the tree-lined ribbon of pavement meandering in front of them, it was easy to understand the appeal.

Unfortunately for one of these Breed families, today this peaceful suburban ideal had proven to be only an illusion.

"The address we're looking for should be about a thousand yards up on the right," Mira said from the passenger seat beside Aric. "Park here on the side street. We'll hoof it the rest of the way, so the crime unit reporting in from JUSTIS doesn't spot our vehicle and get their panties in a wad."

He nodded to the Order team captain and pulled off the main street to where she indicated. In the rearview mirror, Kaya's grim gaze met his from the backseat of the SUV.

"Do we know anything about the Breed family who was attacked?"

Mira pivoted around to answer. "The Order ran an ID, but there's not much to tell. Jonathon and Elena Champlain, mated for nine years. He's an accountant with a Breed-owned firm downtown. She's a teacher—or, rather, she was. According to her work records, she's been on leave for the past four months since the birth of their second child. Their other son is seven."

"Two young children at home," Kaya murmured, her voice heavy. "Is there a chance we'll find either of them alive?"

Mira shook her head. "I don't think so. From what Niko was told, it doesn't sound like there were any survivors."

No one spoke as Aric parked the vehicle. The three of them climbed out in silence, all garbed in black patrol fatigues and armed for combat. It was the second time Aric had been tapped for special duty because of his ability to daywalk. The second time he'd been partnered with Kaya in as many days, even though it seemed as if they'd known each other forever as they fell in with Mira at the lead and headed for the red-brick Tudor residence and whatever carnage awaited inside.

Her dread was palpable. Aric jogged alongside her, barely resisting the urge to reach out for her hand in reassurance. To think, just hours ago they'd been making love under the rising sun while elsewhere in the city a family was being slain in their home. Now, instead of holding Kaya in his arms back at the command center, they were dressed for war and speculating on probable body counts of murdered innocents they were already too late to save.

Such was the life of a warrior.

Aric had the stomach to deal with everything his role with the Order demanded, but damned if wanted to see Kaya subjected to the same ugliness. After the childhood she'd described to him, all he wanted was to protect her. To make sure she never suffered a moment's pain or sorrow ever again.

Not that he stood any hope of doing that from D.C.

And not that Kaya wanted any such thing.

Gone was the apprehension that filled her face back in the vehicle. Now, she wore a look of steely purpose as they approached the Darkhaven. Mira motioned them to follow her around to the rear of the large house, sending Kaya into place as a corner sentry while Aric was directed toward a shuttered sliding glass door on the back of the residence.

He nodded without her telling him what she wanted him to do. The locks and steel-reinforced UV blinds took less than a second or two for him to disable. Once he had the obstacles out of the way, he gestured that he would go inside first, check things out.

The stench of spilled blood hit his nose the instant he crept over the threshold and into a warmly appointed living room. Peering toward the front of the house, he noted a large male body that lay unmoving in the foyer. Human, if he had to guess by the sharp copper bite of the dying hemoglobin that tainted the air. But there was another blood scent in abundance here too. Something sweeter than human red cells.

Fuck. Not a good sign.

Nor was the fact that the Darkhaven stood as still and quiet as a tomb.

Aric motioned an all-clear to Mira and Kaya. They entered behind him, slipping into the house in silence.

"Everyone's dead here," he murmured in a low whisper.

They didn't ask if he was sure. His Breed senses were far more acute than both of theirs put together. He jerked his chin in the direction of the foyer and the front door, which hung ajar, swaying faintly in the soft morning breeze.

"Holy shit." Mira's mouth flattened as she strode past him, her long blond braid thumping at her spine as she walked toward the human corpse near the entrance.

Kaya fell in beside Aric, silent, barely breathing. The trio paused just beyond the perimeter of the odd crime scene, no one saying a word for a moment as they each soaked in the details.

The dead man wore a delivery service uniform. Near the bulky shape of his crumpled, semi-prone body was a crushed package and a large spill of coarse black dirt. Blood leaked out from under the human's corpse, coagulating in a dark puddle on the creamy rug and hardwood.

Mira toed the body with the tip of her combat boot, rolling the man onto his back. "Jesus Christ."

His throat and chest had been slashed wide open. Four symmetric lacerations delivered with enough force it was a wonder he hadn't lost his head.

Mira frowned as she glanced over at Aric and Kaya. "What do you guys think? Whatever was in that box must've really pissed off the owner of this Darkhaven."

"No." Kaya's gaze drifted down to the smashed box. "There was nothing in it. Look closer. It's an empty box."

"She's right," Aric agreed. The pieces were starting to fall in place now, painting a picture of cowardice and deception. "The delivery was a setup. It was the only way to get the Darkhaven door open with a minimum of effort."

Mira's face blanched. "At this hour, with the sun blazing over the lawn, there are few Breed who would risk exposure by opening the door to anyone."

"Right," Aric said. "And this dead fuck right here was counting on that fact. He wanted Jonathon Champlain's Breedmate to answer the door because he needed to overpower her in order to get inside."

Mira nodded. "But he came down to protect her. He would've been here in an instant. Less than an instant. Those wounds on the body are evidence enough of that."

"There's a lot of blood on the stairs," Kaya pointed out. "It goes all the way up to the second floor."

Aric nodded grimly. "It's hers. I can smell it from here."

Mira stepped away from the dead man and the mess surrounding his corpse. "So, where is Jonathon Champlain?"

Aric's gaze fell to the strange spill of black dirt at their feet. A chill washed over him, settling in his marrow. "Ah, fuck. No."

He crouched on his haunches and reached for the empty package, moving it to the side so he could have a closer look at what his instincts were telling him but his brain refused to accept as reality.

An acrid odor rose up as he moved the box out of his way. The odd stench was unlike anything he'd ever experienced before, yet every cell in his body recoiled as the smell of ashed Breed remains—not dirt—wafted into his lungs.

Something gleamed within the pile of black cinders. He retrieved it, holding the strange bullet casing up so he could examine it. The round was formed of silvery metal caged around a diamond-hard glass shell that would have contained something far more powerful than gunpowder. A specialized kind of round that served only one purpose.

Killing members of the Breed.

Mira gasped. "Is that what I think it is?"

"An ultraviolet bullet," Aric answered woodenly. "Whoever came in behind the delivery man came in prepared to kill."

Kaya's gaze bounced between them, confused and stricken. "I don't understand. A UV round? How can something like that exist? And since it obviously does, where the hell did it come from?"

"A few weeks ago, a scientist who pioneered major advances in ultraviolet technology was murdered by members of Opus Nostrum," Aric explained. "Opus got their hands on his work and they quickly began developing it into weaponry."

"Breed-killing weapons," Kaya murmured, her hand coming up to her mouth. "Oh, my God."

"The Order has kept all of this under wraps," Mira added. "You know about the UV bomb that Opus tried to detonate at the GNC peace summit earlier this month?"

"Yes," Kaya said. "If you and Kellan and the rest of the Order hadn't killed the Opus member responsible for that bomb, hundreds of Breed diplomats and most of the Order would have been ashed in front of the entire world."

Mira's nod was understated, especially considering the magnitude of what she, along with her mate and the Order, had accomplished that night. "Killing Reginald Crowe and disabling his bomb only stopped one disaster from happening. By then, we'd also learned that Opus was manufacturing large caches of ultraviolet arms and ammunition."

"The Order tracked down a large supply of both in Ireland," Aric told Kaya. "We took out the Opus member who'd been stockpiling the shit and detonated all but a few samples of everything we found, but there was no guarantee that some of it hadn't already leaked out to Opus operatives."

Mira slanted a look at the dead human. "I guess we have an answer to that question now."

Aric nodded, but his mind was already filling with further questions in need of answers. Opus Nostrum may have played some role in this killing, but the selection of a civilian Darkhaven seemed too random. Opus tended toward high-profile targets, not suburban families, Breed or otherwise.

Aric glanced at the stairs and the blood trail that Champlain's Breedmate left behind. Although his senses told him he wasn't going to like what he found up there, he headed in that direction, leading the way for Kaya and Mira.

His gut clenched at the sight of another pile of ashes at the top of the stairs. This one was considerably smaller than the one in the foyer. Aric tried not to picture a seven-year-old Breed boy racing out of his bedroom in terror as his parents struggled with the intruders downstairs.

Kaya's strangled gasp behind Aric told him that she'd spotted the child's remains too.

"Oh, God," Mira whispered. "The mother's bloody footprints lead all the way to the bedroom at the end of the hall."

"Yeah," Aric answered, his booted feet moving leaden beneath him as they approached the pastel-colored room that stood as silent as the grave ahead of him.

In his mind, the logical sequence of the attack played out in horrific detail. The morning delivery, used as a trap to lure Elena Champlain to the door alone. The first assailant pushes his way inside, dropping the ruse of a package and crushing it under his boot as he knocks the female down with his fist, splattering her blood on the wall.

Her mate flashes downstairs in that next instant, the blood bond and her likely screams alerting him to the danger. He kills the delivery man to give his Breedmate a chance to run for safety—but the assailant wasn't alone. The others push inside now, at least one of them armed with ultraviolet weaponry. They ash Jonathon Champlain. Another ashes their young son, who would have been just old enough to be a threat to an unarmed human. To a man carrying an ultraviolet weapon? The child would be as inconsequential as a gnat.

Any Breed male allergic to sunlight, no matter his size or skills, would be no match for a tiny bullet filled with liquid UV.

As for the lady of the house, Aric had a sickening feeling that her death was far less merciful.

The door to the nursery was wide open. He entered, and it was all he could do not to stagger back on his heels.

The female lay on the floor, brutalized, her clothing torn off. Stab wounds and slashes all over her body. In the crib, her infant son had been reduced to a blackened scorch mark against the soft white sheets and smiling stuffed animals.

And on the walls, written in the Breedmate's blood, were shocking messages of hate.

Breed whore!

Death to the bloodsuckers!

Ash them all!

There were dozens more, each more graphic and uglier than the next. Aric didn't bother to read them all.

But Kaya and Mira were.

He saw their horror reflected in their eyes as the entirety of the slaying washed over them.

Kaya looked as though the slightest touch would knock her over. Her face was bloodless, shell-shocked. Her dark brown eyes were glazed and welling with unspilled tears.

Mira blew out a soft curse. When she spoke, her voice was hardly more than a whisper. "Please collect all of the spent UV rounds, Aric. We should bring them back for Niko to analyze. I'm going to . . . I need to go outside for a minute."

"All right." He nodded once, accepting his grim task with total solemnity. "Kaya, you should go too."

At first, she didn't move. Didn't so much as blink.

Aric reached out for her, his touch landing lightly on

her shoulder. She flinched, a bone-deep jerk of movement that seemed to startle her out of the horrified daze that gripped her. Her gaze lifted to his, bleak and unreadable. He couldn't resist cupping her trembling jaw in his palm.

"Go on with Mira," he gently instructed her. "You don't need to see any more of this."

She gave him a wobbly nod. Then, unspeaking, she pivoted and left him to finish his work.

CHAPTER 15

Kaya hung her head over the sink in her quarters' en-suite bathroom and splashed a handful of cold water over her face. Her stomach heaved, threatening to revolt for the second time since she had returned with Aric and Mira from the Darkhaven in Pointe-Claire.

They'd been back at the command center for a couple of hours and she still couldn't purge the horrific scene from her mind. The blood and death and hatred. The unimaginable cruelty of the ones who'd perpetrated the slaughter of that innocent family in their home.

But her stomach turned for another reason too.

One that put a coldness in her veins as she gathered her shower-damp hair into a long ponytail, then donned running gear and headed out of her room to the mansion corridor outside.

She had to get away from the confinement of the command center's walls, if only for a short while. She needed space and time to process everything that had happened, not only today but ever since Aric showed up in Montreal.

More than anything, she needed to look for some clarity . . . no matter where that search might lead her.

Aric was coming out of a guest room at the other end of the hallway as she headed for the central staircase that led to the large foyer. He held a tablet in one hand, his comm unit in the other.

"Hey," he said, his deep voice soothing with just that simple greeting. "I was on my way to check on you. Thought I'd head down to the war room to dig back into the reception images and look for Mercier's Opus contact."

"Oh. Right." It seemed like a week had passed since they'd begun that task together. If only it felt so long since she'd lain naked and pleasured in Aric's arms. She could hardly look at him now without reliving the bliss of his touch . . . and the erotic power of his body as he moved inside her. She cleared her throat. "I was, um, just going out for a little bit. After this morning, I could use a long run."

"You want some company?"

"No." She only hoped her reply didn't sound as abrupt as it felt on her lips. "I won't be gone long. If anyone asks for me, will you let them know I've gone out?"

"Sure." He nodded. "When you get back, come down and join me. We need to nail this Opus bastard now more than ever."

She wouldn't deny the importance of excising a cancer like Opus Nostrum. If they had supplied the UV ammunition used in today's slayings—and there seemed to be zero doubt about that—then the Order should show no mercy to anyone with ties to the terror group or their sympathizers. On that, she and Aric were agreed.

But it was the idea of teaming up with him again in close quarters that made a knot of reluctance form in her breast. It had been a mistake letting her guard down around him. An even bigger mistake making love with him, no matter how incredible it had been.

She couldn't allow herself to make that mistake again. She needed to keep her head on straight. Stay focused on the things that mattered. If she had let her priorities slip since meeting Aric Chase, what she witnessed at the Darkhaven today had been a stark wakeup call.

And that meant keeping her distance from the Breed male as much as possible between now and the time that he would be returning to his life in D.C.

"Kaya." He said her name softly, concern etched on his handsome face. "Are you okay?"

"Fine." She nodded. Forced all of her misgivings and regrets deep down in order to give him a casual shrug. "I'm fine. I'll see you when I get back from my run."

She stepped around him, feeling his gaze at her back as she jogged down the stairs and exited the mansion. Outside, the summer afternoon was bright and warm and clear. She soaked in every bit of it as she set off at a comfortable pace, through the command center's main gate and out to the private road that descended from the peak of the broad, highly secured hill to the main street below.

Ordinarily, her route might have taken her around the base of the hill on Summit Circle. But today, instead of taking the familiar path, Kaya turned away from it and jogged in another direction. About half a mile down was a large boulevard that would eventually take her into the heart of Montreal. She followed the divided stretch of pavement for several blocks, until she spotted a taxi heading her way.

She signaled to the driver, glancing anxiously around her as the car slowed in front of her. "I need to go to Dorval, please."

At his nod, she climbed in. Twenty minutes later, the driver had delivered her to a depressed section of the city southwest of Montreal's downtown. The area hadn't been a stellar place to be at any point in history, but during the wars that followed First Dawn, this patch of urban sprawl had become a magnet for gangs and rebels of all stripes. Now the ruins of old warehouses and factories long vacated stood drab and dilapidated on either side of the street. Panhandlers and addicts camped at nearly every intersection, including the one where Kaya instructed the taxi driver to drop her off.

"You sure you wanna be down here, miss?" The middle-aged man ran his palm over his grizzled jaw. "If you want me to wait for ya, in this section of town, I gotta add twenty bucks surcharge for every five minutes I risk my vehicle standing at the curb."

Kaya shook her head as she handed him the fare for the drive. "I can find my own way back. Keep the change."

He took her money and wasted no time pulling away after she got out of the car. Not that she could blame him. There were few people who chose to spend time in this area of the city. And usually, if they were lucky enough to get out, they made a point never to come back.

Kaya should know. She'd been one of them.

She walked up the street toward a rat hole bar with a sagging roof and a facade of weathered brown wood scarred with old gunshots and tagged with layers of painted gang graffiti. There was no signage on the door or visible from the street.

Then again, no one who belonged anywhere near this place needed to be told who owned it.

Those who didn't belong were never given a chance to make the mistake twice.

Kaya counted herself in the latter camp, especially now that she had pledged herself to the Order. Nevertheless, she reached for the black iron latch on the door and pulled it open.

The place was empty and dank. It reeked of stale cigarette smoke and spilled liquor. In the light shining in from behind Kaya as she entered, she saw a dark-haired woman hunched over behind the bar with a mop and bucket.

"We ain't open yet."

The young woman's weary voice held a rasp that made her sound as derelict and forsaken as her surroundings. Kaya disregarded the unwelcome greeting and walked inside anyway.

As the door thumped closed at her back, the woman behind the bar huffed out a curse and swung around with a scowl. "I said we ain't—"

Her words cut short the instant her eyes met Kaya's. Astonishment flashed in her gaze, followed by disbelief . . . then a cold, hard suspicion.

Kaya felt all of those things as she looked at her too.

She hadn't seen this woman's face in years, since she was sixteen.

But no, that wasn't quite right.

She saw this face every time she looked in the mirror.

Her twin sister had aged considerably since then, her dark brown eyes narrowing on Kaya as if she were the enemy. And maybe she was.

"Hello, Leah."

"What are you doing here?" No trace of warmth in that accusing question. Only mistrust. Animosity, even.

Kaya steeled herself to the twinge of hurt she felt at her sibling's glower. "I need to talk to you."

Leah glanced nervously over her shoulder, toward the swinging door that led to the back of the bar and the kitchen. She stayed right where she stood, with the bar between her and Kaya like an impenetrable wall. "We've had nothing to say to each other for the past four years. How the hell did you know where to find me?"

"I ran into someone who knows you—or did, anyway. His name was Jacob Portman. He was working security at the Rousseau-Mercier wedding."

Leah's glare morphed into a confused frown. "You spoke to Red?"

"We exchanged a few words," Kaya replied, feeling no emotion for the human who had opened fire on Aric after attempting to attack her too.

She'd read his mind in those frantic moments and knew the hatred he had for Aric on sight, simply because he was Breed. She had registered his alliance to violent rebel gangs like the ones who frequented this bar, and the ones who'd carried out this morning's slayings just a few miles here.

"Portman's dead," she told her sister. "I killed him."

Leah gaped. "Are you insane? Red was one of Angus's men from back in the day."

"Well, now he can meet him in hell."

"You're crazy." Her twin let out a sigh and gave a hard shake of her head. "You can't be here, Kaya. I don't want to talk to you. I don't ever want to see you again."

"Why not? Do you have a reason to be afraid of me now?"

"Fuck you." The response flew at Kaya like a slap to the face. She should have seen it coming. That was always her sister's method for dealing with difficult conversations and hard choices. Lash out with cutting words and claws bared. "Why are you here? If you're looking for some kind of teary, pathetic reunion, you can forget it."

"No, that's not what I was hoping for," Kaya admitted quietly.

She'd all but given up on that idea a long time ago.

One of the last times they saw each other had been after their mother's murder. The night sixteen-year-old Kaya had shot and killed the man responsible for her death, then fled into the city alone. She had run to the only person she knew and felt she could trust: her twin sister.

But Leah had problems of her own, even then. A runaway from the age of fourteen, she had turned out too much like their mother. Troubled. Addicted. Under the control of bad men. Heartless killers who spewed the same hate and lies the girls had been exposed to all their young lives.

Kaya had refused to stay for more than a handful of days. And Leah refused to leave. It was the last time they had seen each other. Until this very moment.

"I want you to know I'm with the Order now."

Leah reeled back. "With them? What the hell does

that mean?"

"I'm training with them here in Montreal, to become a warrior."

Her sister gaped as if Kaya had just told her she intended to tear someone's head off and drink from the stump of their neck. "I hope you didn't come all the way down here just to tell me that."

"No," Kaya said. "I came to see if you know anything about a Breed family who were murdered this morning over in Pointe-Claire."

Leah's face was unreadable. "Why would I know anything about that?"

"Because whoever did it left quite a calling card. They broke into a Darkhaven and slaughtered the entire family—the parents and two little boys, one of them just an infant."

Leah swallowed at that, the first reaction she gave that even hinted at emotion.

Kaya pressed on. "They savaged a young mother, Leah. Using her blood, they wrote awful things on the wall above her body. Things I used to hear quite a lot when our mother was alive. Things I heard from the people you call your friends—ignorant assholes like the one who owns this bar."

Leah's gaze flicked over her shoulder once more. She lowered her voice to a tight whisper. "If you're trying to shock me by insinuating Angus or his men had something to do with a killing like that, save your breath. I know what he's capable of."

"And yet you stay with them. All this time, Leah, you've stayed."

She didn't respond, but a storm churned within the dark brown eyes that were so similar to Kaya's own.

There was torment in her gaze, but she refused to give it voice.

"If you know something about the attack on that Darkhaven, you need to tell me."

Leah crossed her arms. "I don't. But even if I did, talking to the Order is the last thing I would do."

Kaya blew out a curse in frustration. "Don't you care about what's right or wrong? Doesn't justice mean anything to you?"

"You have no idea what matters to me," she shot back now, angry and defensive. "You never did. You were always the strong one, the smart one. Always whispering to me about your dreams and plans for your future, even when we were little kids. The only thing I ever wanted out of my fucked up life was to survive it."

"At the end of the day, that's all anyone wants," Kaya replied.

She'd heard the pain in her sister's voice. She understood it the way only a twin could, connected on a level that went deeper than basic siblings. But Leah wasn't reaching out. She was pushing back, barring Kaya as if she were a stranger.

And maybe after all this time, that's all they were to each other now.

Kaya recalibrated her feelings for her sister, resolved that she wasn't talking to her twin but questioning a member of a hate group so tight-knit and steeped in doctrine it might as well be labeled a cult.

"Do they know you're one of us too?" Leah's question caught her off guard. It held a curious edge, but there was no mistaking the accusation in it, either. "Is that why they sent you here?"

"They didn't send me. And I'm not one of you,"

Kaya replied, but the denial lacked the venom she wanted it to have. "I haven't been part of this world for a long time."

Yet she'd been born into it, raised within it. For the first sixteen years of her life, all she'd known was the abhorrent, violent world that somehow still held her sister in its thrall. As much as she wanted to deny it, Kaya's shame over that fact ran deep. It would likely never fade.

"Oh, my God," Leah whispered, openly astonished. "They don't know."

Kaya felt her jaw clench. "Don't try to make this about me. If you know anything about those killings today, I need you to tell me. Please, Leah. Whoever did it showed up prepared to take out any Breed male they came in contact with. The Order is investigating. It's not going to take them long to come around here asking the same questions I am."

Leah glanced away from her now, her mouth flattened in a hard line. She picked up a damp cloth and began scrubbing the scarred countertop of the bar. "This conversation is over. I want you leave now, Kaya."

Instead of doing what she asked, Kaya stepped forward. "Have you ever heard Angus mention Opus Nostrum?"

Leah's hand stilled. Her face paled a bit, blood draining from her cheeks and lips. At that same moment, a thump sounded from the back room of the tavern. Someone had just come in from the alley at the rear of the place. Kaya didn't have to guess who it was.

"Shit," Leah hissed. "Get out of here, Kaya. Don't ever come back, do you understand? Angus will kill me if he sees me talking to you."

"Then come with me."

She blurted the offer before the thought had barely formed in her mind. But she meant it. Never mind everything that had passed between them four years ago or at any time before or after. Leah was her sister, her twin. She couldn't walk away without trying to reach her, to appeal to any thread of humanity still remaining in her.

"I mean it, Leah. You can leave with me, right now. I promise you, the Order will keep you safe."

"Shut up." Leah gave a vigorous shake of her head, sending her dark brown hair sifting around her shoulders. "Shut up and get out, Kaya. I don't want your help. I don't want anything from you."

More noise sounded from the other area of the bar. Then a voice as jagged and cold as gravel called out. "Raven! Goddamn it, woman. Where the fuck are you?"

When Leah flinched, Kaya reached for her hand. "Come with me before it's too late."

"Too late?" She scoffed, brittle and angry as she wrenched out of her loose grasp. "You have no idea what you're saying. Now, get out of here."

Pain stabbed her as she watched her sister withdraw. "If you refuse now, I may not be able to help you later."

"Go, damn you!" Leah snapped in a harsh whisper. When Kaya's feet refused to take the first step, Leah threw down her wash rag and finally circled the bar. "Get out of here. Before I call him up here to make sure you never come back."

Kaya's gaze snagged on the subtle fullness of her sister's belly. She sucked in her breath and it sounded more like a sob than a gasp. "You're pregnant. Oh, God . . . Leah. Please tell me it doesn't belong to Angus."

But her sister gave her no such reassurance. Her unblinking gaze stayed fixed on Kaya, bleak and hard. Her face was shuttered, inscrutable. Unknowable, even though it was a mirror reflection of Kaya's own features.

"Leah, please—"

"Angus! I'm out here."

Her shout broke Kaya's heart. She backed up a couple of paces, edging toward the door as the clomp of heavy boots vibrated in the floorboards. Her sister turned away as Kaya reached the tavern door.

The last thing she saw of Leah was her stiffened spine before Kaya pivoted and bolted out to the street to make her escape.

CHAPTER 16

Aric dropped an image file into a growing folder of possibles for Kaya to review, then moved on to the next hundred photos that waited on his tablet. It was painstaking work, visually scanning every image from the wedding for a glimpse of a dark head on a portly man who might turn out to be the one she saw leaving the reception. As tedious as the search was, without her having read Mercier's thoughts, the Order wouldn't even have this small advantage in their pursuit of Opus's members.

He let out a heavy sigh, frowning when he considered the way Kaya had acted around him this morning.

They had shared an incredible night together. Hell, sunrise hadn't been half-bad either. He might have been tempted to call it pretty damned close to perfect—if not for the dreadful news that had greeted them not long after they'd come back inside the command center.

The shocking daytime attack on a Darkhaven had put everyone in a grave mood.

In particular, Kaya.

For what wasn't the first time, Aric checked the clock and wondered if he should have insisted on accompanying her for her run. It wasn't that he worried for her safety necessarily. She had been trained to handle herself by some of the most capable members of the Order. She was strong-willed and physically fierce, but she was also shaken to her core by what they had witnessed today. He'd seen that in her eyes after they had returned from the crime scene, even though she had insisted she was fine.

When footsteps approached in the corridor, Aric glanced up, hoping it would be her. But the gait was all wrong, too heavy to be her graceful stride.

He exhaled a curse, leaning back in his seat as Rafe strode into the war room.

His comrade cocked his blond head in question. "Something wrong?"

"I thought you might be Kaya. I'm making some good progress on the photos and I need her help to put this task to bed."

Rafe grunted, then pulled out the chair next to Aric and plopped into it uninvited. "You sure that's the only thing you want to put to bed? You two seemed awfully friendly last night. I've seen you seduce your way around other females often enough to realize there's something unusual going on with this one."

"You're one to talk," Aric volleyed back. He wasn't ready to think about how he really felt about Kaya, much less discuss it with Rafe. Instead, he opted for deflection.

"Just how serious are you about this Siobhan O'Shea?"

"Shit," Rafe said, going quiet for a long moment. "It's serious. I've never met anyone like her, man. She's beautiful and sweet and so damned innocent. I swear, there are times I wonder how someone as pure and lovely as her can be real. And the way she looks at me . . . like I'm her personal hero or something. It's heady stuff."

Aric smirked, reaching out to cuff his friend's shoulder. "My condolences, brother. Sounds like you've got it bad."

"Yeah. I guess I do." He blew out a laugh, but his gaze was as solemn as Aric had ever seen it. "You want to hear something crazy? If I had to construct the perfect woman for myself, Siobhan is it to a T. I don't know why fate decided to put her in my life, but now I can't imagine letting her go."

Aric chuckled. "Coming from you, that does sound crazy."

In all the times they'd caroused together in Boston and more recently in D.C., Rafe had hardly given a second look to any of the countless women who'd tried to catch his eye. His blond mane and aquamarine eyes that turned heads everywhere he went had come from his beautiful mother, Tess. His magnetism with the fairer sex had been a gift passed down from his father, Dante, one of the Order's most dangerous and revered commanders. With his fallen angel appeal and the dark charm and swagger of the devil himself, Rafe could have any woman he desired.

That the golden warrior was smitten with a timid little waif like Siobhan O'Shea made little sense to Aric, but who was he to question his friend's heart?

"Gotta say, never thought I'd see the day you let a woman get under your skin like this," he told him. "Be careful, brother, or you might end up falling in love."

The fact that he didn't deny it or at least come back with a smartass reply told Aric just how captivated he was with the Irish Breedmate.

"I just want to keep her safe," Rafe murmured. "After the hell she's been through, she deserves some happiness. I want her to know she can trust me to protect her."

Aric nodded. He was getting a taste of that feeling himself when it came to Kaya. Except her trust seemed hard to win—maybe even impossible. And while she had definitely survived an awful past, she was far from in need of anyone's rescue. It was a fact that made him respect her even more than if she had been a delicate innocent in search of a hero to save her.

In fact, if he had been pressed to describe his ideal mate she would be a lot like Kaya. Smart, driven, independent. Someone strong and resilient like his own mother, Tavia, or Renata, women who were indomitable despite their scars.

And it didn't hurt that Kaya was a stunning brunette beauty with a killer body and legs that went on for days.

But he wasn't looking for a mate. Unlike his friend Rafe, he wasn't about to let himself careen head over heels just because he was having a good time with a woman any male would be damned lucky to have in his bed.

Or as his blood-bonded Breedmate.

Why the thought of Kaya with anyone else should set his teeth and fangs on edge, Aric didn't know—and didn't care to examine, either.

He was here to do a job, then get on with his life.

Which meant getting his ass back to D.C. as soon as possible, before he was tempted to let things get complicated with Kaya. So far, their relationship was simple. They worked well together. God knew they fit well together physically too. But that was as far as he could allow it to go with her. One and done. No strings attached and no promises of anything more.

Fortunately, Kaya seemed to feel likewise.

Aric told himself it was a good thing.

He glanced at Rafe, arching a brow. "So, what are you saying? You think she might be The One?"

"Like I said, crazy, right?" Rafe grew quiet, then expelled a long breath and stood up. "Listen, I didn't come all the way down here just for relationship counseling."

Aric snorted. "That's a relief."

"Niko wants to see us in his office in about ten minutes. Sounds like we're going to be staying in Montreal until after the baby is born."

"Shit. That could be days." Just what he needed, more time under the same roof with the temptation of Kaya Laurent too close for his peace of mind.

Rafe studied him. "You got somewhere else pressing that you need to be?"

"If I were smart, anywhere but here," he muttered under his breath as he rose from his chair.

They exited the war room and headed up the corridor that would take them to the living quarters of the attached mansion.

"I doubt it's going to be days before the baby arrives," Rafe told him as they walked. "The way Renata looked in the meeting yesterday, she could go anytime.

Niko's already asked to put me on standby to help out if she goes into labor before my mother and the rest of the Order arrives for the birth."

Aric chuckled. "My sympathies to Renata and the baby, if you're their best option for a midwife."

"Fuck you very much," Rafe said, grinning at the jab.

As they headed out toward the residential wing of the mansion, Rafe's demeanor turned somber. "Speaking of infants and new mothers, Mira told me about the situation at that Darkhaven this morning. Jesus, what kind of monster ashes a baby in its crib?"

Aric's blood seethed at the reminder. "The soon-to-be-dead kind, if I have anything to say about it. People like that won't stop until they've seen our entire race scorched from existence."

"People like Opus Nostrum," Rafe said grimly.

Aric shrugged. "Opus may have supplied the ultraviolet rounds, but I'm not convinced they ordered this hit. Someone did this for kicks. Out of a sadistic glee. And if bastards like that have access to UV weapons, today's slayings won't be the last."

"Nikolai's already been in contact with headquarters," Rafe informed him. "He and Gideon are trying to trace the bullet casing you retrieved from the Darkhaven attack to the samples we took from our raid on Fineas Riordan's place in Dublin last week."

"They'll be a match," Aric said. Every instinct he had told him there was little doubt on that score. "There's no telling how much of that shit he'd been able to push out to other Opus members before we destroyed his stockpiles. Now, we have to worry that Opus could be putting this kind of firepower into the hands of rebels and hate groups who've been itching for the chance to start wiping us out."

He and Rafe were in the hallway just outside the mansion's kitchen. The aromas of fresh fruits, baked goods, and coffee wafted out, along with the sounds of female voices. Kaya's among them.

Rafe detoured without explanation—not that Aric had to guess what drew the warrior into the room. Siobhan sat beside Renata at the counter of the kitchen island, a dainty teacup clutched in her hands. The instant she saw Aric's friend, her pretty face lit up with an adoring smile.

"Hey, beautiful." Rafe walked up to her and pressed an intimate kiss below her ear.

Oh, yeah. He was doomed, all right.

As for Aric, he wasn't sure what to think when his gaze collided with Kaya's. Still dressed for her run, she stood on the opposite side of the island from Siobhan and Renata, eating an apple. She set down the fruit, looking uncomfortable as he followed Rafe into the kitchen.

"I was just about to go down and find you."

Her eyes flicked away from him as she spoke. Aric didn't have her ability to read minds, but he didn't need it in order to tell that she was avoiding him for some reason. He'd gotten the same sense earlier, but now everything about her body language and anxious gaze said he was just about the last person she wanted to talk to.

Before she had left the command center, he'd been willing to dismiss her withdrawn demeanor as merely aftershocks of the horror they'd encountered at the Darkhaven crime scene. Now, though, he wondered if there was something more he wasn't seeing.

Maybe her run had given her time enough to regret letting him make love to her.

Hell, he probably ought to regret it, too, but that wasn't the feeling he had when he looked at her. After reassuring himself for most of the morning that one taste of Kaya's sweet body would be enough to sate him for the duration of his time in Montreal, he stood there now, riveted to the sight of her flushed cheeks and the pulse that ticked in a frantic rhythm at the base of her throat.

Renata glanced between them, her gaze shrewdly curious. "Are you two making much progress on the photos from the wedding?"

"As of now, we've got them narrowed down to a few hundred potentials," Aric replied. "Assuming we can find Mercier's Opus contact among the crowds of attendees in the images, all we'll need to do is run a comparison against the guest list and we'll have our man."

"Unless the bastard wasn't invited," Rafe said, his fingers toying with a tendril of Siobhan's strawberry-blonde hair.

"The wedding and reception were locked down as tight as a presidential visit," Kaya interjected. "No one got through the gate without a thorough security check."

Aric gave her an ironic look. "Not unless they had someone like Gideon to construct a reasonable cover for them, that is."

Renata nodded. "And infiltrating an event like that wouldn't be the boldest thing Opus has ever done. Their loyalists could be anywhere."

"Even among the security detail at the Rousseau estate," Rafe pointed out. He glanced at Kaya. "For all

LARA ADRIAN

we know, that guard who confronted you and shot Aric could have been allegiant to Opus—or working as an operative. That could explain why he said he thought he knew you. The Order's only been aware of Opus Nostrum for a few weeks, but that doesn't mean they haven't been studying us for far longer. Maybe they have more intel on the Order and our members than we realize."

"Maybe," she answered quietly, giving him a faint shrug.

Renata let out a curse. "It's one thing for the bastards to come after us. What happened at that Darkhaven today has crossed a hard red line. If it turns out that Opus is putting ultraviolet rounds and weaponry into the hands of rebels or other hate-mongers, then we need to unleash hell on all of them."

Siobhan glanced up at Rafe. "UV weapons? Oh, my God. What happened today?"

"Something terrible," he answered gently. "But Opus and the rest of the animals who did it are going to pay—with a lot of blood and death if the Order has anything to say about it."

As he spoke, Mira strode into the kitchen with Kellan, both of their faces lit with excitement.

"We just got a positive ID on our shredded delivery guy over in Pointe-Claire." She held up a tablet displaying the face of the human corpse they'd found in the Darkhaven foyer this morning. "Rahul Gales. Or, 'Repo,' as he's more commonly known to both law enforcement and the scumbags he runs with on a regular basis."

Mira set the device down on the island countertop for everyone to see. Aric scrolled through the collection of mugshots, rap sheets, and other reports documenting a life of poverty, larceny, drug abuse, and assorted hate crimes.

"Do we know anything else about him?"

Kellan nodded. "Last week, Gales got picked up by JUSTIS for selling narcotics down in Dorval. The guy who bailed him out, Angus Mackie, is a real piece of work too. Most of his underlings call him 'Big Mack.' He owns a seedy bar in Dorval, a known hangout for gangs and other criminals."

"Right," Mira said. "Mackie's only been in Montreal for the last decade, but he's got a long record too."

She touched the screen and brought up another photo and arrest record. Numerous felonies filled the display, everything from assault to murder. The fact that a killer like him wasn't rotting in a prison cell somewhere was a question for another day. Because what struck Aric more than anything else was one of the evidence photos taken of Angus Mackie following one of his arrests.

The image showed the human bared from the waist up, covered in bruises and lacerations. A collection of tattoos rode Mackie's chest and arms, crosses and stars and Gaelic symbols. But there was one tattoo on the criminal's right pectoral that made Aric's blood run cold.

He glanced up at Rafe. "Jesus Christ. Do you see that?"

"Holy hell." His friend's face hardened with grim realization. "A black scarab."

Aric nodded. "He's one of Riordan's men."

"Fineas Riordan?" Siobhan's eyes went wide at the mention of the infamous crime lord from Dublin. "I thought he was dead. I thought the Order killed him recently."

"We did," Rafe replied, stroking her arm. "And if this Angus Mackie turns out to have received UV weaponry from the bastard before we took Riordan out, then Big Mack is next on the list for extermination."

Renata eased herself up from her seat at the island. "I'll go tell Niko what we've found. He'll want to alert D.C. right away."

"Hang on, Rennie. I'll go with you," Mira said, more than likely an excuse to ensure the pregnant Breedmate made the long walk without issues.

The prospect of closing in on someone not only involved in the Darkhaven attack but also linked to a known Opus member had Aric's warrior instincts itching with the need for combat. But he couldn't dismiss the fact that Kaya was still pointedly avoiding his gaze.

She tossed her half-eaten apple into the trash. "I should go clean up and get back to work on those photos."

Aric nodded in acknowledgment, but when she slipped out of the kitchen without another word, he couldn't resist following her to the hallway. He reached out and loosely caught her arm.

"Kaya. You okay?"

"Sure." Her attempt to seem nonchalant was just that—an attempt. She drew out of his grasp and folded her arms over her breasts. "Sorry my run took a little longer than I planned. I hope I didn't hold you up."

He shrugged. "Don't worry about me. Seemed like you needed to sort a lot of things out today."

"I guess I did." She gave him a faint nod, then started to walk away.

"So, did you?" He knew he should let her go, not

only right now but in all the other ways that mattered as well. But her walls had gone up like skyscrapers between the time they'd come back from the crime scene in Pointe-Claire to now.

Especially now.

She paused, turning a frown on him. "Did I, what?"

"Sort everything out."

"I'm working on it."

He advanced toward her, unable to stop his feet from closing the distance. He couldn't resist touching her again, too, just the lightest stroke of his palm against her cheek. She drew away, slowly, yet resolutely.

He scowled. "Are you upset with me?"

"Of course not."

"Then what's wrong?"

"Nothing." A clipped reply, too abrupt to be believed. "I'm tired and I have the stink of the city on me. I just want to go and take a long, hot shower."

He stared at her, certain she wasn't being honest with him. He had seen Kaya operate at her determined maximum before, and he realized that's what she was doing now. She couldn't get away from him fast enough, but why, he wasn't certain.

"Are you acting like this because of last night?" Damn it, he hadn't meant for it to come out like a demand, but there it was. He uttered a low curse, then tried for a more controlled timbre. "Is this about you and me having sex, Kaya?"

She exhaled a sharp breath and shook her head. "Don't flatter yourself, warrior. It was just sex. I thought we both understood that."

"Yeah, it was," he answered, cautious in the face of how cool she was reacting toward him. It didn't help that some part of him he didn't recognize balked at the idea that the time they spent talking and making love on top of that steep ledge hadn't changed them both somehow.

"Good," she said. "Now that we've got that out of the way, will you please let me go?"

Damn. She really meant it. As passionate and responsive as she'd been with him when they made love, now she was shuttered and distant. Completely closed off to him.

Aric stepped back without another word, giving her space to leave.

And she did.

Pivoting on her heel, she left him standing there stonewalled and confused, like the idiot he apparently was.

CHAPTER 17

The shower hadn't helped at all. Kaya's guilt and fear about her past and the people in it was a pain that clung to her no matter how long she'd soaked or how hard she'd tried to scrub it all away.

Seeing Leah after four years apart had confirmed everything she'd been dreading—that her sister was still living among lowlifes and killers like Angus Mackie and his criminal associates. She was still one of them, even after all this time.

Worse than one of them—she was also going to bring a baby into that toxic, violent environment.

The reality of that fact put an ache inside Kaya that she felt to her marrow. She and Leah had been so close once, albeit a long time ago. As little girls, they had been as entwined as identical twins could be, two halves of one soul. But then Leah grew up too fast and life continued to pull them further and further apart.

That slim tether that had connected them was severed, and Kaya had worked hard to convince herself that she was okay with that loss. Even now, she desperately wanted to divorce herself from caring for the sister whose life seemed destined to become a tragic repeat of their mother's.

But she couldn't do it.

As much as she wanted to deny the fact that Leah's rejection had hurt her, she was heartsick over it. And as much as she wanted to rationalize that the Leah she knew as a child had been lost for good at least a decade ago, the hell of it was she still loved her twin.

In some weak, pathetic place inside her, Kaya still felt an unbreakable loyalty toward her only living kin. She felt protective of Leah and concerned for her wellbeing, especially now that she realized her sister was pregnant.

Had Angus Mackie raped her? Kaya wouldn't doubt it for a second. Her sister had made some poor decisions in her life—much like their mother—but Kaya refused to believe that Leah might have willingly allowed a sadistic animal like Big Mack to touch her.

Then again, what did Kaya really know about Leah now?

That she feared Mackie was obvious. She'd have to be a fool not to. But had Leah's self-worth slipped so far that she might actually have developed some kind of relationship with the vicious gang leader? Kaya could only pray not. Her sister had to be saner, smarter than that.

And if she wasn't?

What if it turned out that Leah's brainwashing and abuse within the commune of criminals had consumed every last shred of her humanity? Kaya didn't want to consider it.

But she had to consider it, because it wouldn't be long before the Order answered the question for her.

There was no doubt they would be moving in on Big Mack and his cronies—and soon. With the existence of ultraviolet weaponry a very real, very lethal threat to all of the Breed, combined with an evidential link between Angus Mackie and a recently terminated Opus Nostrum member, the Order would waste little time before formulating a plan of attack and then executing it.

Which meant Leah would soon be in the crosshairs of the Order's wrath as well.

Not to mention her unborn child.

The weight of Kaya's concern sat like an anvil on her chest. She exhaled a heavy sigh. "God, Leah. How did you end up like this? Why didn't you let me help you?"

Now, it might be too late to fix anything in her sister's life.

After today, it might be too late for Kaya to fix things for herself too.

She should have spoken up as soon as Mackie's name was mentioned. Fear had stalled her tongue. What would her teammates think of her, hearing she'd been on Big Mack's turf as recently as this morning?

How could she expect to remain in the Order's fold if they ever learned that she herself had once been part of the very group that had slaughtered an innocent family in their home? That she had been born into that hateful world, raised within it. Still bound to it by her love for her twin.

What would they all think if they knew she'd been withholding those truths from them all this time?

Their faith in her would be shattered, possibly without repair.

Sooner than later, she would have to choose between the only family she had left and the one she was making with her friends and teammates of the Order.

She thought she had made her choice when she began training as a warrior. Now, she wasn't certain her heart was stalwart enough to shut out either one of the things she loved.

But as conflicted as she was about devotion to her blood kin versus duty to the only people who had ever made her feel that she belonged, Kaya's regret for the way she behaved with Aric went even deeper.

To her surprise, he was in the war room when she headed down after her shower to resume working on the photos. She had anticipated being alone to go over the images he'd reviewed while she was gone that morning. Instead, he stood facing a wall of projection glass where an array of pictures from the reception were displayed.

Kaya stood in the open doorway, her gaze more riveted to the man than to the dozens of photos illuminated in front of him. Tall, broad shouldered and hewn of pure muscle, as a Breed male Aric Chase was magnificent. Even standing still he radiated otherworldly power and strength.

As the lover who had touched and kissed and pleasured nearly every inch of her body in the small hours of last night and this morning, just the sight of him made her legs go a bit weak beneath her.

He hadn't deserved her cool rebuff when he approached her outside the kitchen a short while ago. Nor had he deserved her lie that the intimacy they had shared meant nothing to her.

She only wished it meant nothing.

In truth, the hours she'd spent alone with Aric naked in his arms under the moon and stars, and then the rising sun, had been ones she would cherish for the rest of her life.

She would have to cling to those moments, because she could never give in to the temptation again.

Even if that meant pushing him away.

He glanced over his shoulder, aware of her presence even without her saying a word. "It should be easier to compare the photos here instead of at the table."

His tone was level and professional, as if she were simply one of his comrades now. Why that didn't give her more relief, Kaya refused to acknowledge.

The one thing they both agreed on was the fact that their partnership was temporary. When it was over, their lives would continue on separate paths. No expectations of anything more.

Simple, uncomplicated.

Yet when she thought about Aric—every time she was near him—her feelings were anything but simple or uncomplicated.

It was a realization that terrified her as much as any ugly secret from her past or the threat of losing everything she'd worked for with the Order.

Aric Chase made her crave things she never imagined she would have in her life. A confidant. A protector. A lover who gave as much pleasure as he demanded.

A true partner in all the ways that mattered.

Things she could never hope to have so long as her past and the people who still tied her to it were secrets she dared not bring into the light.

How long she could keep the truth hidden from these new people she cared about, Kaya didn't know.

More and more, it tasted like poison on her tongue.

Especially when she was looking at Aric.

"Yes, it should help," she answered, stepping into the room as he put up more images for them to review.

She drifted to his side and tried to concentrate on the hundreds of faces and profiles and nondescript backs of heads—any one of which could be the man they were looking for.

Her eyes scanned the crowds and candid group shots, but all of her senses were fixed on Aric. "I thought you might be somewhere with Rafe and Mira and the rest of the team."

"Thought, or hoped?" He didn't look at her, not even a sidelong glance. As if he hadn't said it at all, he reached out to rearrange the sequence of images in front of them. "The patrol team has their work to do. I've got mine. Unfortunately, I'm not going anywhere until we find the Opus bastard who was at that wedding reception."

And from the steely edge in his voice, it seemed he couldn't finish fast enough.

"What about this guy?" He pointed to a mostly obscured profile on a short, brown-haired man.

Kaya shook her head. "It's not him. The hair is lighter and longer than that of the man I saw."

Aric grunted and moved on. He zoomed in on a different squatty wedding guest with dark hair, pausing to look at her in question.

"Too heavy. And I believe that gentleman is wearing a toupee."

Peering closer at it, he smirked. "Damn. You're

right."

He discarded both images, along with several others containing alternate shots of the same men. And so it went, one photo after another, none of them netting positive results for the Order.

Kaya sighed. "At the rate we're going here, it could be days before we find Mercier's contact."

"We don't have days anymore." Aric's voice was sober. "If the UV bullet casing we recovered isn't bad enough, that black scarab tattoo on Angus Mackie changes everything."

She swallowed, her nerves jangling with dread. "What do you mean?"

"The Order isn't about to stand by and watch Opus Nostrum or anyone with alliances to them create panic among the Breed with the threat of ultraviolet weaponry. Big Mack's going down."

"Goddamn right he is."

Nikolai's voice was a low growl behind them. Both Kaya and Aric swung around to look at the Breed elder, who was suited up in black fatigues and combat boots. Around his hips was a belt studded with all manner of weapons: guns, blades, throwing stars.

Aric flashed a cold grin and a hint of his fangs. "You heading up the team tonight, Commander?"

He gave a short nod. "Lucan wants this asshole taken alive so we can question him. And if he's got UV on hand, we need someone to bring that shit in safely and lock it down."

Frowning, Aric glanced at Kaya then back to Niko. "Someone who isn't going to get ashed, you mean."

"Ideally, yes." Nikolai smirked. "So, consider this your official graduation to the team, both of you.

Congrats on making the grade. Now, suit up and get your asses down to the weapons room. Sundown's in two minutes. I want wheels rolling on pavement the second night falls."

CHAPTER 18

The surprise raid on Angus Mackie was a bust. Aric sensed it even before he entered the gang leader's seedy tavern in the armpit of Dorval. He and Kaya and Rafe had accompanied Nikolai into the vacated establishment while a few miles away, Mira and her three warrior teammates had just called in the same disappointing situation when they closed in on Big Mack's rundown house near the river.

"Find anything back there?" Niko asked Aric as he came out with Rafe after their search of the empty rear office and store room.

"No trace of Mackie, but yeah, we found something."

Aric held out his hand. Resting in his palm was a bullet that made even a seasoned warrior and custom-crafted munitions expert like Nikolai take a step back. This was no spent casing like the ones they had recovered from the Darkhaven murders; this was a live round. Inside the diamond-glass body of the bullet glowed a small, but lethal dose of liquefied ultraviolet light.

"It was lying near the back door that dumps out on the alley."

"Holy hell." Niko slowly shook his head, his gaze riveted on the milky blue color of the fluid within the small cylinder. "I guess we don't need to wonder if any of Riordan's UV arms and ammo made it out of Ireland anymore."

"No," Aric said. "The only question is, how much are we talking about? There are muddy wheel marks from a hand truck rolling over the dirt and concrete out there. Someone made a lot of trips back and forth carting something out of here in a hurry today."

"Shit." The commander scraped a hand over his squared jaw. "All it takes is one of these rounds to ash even the strongest of our kind. Every bullet our enemies hold is one too many."

On that, they all agreed.

Even if Aric's memory wasn't as flawless as his mother's, he would never forget the sight of black ash piles that had once been living, breathing Breed civilians. Aside from a rare handful like him who'd been born impervious to sunlight, for most of their race there was no coming back from a UV assault.

Fury smoldered in Rafe's eyes. "Mackie was tipped off that we were on to him."

"Probably," Nikolai muttered. "But there's a chance he pussied out and ran after his comrade got fileted during that Darkhaven assault. It's no secret that the Order was on scene at Mercier's wedding where another of his longtime cronies ended up dead, so even a blunt instrument like Big Mack might've been able to guess we'd come knocking on his door with questions sooner or later."

Rafe grunted. "Hell of a lucky guess, in that case. Rats like Mackie run in packs, and we all know hate is an insidious bitch that can hide in any crowd. It'll even have the audacity to smile at you while it hides a blade behind its back."

"Or a gun loaded with these," Aric replied.

Nikolai gave a grim nod. "Okay, we're done here. We don't need anything more to know we're on the right track with Mackie. The son of a bitch just made himself our top priority. Let's head back to base and—"

"Commander," Kaya said from behind the bar, her voice grave. "I found something. There's a safe hidden down here."

She had seemed to be doing her best to avoid Aric since the teams departed tonight. Pensive on the ride out to Dorval, she'd sat in back with him in silence while Niko drove and Rafe rode shotgun in the Order's black SUV. In spite of the fact that she was surrounded by a team of three Breed warriors, she seemed equally solitary now, continuing her search of the establishment while Aric and their comrades conversed on the other side of the room.

Nikolai pivoted an approving glance at her. "Good eye. Let's crack it open and have a look inside."

She stepped back to let him move in. Aric and Rafe followed, watching as Niko hunkered down and disabled the combination lock with a mental command. He started to open the safe's door, then paused. His cool ice-blue gaze flicked up to Aric. "Maybe you ought to do the honors. Just in case there's any more of that shit in here."

"Sure." Aric returned Nikolai's grin as he carefully laid the UV bullet on top of the bar's scarred surface. There would be no quips about the Order elder's caution. As one of the Breed, only an outright fool or a tragic hero would be cavalier enough to dismiss the killing power of that kind of weaponry. In the end it wouldn't matter which category applied because either one would leave behind nothing but ashes.

Aric waited to investigate until Niko and Rafe had stepped around to the safety on the other side of the long bar. Kaya remained, and he heard her indrawn breath as he pulled open the safe's door.

"Be careful," she whispered, the first words she'd spoken to him since they arrived.

He nodded, struck to see true concern in her expression. It warmed him more than he wanted to admit. How had he gotten so tangled up in this female that a simple utterance of kindness from her as his fellow comrade should affect him as profoundly as her embrace?

With more effort than it should have required, he put aside his awareness of her and concentrated on doing his job. He peered inside the safe.

"Couple of handguns," he reported as he pulled out the weapons and inspected them. "Basic nines, standard rounds. No UV."

"Thank fuck for that," Rafe muttered.

"There's something else in here." Aric reached toward the back, his fingers closing around a brick-sized block of substance that was wrapped in thick cellophane. "Narcotics. Ah, shit," he said once he had the object out of the safe and in his hand. "It's Red Dragon."

Nikolai hissed a curse in his native Russian. "How much you got?"

"About a kilo," he guessed, judging by the weight of the package in his palm. He stood up and placed it on top of the bar next to the live UV round and the pair of pistols.

"Christ." Rafe's mouth pressed flat as he picked up the brick and stared at the packed red powder concealed within the plastic shrink wrap. "Like with UV, it doesn't take much of this shit to do the job."

Kaya glanced at it, too, her fine brows pinched with confusion. "What's Red Dragon?"

"Instant bloodbath," Rafe replied. "If you want to turn the mildest Breed civilian into a violent killer, give him a dose of this garbage then stand back."

"It's a drug we've recently linked to Opus," Aric explained. "When the Order took out Fineas Riordan, they blew up a large cache of ultraviolet weaponry and cartons of sealed narcotics like this one. We know some of it is already in circulation around the world for the simple fact that we've been seeing an uptick in Rogue activity lately. There have been Breed slayings of humans in different areas all over the world."

"Oh, God." Her face went a bit slack. "You're saying this red powder is making law-abiding Breed vampires turn into bloodthirsty murderers?"

Aric nodded. "Nothing Opus would like better than to fan the flames of paranoia by creating an epidemic of Breed-on-human attacks."

"Which usually results in retaliation from the other side," Rafe added. "Not to mention the power it gives to hate-based gangbangers like Angus Mackie to keep bringing in fresh recruits to their cause."

Nikolai grunted. "Vicious circle. One we've been fighting for a long damned time."

Aric and Rafe agreed in unison. Although they were new to the battle, both of their fathers had been engulfed in it along with Niko and the rest of the Order since the beginning.

The Order's work had been tremendous, as was their success, but the war was far from over. Aric had a feeling this new fight was going to get a hell of a lot uglier than anything the world had seen before. He intended to meet it on the front lines, and that was just one more reason to be glad that Kaya had slammed the brakes on whatever it was that had been taking shape between them.

Still, that didn't keep his gaze from straying to her as she stood next to him behind the bar, her arms crossed and pretty brown eyes distant, troubled. As haunted as he'd ever seen them.

"Nikolai," she murmured after what seemed the longest time. "Do you think I could talk to you priv—"

The commander's sudden, sharp groan cut her question short. His expression constricted into one of agony. "Ah, Christ." He bit off a curse and thrust out his hand, gripping the edge of the bar.

"Are you okay?" Rafe reached for his arm. "Niko, let me help you."

"Can't." He shook his head, pain radiating off him.

"What's happening?" Kaya asked, rushing around from behind the counter with Aric.

The immense Breed warrior staggered, sweat popping out on his brow. "Renata." He uttered his mate's name through gritted teeth and fangs. "Holy hell.

It's the baby. He's coming. Right now."

Aric shot an urgent glance at Rafe. "I'll get the vehicle."

"No time." Niko gave a harsh shake of his head. And through his anguish, an excited grin pulled his lips away from his emerged fangs. He chuckled, wonder shining in his ice-blue eyes despite the intense physical pain he shared with his Breedmate through their blood bond. "Holy fuck, it's really happening. I'm outta here. I'll get home faster on foot."

He didn't waste another second. In a blur of movement, Nikolai bolted out of the bar and vanished into the night.

CHAPTER 19

Nikolai didn't slow his speed until his boots hit the polished marble of the command center's foyer. His Breed genetics had carried him in a few scant minutes across the miles of pavement between Dorval and the mansion at the top of Summit Hill; now his blood bond to Renata sent him rushing through the residence and down to the infirmary housed in the Montreal base's nerve center below.

Kellan stood in the corridor outside the medical room, his comm unit in hand. "I just tried to call you to let you know it's showtime." The younger Breed warrior gave him a sympathetic smile. "Should've known your bond would give you the heads-up before anyone else needed to. Everything happened so fast."

"How is she?"

Kellan chuckled. "Been issuing orders like a drill sergeant since her water broke a few minutes ago. And threatening to skewer you with all four of her favorite blades if you didn't make it back here before the baby does."

In other words, Renata was fine. Niko heaved out the breath he hadn't been aware he was holding. "That's my girl."

Kellan nodded. "As for your other girl, I called Mira right after I tried to reach you. She's on the way back now with her team."

"Thanks." Niko clapped his adopted daughter's mate on the shoulder. "Now, I'd better haul my ass inside before my female decides to carve me a new one."

His gaze strayed past the male to halfway up the passageway. Siobhan carried a large stack of folded towels in her arms as she hurried toward Nikolai and Kellan.

"I thought these might be helpful," she said, the petite Breedmate nearly out of breath as she approached. "Is there anything at all I can do? You've all been so kind to me, and I just feel a bit useless and in the way since I've arrived here."

The commander in him was on the verge of informing the doe-eyed civilian that she was in an area restricted to members of the Order, but she looked so earnest with her offer of help that Nikolai checked the impulse. Barely.

Giving her a curt nod of acknowledgment, he glanced pointedly at his comrade.

Kellan smoothly stepped in. "I'll take those for you, Siobhan. Come on, I'll show you the way back upstairs to wait for Rafe and the others. Awfully easy to get lost down here if you don't know where you're going."

Niko appreciated the diplomatic assist. Right now he

didn't have the patience for anything but getting to Renata's side. The shared pain of another of her sharp contractions tore through him as he stepped away from Kellan and Siobhan to reach for the latch on the infirmary door.

Gritting his teeth against the burn of her agony, he entered Renata's delivery room.

"Hey, baby."

She sat in a semi-reclined position in the middle of a railed hospital bed. Her fingers gripped those rails in a white-knuckled grasp and she roared as the worst of the labor pain poured over her. Nikolai felt it too. Not only because of their blood bond, but because of the depth of his love for the woman who suffered this racking torture because of him.

For him.

And for their child.

He went immediately to her bedside. A collection of terry washcloths rested on the table next to her. He wet one from the pitcher of ice water that sat there too, then pressed the cool compress to her sweat-beaded brow.

"He's coming so fast," she panted between contractions. "I can't slow him down."

Niko grunted. "First our boy makes us wait nine long months and then some, and now he's in a rush to get here. Definitely gonna have to talk to him about timing."

Renata managed a laugh, but her gaze stayed locked and solemn on his beneath the dampened tangles of her chin-length ebony hair. "When you left tonight, I had a feeling he was coming soon. I was afraid you were going to miss it."

"Never." Niko shook his head and caressed her warm cheek. "There's not a damned thing that would stand between me and this moment. You know that, right?"

She managed a wobbly nod before bearing down on another wave of staggering pain. Her cry ripped through every fiber of his being. God, he wished he could bear it all for her. All his jokes about keeping her pregnant with more of his sons dried up like sawdust in his throat as he mopped her face and stood feebly by, humbled and awed by the sheer tenacity of his lovely, strong Renata.

"You're doing great, sweetheart." He leaned down and kissed the top of her head as the contraction subsided. "Christ, you're so brave. So beautiful."

She snorted. "I'm drenched in sweat and my belly's as big as a house. I feel like a tick about to burst wide open."

Niko smiled. "Well, you look like a goddess to me. You are a goddess. *Mine.*"

"You're crazy," she said, but she allowed him to kiss her parted lips. "I love you, Nikolai."

"Ah, baby." His voice was choked with emotion he couldn't contain. "I've loved you from the first minute I laid eyes on you."

"Even in that second minute when I mind-zapped you and dropped you on your arrogant ass?"

"Especially then."

He grinned, reflecting back on how he'd met the tough black-haired Breedmate with the uniquely powerful psychic ability. He pressed his forehead to hers, holding her watery jade-green gaze. That this extraordinary woman was his, he could hardly reconcile the fact. Nor would he ever want to take a breath without her at his side.

Another contraction buffeted her and she rode it

out, settling into the pain. Owning it. Niko could only curl his fingers around her hand and hold fast, willing all of his strength to her even though his warrior of a woman seemed to have an endless reserve of her own.

In the brief lull that followed, she lay back and closed her eyes, shoring up for the next round.

"Talk to me," she murmured softly. "Tell me about the mission tonight. Did we smoke that son of a bitch down in Dorval?"

He chuckled under his breath, shaking his head. "There really is no stopping you, is there?"

Her mouth curved in a slow smile. "Would you have me any other way?"

"My love, I'd take you any way I can." He stroked her beautiful face. "And I have, if memory serves."

Now she laughed, and the sound of her comfort with him—her complete trust in him as her mate and her partner in every other thing they faced together—made his heart swell in his chest. He continued to caress her, needing the tactile contact as much as she seemed to. And if hearing about Order business might give her some measure of ease in the midst of her labor, who was he to argue?

"We were too late closing in on Mackie or his gang. The bar and his residence had both been cleared out not long before we arrived." Niko sighed, letting his curse leak out of him on the exhalation. "He knew the Order was on to him somehow and he had time enough to evacuate—along with what appears to be substantial amounts of UV munitions. But he did leave us a couple of consolation prizes."

Nikolai gave her a quick rundown about the live round Aric and Rafe recovered, and the brick of narcotics that was all but certain to be Red Dragon.

"Lucan's not going to be happy to hear we lost Big Mack tonight," he confided. "Hell, I'm not happy about that either."

"You'll get him," Renata assured him, her inky lashes lifting to reveal confident, determined green eyes. "*We'll* get him, Niko. Because we're not going to stop until every last member of Opus and their followers are erased from exist—*agh!*"

The contraction rolled over her like a freight train, the worst one yet. Nikolai hated the pain she was in, hated that he had played a role in putting her through it when he planted his child inside her. He murmured tender words of encouragement as her body struggled and fought to the other side of the agony.

Niko swept the cool cloth over her face and neck as she relaxed once more, so caught up in Renata he hardly heard the knock on the door. Rafe slowly opened it and took a step inside.

"How's it going in here?"

Nikolai had only one answer. "I'm mated to an incredible woman."

Rafe smiled. "No one would ever argue that point with you. Renata, can I do anything for you?"

She shook her head on the pillow, her fingers still entwined with Niko's. "I'm good. The baby's almost here now."

Rafe glanced at Niko for confirmation. Although it wasn't unusual for Breed births to occur privately at home, without medical attendants, having a healer present at the command center was a comfort Nikolai could not deny. But he was loathe to share Renata and this moment with anyone else.

Almost anyone.

"Rennie?" Mira peeked in around the half-open door.

"Mouse." Renata's face lit up at the sight of the former orphan who had become a daughter to both Nikolai and her in the past twenty years they'd been together. She held out her free hand to Mira. "Come in with us. You belong here too."

They were family, the three of them. More recently, Kellan had brought their number to four.

And soon, a few minutes at most, they would welcome another into the fold.

"We should call D.C.," Mira said to Rafe as she stepped inside the room. "They'll want to know the baby is finally coming."

Nikolai smiled at the air of command in her. She hadn't been born from Renata's body, but Mira had grown up under her wing and guidance to become a force to be reckoned with.

Rafe smirked. "I made the call on the way here. Lucan's had the jet fueled and on standby for more than two weeks. They're already en route as we speak."

Niko nodded at Rafe and his daughter. "Thank you. Both of you."

The warrior healer departed in silence, closing the door behind him. Mira rushed to the other side of Renata's bedside and pressed a loving kiss to her temple.

"What can I do?"

Renata smiled tenderly. "Take my hands, Mouse." Then she glanced over meaningfully at Niko and gave a mild nod. "He's coming now."

There was barely a moment before the next contraction seized her. Together, he and Mira helped her through the last of her ordeal. Then, when it was time, Nikolai was the one to receive the slippery, squalling miracle that was his son.

He held the crying baby in his palms, rendered mute and practically useless for the wonder of what he had just experienced with the two women he cherished more than anything else in his long life . . . and now this, the precious gift he cradled in his hands.

Renata told him what to do next, somehow clear-minded enough to think and talk and do the right things for their child after all she'd been through, while Niko could hardly do more than stare and marvel, silently thanking whatever god would hear him for the blessings he could never hope to fully deserve.

"Our son," he said as he carried him to Renata and carefully placed the cleaned, naked infant on her chest. Nikolai didn't care that his cheeks were wet with tears. He felt no shame in his weakness when it came to this woman . . . and now, this child.

He glanced over at Mira, whose own eyes glistened with wells of tears. Nikolai nodded, overwhelmed with emotion when he looked at this grown child of their heart too. "Mouse, meet your little brother."

"I love him already." She beamed, cupping the baby's head in her hand. "I'll let you two enjoy him while I let everyone know he's finally arrived."

CHAPTER 20

The Montreal command center vibrated with energy in the couple of hours following the birth of Nikolai and Renata's son. As if the baby wasn't enough to send a ripple of excitement through the place, preparations were also being made for the arrival of the Order's founder, Lucan Thorne, and several other warrior elders and their mates currently on the way to celebrate the birth in person.

Kaya was thrilled for Niko and Renata. She was thrilled for her friend Mira, too. The tenacious team captain had immersed herself completely in her new role tonight—that of the elated older sister. Mira had been practically walking on air since she emerged from her adoptive parents' sides in the infirmary to announce the baby had made his long-awaited entrance.

As for Kaya, she couldn't help but think of her own sister and the child she carried.

In truth, she'd been thinking about Leah constantly all day. Even more so, now that Angus Mackie and his entire gang had apparently gone to ground ahead of the Order's raid.

Standing alone in the mansion's kitchen, Kaya put a kettle of water on the burner, guilt raking her when she relived tonight's mission. Not only because it was likely her visit to Leah at the tavern that had spurred Big Mack to run, but because of her silence about that visit when she and the other warriors prepared for the raid.

For one of the first times in her life, she had behaved like a coward.

Yet there was a part of her that was profoundly relieved that her sister had escaped the Order's discovery. And their wrath.

Kaya knew her day of reckoning was coming. She had been preparing herself for that moment earlier tonight, before Nikolai had come down to the war room and informed her and Aric that they had both finally made the grade as warriors. Kaya should have been celebrating the achievement she'd worked so hard to earn. Instead she'd ridden to Angus Mackie's bar feeling as though she were on her way to the gallows.

Then, when she'd finally shored up her courage to try again, her blurted request to meet privately with the commander was thwarted by the urgent arrival of his son.

She exhaled a humorless laugh, miserable with the irony of it all.

And if she were headed for her grave as far as the Order was concerned, it was a hole she alone had dug for herself. Fear of being rejected by the only people who'd ever showed her any kindness had kept her silent about her past and the people in it. Now it was that fear and silence that would ensure she'd lose this new family she cared for so deeply.

Including Aric.

Although to be fair, he wasn't hers. Imagining a world where he might be only made the regret and futile longing inside her worsen.

How had the arrogant Order prince she was certain she'd despise turn out to be the only man who had ever gotten close enough to see past the steep walls she'd built around her heart? How could she be in danger of losing her heart to a man who couldn't wait to leave her in his rearview mirror?

How could she crave Aric Chase regardless of all those things?

Kaya slowly shook her head. "Because I'm a fool, that's why."

The kettle began to whistle, pulling her thoughts away from dreams she'd never so much as pretended she would ever have until she met Aric. Kaya poured the boiling water, staring into the twisting plume of tea-infused steam that rose up over the rim of her mug.

She had no more time to waste on soft feelings and foolish fantasies. As soon as the fervor over the baby's arrival and the visiting warriors were gone, she and Nikolai would have their talk. And then, she was certain, her short career with the Order would be over. Before that happened, she wanted to do something useful with the time she had left.

She couldn't be more disappointed in herself, but she'd be damned if she failed the Order any further by letting up on her mission to identify the Opus member she'd linked to Stephan Mercier.

Mug of hot tea in hand, she walked over to the large kitchen table where she'd laid out printed photos and a tablet containing image and video files from the wedding. Aric had helped her narrow the search considerably since they started, but there was still hours of work ahead. Possibly days.

Her heavy sigh was met by a subtle shift in the air behind her. Although Aric was silent, a born predator, the power of his presence registered within her senses like a physical caress.

"Quite a night," he said, his deep voice a vibration she felt in her veins.

"Yes, it has been." Kaya pivoted to look at him as he approached.

They had both changed out of their patrol gear. Gone were his black fatigues, in their place he wore low-slung workout pants and a dark tank that showcased his strong arms and shoulders while clinging to every ridge and muscle of his magnificent torso.

Kaya nearly groaned at the way she ached just looking at him. Her skin felt tight and hot beneath her loose clothing. She had opted for comfort as well, dressed in yoga pants and an oversized T-shirt that Balthazar had loaned her a week ago after one of their paint-gun training sessions ruined hers. Her comrade hadn't asked for it back, and while she'd thought nothing of wearing it when she put it on tonight, seeing Aric's gaze narrow disapprovingly on the warrior-sized garment made her cheeks flush with unwanted heat.

And her face wasn't the only thing suddenly growing too warm as he came to stand beside her.

She cleared her throat. "How are the new parents doing?"

"I just left the infirmary a few minutes ago," he said, his sensual mouth curving in a smile. "Renata's already up and on her feet. Which is good, because Nikolai's legs still look a little shaky."

Kaya laughed, trying to picture the fearsome Siberian-born warrior as anything less than in full command of any situation. Much like the handsome Breed male currently at her side.

"Mira told me she thought Niko was going to pass out after he delivered the baby. I didn't realize he and Renata would be handling the birth on their own."

Aric nodded. "Rafe was on standby in case anything went wrong and they needed a healer, but complications are rare among the Breed. It's up to the parents to decide who they want in the room with them. For a lot of couples, births are as sacred and intimate as their blood bond."

"Is that how it was with your parents?"

His grin deepened. "Once you meet them, you won't need to ask. They should be here anytime now."

Kaya swallowed, her stomach lurching at the idea that she would soon be standing in the same room with his mother and father and several other Order elders and their mates when the time came to present the baby and announce his name. Mira had filled her in on the basic details of the ritual the Breed practiced following the birth of a child, and Kaya couldn't deny that she was excited to be part of it.

The arriving Order leaders would be meeting her as a member of the Montreal team, a distinction that she felt honored to hold no matter how temporary it might end up being. But most of her anxiety stemmed from the simple fact that she wanted Aric's parents to like her.

A ridiculous thing to hope for, and selfish too.

Yet that didn't make her want it any less.

Knowing Aric would be on the plane with the rest of the Order when they returned home to D.C. didn't make her want him any less, either.

Particularly when he was looking at her with steady eyes that smoldered with dark promise.

Kaya mentally shook herself out of her pointless yearning and pivoted back to the photographs. "Who do you suppose will be named the baby's godparents?"

"Rio and Dylan," he answered without hesitation. "There was never a doubt about that. Niko and Rio's friendship goes back twenty years, back when the Order had only a handful of warriors and was based in Boston."

She glanced at him as he moved in closer, joining her at the table. "Boston," she remarked. "That's where your father's family is from."

He nodded. "The Chases have been in that city for countless generations."

"But you're heading to Seattle now that you've been promoted up to warrior?"

"Eventually," he said. "Ideally, I want to be wherever the action is. Wherever I can best serve the Order."

Kaya looked back at the images of all those wealthy, happy people. People who could make their own futures, choose their own destinies. People who weren't tied down by poverty or neglect or choices that would saddle them for all their lives. People like Aric, who held the world by the tail simply by virtue of his birth.

"What do you want, Kaya?"

She didn't dare look at him. She, the girl who taught herself to fear nothing, now stood there terrified that she might let him see how afraid she was of wanting him.

She shook her head, hoping he'd let the question go.

But this was Aric Chase she was dealing with. He was as tenacious and determined as she was. He reached out and gently caught her chin on the tips of his fingers. "Tell me."

"I used to think I wanted to see the world," she murmured, recalling how desperately she prayed for wings to fly her out of the hell of her childhood. "I wanted to be anywhere but this city. As far as I could go. One adventure after another."

His smile was tender, his nod mild with understanding. "And now?"

"I don't know."

"I think you do." His palm glided along the line of her jaw, his long fingers splaying into her hair. "Tell me."

A strangled moan escaped her before she could call it back. "Aric . . . I can't."

"Then tell me why you can't."

She closed her eyes. "Why are you doing this to me?"

"Because I think something's got you terrified, and it's not me." His caress gave her no choice but to open her eyes and meet his smoldering gaze. "I don't know what's going on in that beautiful, stubborn head of yours but I want you to know that you can tell me, Kaya. You can trust me."

"Trust you? I hardly know you." The protest sounded weak, despite the force with which she pushed it past her lips.

"You really want me to believe you feel that way? Because I've been trying to convince myself that's how I feel about you, and it's not working. Not one damned bit."

Her heart leapt at his confession. She could not allow this hope to bloom, though. Not when the secret of her past was all but certain to crush anything Aric felt for her, along with his trust.

Yet she couldn't move.

She couldn't speak, neither to confirm nor deny what he was saying.

She stood there, torn between wanting him to kiss her and knowing she should push him away. But she couldn't push him away. Inside she was a mess, and Aric was the only thing grounding her.

He stroked his fingers along the side of her neck, his penetrating gaze locked on her. "Tell me again that you hardly know me. That you really feel there's nothing between us."

His voice was low and quiet, but filled with a masculine power that spoke to everything female inside her. And, God, she couldn't think when he was touching her. Those leaf-green eyes captivated her too, made her remember how good it felt to be drowning in his hungry, molten stare while his body moved against hers, inside her.

She wanted to feel that pleasure again. Wanted to tell him that she would never be the same now that she knew the fire of his touch, his kiss, his passion.

With this man, she simply . . . wanted.

"I didn't say there was nothing between us, Aric." She shook her head, miserable for all of the longing he stirred within her. "I only wish I had the strength to tell you that."

"Finally, honesty," he murmured. "Was that so hard?"

It should have been. Kaya didn't trust easily. She

didn't let people see past the wall that protected her heart, let alone allow them to breach it. Yet she never felt safer than when she was with this dangerous Breed male. She didn't resist at all when his hand moved around the back of her neck, warm and possessive. He drew her closer, his gaze flickering with amber light as he lowered his head toward her parted lips.

At that same moment, Rafe's deep voice sounded just outside the kitchen entry, a low murmur that Kaya couldn't quite make out. It was followed by the soft titter of Siobhan's giggle as the pair entered the room.

"Oh, shit," Rafe blurted. "Are we interrupting?"

Aric's reply was no better than a growl. "Yes."

"—No," Kaya answered at the same time. She slipped out of his reach and turned back to her work spread out over the table. "I was just going over the intel from the wedding and reception."

"Ah," Rafe said. "Getting anywhere?"

Aric's grunt held a sardonic tone. "We were starting to, but then you showed up."

Kaya didn't miss the questioning look he gave his comrade as Rafe brought the shy Breedmate to one of the tall stools at the island counter, then headed over to the stove. "Siobhan's hungry, so I told her I'd make something for her to eat."

Aric leaned against the long counter and cocked his head, then glanced at the female. "Has he mentioned to you that he's Breed? My man over here has never cooked a day in his life, nor tasted anything he's made. His diet is the same as mine: human red cells only."

"And even that's losing its appeal lately," Rafe said, flicking a meaningful look at Siobhan. "Anyway, I think I can manage to scramble a couple of eggs and throw in some chopped vegetables. Kaya, would you like some too?"

"No, thanks." Unlike the other Breedmate whose flushed face and throat and dusky, heavy-lidded eyes threw off an unmistakable post-sex vibe, Kaya had no appetite for food. Her stomach had been in a knot for days—ever since Aric Chase had sauntered into her life.

She felt his gaze return to her as she busied herself with the stacks of printed photographs and the surveillance videos stored on the tablet. The mention of blood and hunger only made the heat of Aric's stare feel more intense. Try as she might not to imagine any of the human blood Hosts he was required to feed from—especially the females—the thought of Aric sinking his fangs into the soft flesh of another's throat sent a dark lick of curiosity through her veins.

And a profound, shocking envy.

She couldn't have been more relieved when Rafe drew Aric's attention away from her, even though the conversation centered on the disappointing raid on Angus Mackie and the troubling evidence they collected at his bar.

"Too bad we weren't able to grab the son of a bitch and haul him in for interrogation," Aric snarled. "I'd have liked to see how long Big Mack would last in front of a room full of Breed warriors before he started spilling everything he knows."

"Not to mention a lot of his bodily fluids," Rafe added with a smirk.

"Will all of the Order's commanders be here tonight?" Siobhan asked in between bites of her omelet.

Rafe shook his head. "Not all. Lucan Thorne and his mate Gabrielle are coming, of course. Along with Aric's parents, and mine."

"Carys too," Aric put in. "She called me as soon as she heard about the baby's birth. She and her mate Rune are on the jet with the others. Darion Thorne's with them as well."

"Don't forget Rio and his Breedmate, Dylan," Kaya added.

Aric gave her a warm nod. "That's right. The ceremony doesn't start without the godparents being present."

"As for the others," Rafe said, "Gideon and Savannah will be holding down the fort in D.C. along with Brock and Jenna. Commander Hunter and his mate Corinne have just returned to New Orleans to deal with a Rogue outbreak in that city. Kade and Alexandra are back at the command center in Lake Tahoe for the same reason. Unfortunately, our European commanders have fires of their own to put out as well, so neither Mathias Rowan nor Lazaro Archer will be at the ceremony, either."

"What about Tegan and Elise?" Aric asked.

Rafe shook his head, his face oddly grim. "They're on the way to Budapest."

"Isn't that where Micah was sent recently? Some kind of black ops mission for the Order?"

"That's the last we heard," Rafe confirmed. "Apparently, there's been a development."

The way the warrior said that word gave Kaya the sense that it wasn't anything good. The fact that Micah's parents had gone after their reputably formidable warrior son only confirmed the unease she felt.

Siobhan, being civilian, seemed to miss the gravity of the conversation. "Well, even without the ones you mentioned, it sounds like quite a full guest list to me."

"It's too bad everyone won't be here." Rafe gently covered her hand with his. "Sooner or later, I'd like all of the Order to meet you."

Kaya couldn't keep her surprised gaze from meeting Aric's. He lifted his thick shoulder in a shrug as his comrade tipped his lover's face up for a tender kiss.

Aric cleared his throat, whether in payback for the interruption Rafe and Siobhan's arrival in the kitchen has caused him or out of the same awkwardness Kaya felt as an audience to the other couple's passion, she couldn't be sure.

"Keep that shit up and we'll be celebrating another howling infant nine months from now," Aric drawled as his friend drew back from his woman.

Rafe chuckled, his eyes still rooted on Siobhan. "We're not blood-bonded yet. Not for my lack of interest in pursuing the idea."

She dropped her gaze and pushed some of the egg around on her plate. "Everything's just moving a little fast for me, that's all."

"I know, angel. Can I help it that I'm absolutely crazy about you?"

Their affection for each other was almost too much for Kaya to take. That Rafe was mad for the female anyone could plainly see. Siobhan seemed equally taken with him, but there were shadows in the Breedmate's hazel eyes that made Kaya wonder how tall and thick were the walls around Siobhan's heart?

Rafe didn't seem to notice. Or maybe he had enough hope for both of them to assume that eventually they would be able to knock those walls down together.

Hope that she and Aric would never have unless she

was willing to come clean to the Order about her past. Bad enough that she had kept it from them all this time. Now, she had the failed raid on Angus Mackie weighing heavily on her conscience.

Reminded of all the obstacles standing in the way of anything she might have with Aric, Kaya went back to her work. As she reviewed the collections of photos, then shuffled and reviewed them again, Aric and Rafe went back to discussing Order business and speculating on the far-reaching tentacles of Opus Nostrum's secret brotherhood.

Siobhan finished her meal and slid off the stool to carry her plate to the sink. On her way back, she paused at the table and glanced at the various groupings of images.

"Still haven't found him, aye?"

"Not yet," Kaya said. "But he's in here somewhere. He can't hide forever."

"No." Siobhan gave a sympathetic tilt of her head. "No one can."

Although the comment wasn't directed at her, Kaya's nape prickled with warning as she watched the Breedmate walk away and fold herself under Rafe's protective arm. Was it possible that Siobhan could suspect her of keeping secrets from the Order? Or was it merely Kaya's guilty conscience that made heart suddenly begin to bang around like a trapped bird inside her rib cage?

God, she was going to lose her mind if she didn't put an end to this self-torment soon.

Unable to concentrate now, she swept the photographs into the file pouch, then reached for another stack she had yet to pore over. In her haste, she knocked the pile of pictures off the table. They scattered in a disorganized mess on the floor around her chair.

"Shit." Kaya dropped to her hands and knees to collect them. Aric was at her side in the next moment. "You don't have to help. I've got this."

"Yes, I know you do," he said, gathering up a handful of the images and holding them out to her. "But you don't have to do it alone."

The image on top of the stack happened to be a candid snapshot taken of the pavilion during the bride and groom's first dance. Aric and Kaya stood on the periphery of the crowd, holding hands and pretending to be a real couple. Except unlike the rest of the gathered onlookers, they weren't watching Stephan Mercier and Anastasia Rousseau sway in the center of the open floor.

They were looking at each other.

And Kaya saw in her own face the expression of a woman already falling swiftly, hopelessly, in love. To her utter shock, she saw a similar tender regard in Aric's handsome face—both in the photograph and in the solemn expression he held her with now.

"Partners, Mrs. Bouchard. Remember?"

She couldn't hold his intent gaze. It was too easy to believe him. Too easy to think the fake relationship that had marked their initial meeting might actually have become something real.

Not only for her, but for Aric as well.

Kaya glanced down . . . and her gaze rooted on another face in the crowd.

"Oh, my God." She grabbed the photo and peered more closely. "Aric. There he is."

"Are you serious?"

She nodded vigorously, her finger trembling as she

pointed to a half-obscured face standing among the wedding guests behind her and Aric. The squatty, dark-haired man had an unremarkable face but Kaya would know his build and carriage anywhere.

"It's him. Mercier's Opus contact."

Across the kitchen, Rafe uttered an excited curse. "Let me see." He and Siobhan both came over to look at the image. "Who am I looking for?"

"Right here," Aric said, marking the place in the photo as he handed it to his comrade.

Then all of his attention returned to Kaya. "You did it. You found him."

As excited as she was, she shook her head, loathe to take the credit when their task was far from finished. "I only found his face. We still don't know his name."

"We will." Aric tapped his temple. "You leave that to me . . . partner."

Before she could say another word, he caught her face in his palms and claimed her mouth in a slow, bone-melting kiss. Kaya didn't fight it. Not even close. Looping her arms around his neck, she kissed him back with all of the desire and emotion—all of the love—she'd been trying so desperately to deny.

Dimly, distantly, she registered that Rafe and Siobhan no longer stood near them. And then she realized why, when someone pointedly cleared his throat just inside the room.

Someone that wasn't Rafe and certainly wasn't Siobhan, either.

Alarmed, Kaya squirmed, but Aric took his sweet time letting go of her.

When he finally did, his beautiful green eyes danced with bright flecks of amber. He swiveled his head to greet the new arrivals, his fanged smile utterly unapologetic.

She glanced toward the entrance of the kitchen too. Standing there were two couples. There was no mistaking the air of authority—and lethal danger—that radiated from the Breed males, both the handsome, golden-haired one in a crisp white shirt and dark jeans and the devilishly good looking brunet who stood beside his well-dressed comrade wearing a lot of sleek black leather and a pair of long, curved daggers sheathed on his belt.

The two Breedmates at their sides were equally stunning for different reasons, each blessed with incredible beauty and a strength that seemed to emanate from deep within.

Aric rose, taking Kaya's hand to bring her up with him from their embarrassing clinch on the floor. He smiled at the tall female with caramel-brown hair and eyes the same spring leaf green as his own. Then he tipped his head in greeting to the golden male at the beauty's side.

"Hey, Mom. Hello, Father. There's someone I want you to meet."

CHAPTER 21

"Lars Scrully," Aric said, dropping a passport photograph and a folder of intel he'd assembled for the four Order commanders gathered with Nikolai in his private office.

The group of Order elders presented an imposing picture, even seated as they were around Niko's large desk, engaged in sober conversation. Gabrielle Thorne and Aric's mother Tavia were also in the room, seated together on an oversized sofa near the fireplace. The other warriors' Breedmates and the rest of the mansion's occupants were catching up elsewhere in the compound with Kaya and Mira and the Montreal team while Renata continued to rest with the baby.

"Scrully wasn't on the wedding guest list, nor in any of the gate check security data Gideon's hacking provided us. But we've got the son of a bitch." Aric gestured to the file of intel he'd collected in the twenty minutes since Kaya had ID'd the squat, dark-haired man in the reception photo. "I knew I'd seen his face somewhere before," he told the group of warrior elders. "There were some news stories from eighteen months ago when Lars Scrully inherited his father's pharmaceutical empire."

"Scrully Pharmaceuticals?" Tavia asked, her distaste for the name evident in her tone. "That's the company that came under fire several years ago for acquiring expired patents on antivirals, cancer treatment drugs, and other medicines, then jacking up their prices by five-thousand percent. People literally died because they couldn't afford to pay his exorbitant prices."

Aric nodded, unsurprised that his mother would be the one to mention that fun fact. If his gift for recollection was flawless, it was only because it was handed down to him through her powerful DNA.

"That's the one," he confirmed. "Lars's father, Simon Scrully, made a fortune off the backs of other people's suffering." Aric pulled out a printed obituary and laid it on top of the folder. "The old man had a severe allergy to shellfish. Apparently, someone forgot to tell the new chef at his favorite restaurant. Scrully ate a bite of lobster sauce on his pasta and dropped dead of anaphylactic shock before anyone could administer his medicine to counteract it."

Dante let out a wry chuckle. "Ironic way to go, considering how the asshole got rich in the first place."

"Or convenient," Aric's father said. "Now that I'm hearing this, I recall some rumors about the old man's death. Some of the gossip at the time seemed to suggest Scrully's son settled into his inheritance with a bit more glee than grief."

Aric nodded. "That's right. And he's been spending money like water ever since. Expensive toys and women. Palatial homes. In fact, just three months ago, he moved into a newly built twenty-thousand square-foot lake estate here in the province."

Nikolai frowned. "And thanks to Kaya, we also know Scrully was making arrangements to pay a cool hundred million to Stephan Mercier on behalf of Opus Nostrum."

"Right," Aric replied. "The question is, in exchange for what?"

His father grunted. "Too bad we can't ask Mercier. Kind of hard to talk when you're missing your tongue and half your throat."

Niko nodded, grim. "No need to guess whose handiwork that hit was. Opus tends to get twitchy whenever we start closing in on any of their weak links in the chain."

"Which means we need to get our hands on Lars Scrully as soon as possible," Lucan said, his gray gaze as cool as gunmetal.

Dante leaned back in his chair, flashing a dangerous grin. "I do love a good old-fashioned interrogation session."

Beside him, Rio chuckled. "I'm with you on that, brother. Especially the part where we each take a piece of this Opus bastard apart with our fists and fangs." The immense warrior with the smooth Spanish accent and a vicious tangle of old shrapnel scars riddling the left side of his face could be a charmer, but tonight he was as lethally serious as the rest of his comrades. He glanced at Aric. "How far is Scrully's place from here?"

"About an hour."

Dante's whiskey-colored eyes lit up beneath the black slashes of his brows. "Plenty of time to be there and back with Scrully before the sun rises."

"Lucan," Gabrielle interjected softly, but firmly. The auburn-haired beauty had the regality of a queen, and now was no exception. All heads turned toward her as she spoke. "I don't think I like this. I've got a bad feeling."

"How so?" The Order's founder looked at his woman, all of his focus fixed on hearing her opinion.

"Opus isn't playing games, Lucan. They've been a serious threat from the very beginning. And now we know for certain they have ultraviolet weapons. A lot of them." She shook her head, true fear written on her pretty face. "Maybe we should take this new intel on Lars Scrully back with us to D.C. when we return, then work on a plan of attack after we've had more time to consider it."

Lucan listened to his mate in sober silence. All of the warriors grew serious and quiet, everyone grimly considering the gravity of the facts she was pointing out.

It took Lucan a moment to reply. When he did, his deep voice was low and gentle. "Yes, Opus does have UV on their side now. But they're going to have it no matter how long we wait to strike. And to wait will only risk letting Scrully or the others in Opus's cabal have more time to get the upper hand."

Gabrielle nodded, but Aric could see that as sound as her formidable mate's logic was, it did little to erase her worry.

Lucan went on, his steely gaze moving to the four commanders who trusted him to lead. "Right now, we have the element of surprise working for us. We should use it to our advantage."

"We hope we have the element of surprise," Nikolai commented. "Lately, it's feeling as though Opus is staying one step ahead of us."

"What are you saying? You think we've got a leak somewhere?"

"I don't see how we could. All of our contacts in JUSTIS and elsewhere have been double and triple checked. They're solid, Lucan."

Rio glanced at his friend, a haunted look in his topaz-colored eyes. "If that's true, then any breach would have to come from somewhere outside of those networks. Possibly someone we trust."

The massive warrior knew a thing or two about that. The scar on his face had come on the heels of the worst betrayal a man could suffer—that of his own mate. It wasn't until Rio met Dylan that he was finally able to heal on the inside. The wounds that marred him on the outside would always serve as a reminder of the pain that came in trusting the wrong person with his heart . . . and his life.

As Rio spoke, Aric thought back on Angus Mackie and the certainty that the gang leader and his followers hadn't merely gotten lucky when they made the decision to vacate not only the tavern and its store room but Big Mack's residence as well.

Sure, they could have guessed that trouble would be heading their way after the headlines Mercier's wedding reception debacle had made. Or maybe they'd had an attack of nerves after the heinous act they'd pulled in ashing that Darkhaven family.

But Aric's warrior senses prickled with unease when he considered all of the what-ifs and the scenarios he was reluctant to put into words.

And then there was Kaya.

Try as he might to deny it, he kept coming back to her remoteness, her emotional distance, following the Darkhaven attack. After her run that same day, she had been even more anxious and withdrawn. Her edginess hadn't improved as she and the rest of the Montreal team had gone with the commander on the mission to grab Mackie. When she asked Nikolai for a private meeting, she looked about as miserable as Aric had ever seen her.

What did she need to talk with Niko about that couldn't be said in front of everyone?

Was it something about the raid?

Then again, maybe it was simply Aric himself who was making her so uncomfortable.

Whatever it was, she didn't seem ready—or willing—to trust him with it.

Not that she should. He hadn't made her any promises. No, all he'd done was pursue her with single-minded purpose then seduce her. They had agreed to no strings or obligations, but the more time he spent with Kaya the less eager he was for his business in Montreal to end.

"So, it sounds as if we're all agreed that we need to act swiftly" Lucan said, then he slid an apologetic glance at Gabrielle. "Most of us, that is."

All four warriors nodded, their faces solemn yet determined. But then a further look passed between them. The exchange was unspoken, until Aric's father took the lead.

"We're agreed that we cannot wait to make our move on this new Opus lead, Lucan. But your mate is right to caution us that this is no ordinary mission. None of them are, now that Opus and their loyalists are in possession of UV weapons."

Lucan Thorne's scowl deepened to one of suspicion. "What are you trying to say, Harvard? If you've got something on your mind, spit it out."

Chase nodded. "We're going in to get Lars Scrully. Tonight. But we're going without you."

A growl erupted from the powerful Gen One. "The fuck you say. If you expect me to sit out on a mission with my dick in my hand—"

"You're not going this time," Dante said, his deep voice as firm as Chase's had been.

Rio nodded. "The risk is too great. You're Gen One, Lucan."

"Yes," he snarled. "And a blast of UV will kill any one of you the same as it will me."

"But you're the founder of the Order," Nikolai added. "We can't afford to lose you."

He bellowed a sharp curse and shoved to his feet. "No. Fuck this. And fuck all of you if you think the Order will stop without me. We can't afford to lose anyone, understood?"

"Lucan." Gabrielle stood up and walked over to him. He stilled as she laid her hands on his broad chest. "They're right. The Order can't lose you. But you're more than just the leader of these fine men and women who serve under your command. You're the chairman of the Global Nations Council. Since First Dawn, whether you like it or not, you have become the voice of the entire Breed nation."

His eyes flashed amber-bright with his barely banked rage. But Gabrielle's words calmed him. It was clear to everyone in the room that this woman grounded him the way nothing else could.

"You're staying behind this time." Her demand was softly spoken, but brooking no argument.

He cupped her cheek in his big hand, his jaw clamped tight for a long moment. Then another low curse rumbled out of him.

Finally, he looked back at his comrades and Aric. "Tell everyone to assemble in the war room in ten minutes to receive their team assignments and mission directives. I want schematics of Scrully's estate now, as in yesterday. Let's go, people."

As they all began to hop to his command, Lucan pointed a finger at Nikolai. "If I'm cooling my heels here tonight, then so are you. I'm not going to risk leaving that baby boy without a father in the first few hours of his life."

Niko scowled, but after a moment, he gave a curt nod.

"Look alive," Lucan ordered them all. "Time's wasting already."

CHAPTER 22

With a low-throated scream, a horned owl swooped off the bough of an immense pine in front of Kaya and her comrades as they crept into place in the forest that surrounded Lars Scrully's enormous lakefront estate.

The warriors had split into three teams once they left the city. With Nikolai grounded alongside Lucan back at the command center, Mira and Sterling Chase were in charge of the unit tasked with surveillance as the other two teams got into place. Kaya, Mira, and Chase watched the northern border of the estate. Keeping an eye on the southern perimeter were Torin and Tavia, along with Lucan and Gabrielle's son, Darion. Although Tavia had limited combat experience, it was the Breed female's immunity to ultraviolet light that persuaded the Order's commanders to permit her along on the mission.

For the same reason—along with the added bonus

of her ability to shadow bend like Aric and her father—Carys Chase had been assigned to the second team of six, which was moving into position at various points around the property, running reconnaissance and waiting for the command to sweep onto the grounds and take out any guards who tried to block the assault. Led by Dante and Rio, the team also had the experience of Rafe and Kellan, both proven warriors. And while Carys's mate Rune was new to the Order, he had earned his fighting skills in illegal cage matches back in Boston before he met her.

Rounding out the mission's operatives was the third team, the vanguard consisting of Aric, Balthazar and Webb. None of the units were cleared to move in until Aric and his partners gave the all-clear.

"Shouldn't we have heard from them by now?" Kaya could hardly keep the edge of worry from her quiet whisper to Mira.

Her friend nodded. "They should be approaching from the lake any minute now."

As if on cue, the team's earpieces crackled with an incoming transmission from elsewhere in the field. But instead of Aric's deep voice announcing that he and Bal and Webb had emerged from the water as planned, it was Darion Thorne's low growl that came over the communication link.

"Alpha. Bravo. We've got a problem down at the southern gate."

Mira's grave stare flicked to Kaya and Commander Chase. "What kind of problem?"

"Two security guards with acute lead poisoning. They've both been shot execution-style."

"Shit." Mira touched her ear and spoke with clipped

urgency. "Torin, can you get close enough to pick up a reading for us?"

"On it, captain." Silence fell for a handful of seconds that felt like days to Kaya. Then the warrior with the ability to psychically detect shifts in the energy forces of a place came back on the line. "I'm sensing a lot of fear and panic radiating from within the residence. There's more death inside there too."

Kaya's stomach clenched. "Something's not right."

"No, it's not," Chase replied. "We're too late. Opus's assassins have already been here."

The sudden staccato report of gunfire ripped through the quiet of the surrounding night. Mira's face went grim. "Holy hell. They're still here."

As she said it, a bolt of lightning lit up the inky black sky near the lake. Then another.

Kaya looked toward the large body of water, where Aric, Webb, and Bal were currently swimming in as an amphibious team to breach the estate's weakest perimeter. More light exploded in that vicinity. The bright illuminations reflected on the lake's surface like fireworks.

Cold dread swept through Kaya's veins. "It's UV. Oh, my God. They're shooting at them with ultraviolet!"

"Abort," Mira called over the comm link. "All units abort right now!"

A reply came back at nearly the same time. "Bal's down." Webb's usually calm voice had a catch to it now, and an edge of fear that Kaya had never heard in the arrogant male before. "Ah, Christ. They just ashed Bal. Fuck!"

Kaya's hand flew to her mouth. A jagged moan leaked past anyway, anguish she couldn't hold in. No.

Not him. Not Balthazar.

Mira's face held the same bleak disbelief, but the captain kept her composure. "Where are you, Webb?"

"Near the dock. Motherfuckers have me pinned down with UV fire."

In the few seconds it took to receive that awful news, Tavia, Torin, and Darion arrived from their lookout points to rejoin Mira, Kaya, and Chase.

"We're pulling out," Mira told them. "If Opus has already been here, I doubt Scrully will be any use to us now. And I'm not going to lose anyone else over that asshole."

"Aric's already inside," Webb reported. "As soon as we came out of the water and ditched our gear, we started taking heavy gunfire and UV. Before I knew it, Bal was down. Then Aric turned into shadow and I lost sight of him."

"Oh, God," Kaya murmured, every instinct she had twitching with the need to go after him. Even though Aric was more than capable of taking on a small army of human assailants purely by virtue of his Breed genetics, the thought of him charging into danger alone was too much to bear. Both the warrior in Kaya and the woman wanted nothing else but to be alongside her partner. "I'm going in too."

"So am I," Tavia and Carys announced at the same time. The pair of daywalking Breed females were united in their fury and their determination.

"You're not going in there without me," Chase demanded, his stance as unyielding as his hard gaze. "Neither one of you leaves my sight."

Tavia's eyes crackled with amber fire. "We're going. And you're staying." The tips of her fangs glinted in the low light of the fading UV rays. "Don't you dare try to override me on this. There's no room for argument here, my love."

The commander's jaw went taut, but the only protest he uttered was a low growl as Tavia briefly touched his rigid cheek.

"All right, that's settled," Mira said. Then she spoke to the other Breed warriors who'd gone silent on the comm link. "The rest of you, stand down too. We're going in."

Carys's Breed gaze glittered with the same fierce determination as her mother's. "I'll go provide cover for Webb."

"Be careful," Tavia said. Then she glanced at Mira and Kaya. "I'll head for the house. Aric knows what he's doing, but he may need some help. I'll look for Scrully while I'm inside."

At the captain's nod, both daywalkers vanished into the woods.

"Let's go," Mira said.

Heart racing, Kaya fell in beside her friend and comrade. They made much slower progress than Tavia, who was likely already at the mansion and finding her way inside. Kaya and Mira raced through the thick forest that hemmed in the expansive limestone brick house and its sprawling footprint.

Up ahead, the rapid chatter of automatic gunfire. More explosions of UV light flashed in and around the house from attackers unaware that those Breed-killing weapons were no good against the daywalkers who had infiltrated the place. Men's voices shouted orders near the stronghold; here and there, a human scream cut short as either Aric or his mother took them out.

With their own weapons in hand, Kaya and Mira reached the edge of the woods and hunkered down, peering out at the frenzy of activity near the mansion. They unleashed a hail of bullets on four guards jogging around from the back of the house, dropping them one by one. Kaya's training kept her focus laser-sharp, her remorse for killing on a back burner.

She only wished she could say her soldier's training was enough to stanch her concern for Aric. But as she and Mira rushed out of the trees and down to the lakefront mansion, all she could think about was the man she loved.

No sense in denying that fact, especially to herself.

She was in love with Aric Chase. The thought of losing him—the mere idea that he could meet with harm at the hands of their enemies tonight—put a hollow ache in the center of her breast.

"Around to the back," Mira said. "The house is nothing but glass looking out over the water. All the easier to blast our way in from that side."

Kaya nodded, reloading with a fresh magazine. "Let's do it."

She and Mira shot out the wall of soaring glass, standing back as the sharp, heavy shards rained down on the bricked terrace where they stood. The breach brought three men running into the large great room inside. Before they could open fire, Kaya and Mira mowed them down then stepped around the corpses to enter the residence.

Just as they did, bullets sprayed at them from the open loft area above. Mira squeezed off a volley of shots as she took cover behind an imposing carved wood bar that dominated one whole side of the room. Meanwhile

Kaya dove out to the adjacent hall just as another armed man thundered her way. Rolling into a crouch, she squeezed the trigger of her semiautomatic pistol and the big human went down like a rock.

"Aric," she whispered urgently into her comm's mic. "I'm in. Where are you?"

His sharp, angry curse was a relief all by itself. "Kaya? Damn it, stay put."

A deafening cacophony of gun blasts ripped over the open link before it went dead silent. "Aric!"

Ultraviolet light couldn't hurt him, but that didn't mean he couldn't be shot to death with enough rounds to the head or vital organs. There were other ways he could be killed too. Possibilities she dared not even imagine.

She started moving even before she realized her boots were chewing up the floor beneath her. From the schematics of the house the team reviewed before leaving base, Kaya recalled the location of a back staircase that led to the second floor. The gunfire she heard over her comm had come from above. If Aric was up there too, she had to find him.

She found the stairs and started bounding up them on silent feet. Halfway to the top, a gunman rounded the corner and spotted her. He swung his weapon up and took aim at her. Kaya fired first, but had no choice other than to leap over the railing to avoid the returned shots.

She dropped to the floor below, bullets spraying her from behind. More than one struck home. The searing pain made her let out a scream.

Blood streaked the floor where she'd fallen and in a path behind her as she staggered on a wounded leg into a sheltered position against the wall of the stairwell. As soon as her assailant peered down to look for her, she raised her gun and filled his chest full of lead, ignoring the fiery protest of her bleeding biceps. The man fell over the banister in a heavy heap at her feet.

To her horror, as she sagged back against the wall, panting from blood loss and agony, three more guards closed in from all sides.

She struggled to lift her bloodied arm to defend herself. But in that next instant all she saw in front her was a blur of shadow and quicksilver movement. When it stopped, Aric was there, standing between her and the broken bodies of three dead gunmen whose necks had all been savagely twisted.

As for Aric, he had never looked more lethal. Eyes blazing like burning coals, his narrowed pupils were all but devoured by the fire of battle rage that lit his gaze. His fangs filled his mouth, bright white, sharp as daggers. The *dermaglyphs* that tracked up his arms and disappeared under the short sleeves of his black fatigues were seething with dark, vicious colors. His clothing was torn and bloodstained, bullet wounds riddling him in too many places to count.

"Aric." She exhaled his name on a broken whisper. "You've been shot."

He didn't answer, just went down on his haunches in front of her and tenderly caught her face in his palms. On a curse, he slanted his mouth over hers and kissed her, slow and deep, as if he needed the contact even more than she did. His Breed gaze traveled over her, his nostrils flaring as he inhaled a shallow breath.

It took her a moment to realize just how quiet the place had gotten. No more gunfire. No more thudding boot falls or sounds of violence. The fighting had ended.

Tavia materialized as if from thin air, her speed of movement far too fast for Kaya to track. "Thank God, you're both all right."

"Kaya's been wounded," Aric said, still hunkered beside her. She didn't miss the odd pitch of his voice as he lingered so near to her bleeding injuries. His voice was rough, unearthly. Filled with an unmistakable hunger . . . and torment.

Sterling Chase strode in from the adjacent hallway now, accompanied by Mira and Kellan. Rio and Dante followed along with Darion Thorne.

"Carys brought Webb up from the waterfront. He took a few rounds, but fortunately he's fine. Rafe is healing the worst of them." The commander glanced over at Kaya. "Better let him have a look at you too."

Aric's answering growl was barely audible, but the possessive, animal sound vibrated against her. Something deep inside her responded with a blooming heat that throbbed through her veins and into her marrow.

"Scrully's dead?" Chase asked Tavia.

She nodded. "I found him in the master bedroom. Someone wanted to make sure he didn't get up ever again. Large caliber round delivered point-blank between his eyes and his throat sliced open for good measure."

Dante blew out a low whistle. "Opus's cleaners sure are messy motherfuckers."

"And they came prepared for a fight from the Order," Tavia added. "There are two crates of UV ammunition sitting in a van parked inside the garage."

Chase cursed, running his hand over his jaw. "Opus's assassins knew to expect us. And they were

214

obviously ordered to take out as many of us as they could."

Aric acknowledged that fact with a grim nod. "They blasted me with UV half a dozen times on my approach. You should've seen the looks on the bastard's faces when I kept coming."

Chase's scowl deepened, then he glanced at Mira. "Captain, your call for us to stand down was a solid one. You probably saved our lives."

"All except one," she murmured thickly.

Kellan wrapped his arm around Mira's shoulders and drew her close to him. "We all signed on for this mission knowing we might not come back. I'm sure Bal would tell you that too."

Rio nodded. "The Order goes into every mission with the understanding it could be our last. But after seeing what happened here tonight? We've never had to be prepared for anything like this before."

Dante slanted his comrade a sober look. "The rules of the game have changed, my friend. Opus is making that point loud and clear."

"Yes, they are," Chase agreed. "And that means we either adapt fast, or die trying."

From his crouch beside Kaya, Aric glanced up at his father and the rest of the Breed warriors gathered in the small space. "If this is our new reality, the Order's going to need more daywalkers."

CHAPTER 23

Following the shitstorm they'd encountered at Scrully's estate, the teams had returned to base haggard from the battle and somber over the loss of one of their own. Aric shared the disappointment of his Order brethren, but it was concern for Kaya that racked him during the couple of hours since they had arrived at the command center.

He'd kept his distance while Rafe tended her wounds on the drive back, if only because the cinnamon and roses scent of her blood was a torment he could hardly bear. His mouth still watered at the thought alone, his fangs still throbbing with the ache of his hunger.

His own wounds would have benefited greatly from nourishment, but the idea of going out to the city in search of a blood Host was the last thing on his mind.

Especially when the only vein he truly thirsted for was Kaya's.

So it was probably a mistake to be standing outside the closed door of her room, yet for the past full minute, that's where Aric had been. He needed to see her, make sure she was all right. Time away from her after nearly losing her in combat tonight was a torment all of its own. Swearing under his breath at his own weakness, he dropped his knuckles against the door.

She opened it without asking who was there, and the sight of her healed and whole, dressed in a soft top and loose-fitting yoga pants, dragged a low sound of relief from him. At least until he saw her dark brown eyes and the pain that clouded them.

"You've been crying."

She swiped at the faint traces of wetness that streaked her cheeks and stepped away from the open doorway, an unspoken invitation for Aric to come inside. He closed the door behind him and followed her to the small living area of her suite. A half-empty bottle of wine and an empty glass sat on the cocktail table between the sitting area and a cozy fireplace that crackled with the embers of a dying fire.

She curled into the corner of the sofa, tucking her legs up and wrapping her arms around her knees. In the short time he had known her, he had seen Kaya Laurent stubborn and tenacious, fearless and unflagging.

Now, he saw a tender vulnerability in the courageous woman that carved a hollow in his chest. He wanted to be the one to protect her from all hurts, physical and otherwise.

It astonished him how deeply he wanted to be the only man she turned to for all of her needs . . . and her desires.

Including the most essential, sacred one that existed

between a Breed male and his mate.

The one he wanted despite the many questions and niggling suspicions he couldn't seem to shake when it came to this female.

Aric sat down beside her. "If your injuries need more care, tell me and we can go find Rafe."

The words tasted like sawdust on his tongue, but it was all he had to offer her. It was a relief when she shook her head in denial.

"It's not my body that hurts, it's my heart. I still can't believe Bal's gone."

Aric nodded, but inside he felt a jolt of uncertainty now. The memory of Kaya wearing a massively oversized shirt that could only have belonged to the behemoth of a male sank sharp talons into him. "Did you love him?"

"Yes." She turned her face toward him when her answer had made Aric's molars clamp together. "Bal was kind to me from my first day at the command center. I loved him like a brother, Aric. Like a friend. I always will."

"Of course," he answered, consoled that he wouldn't have to spend the rest of his days envying a dead man.

Kaya reached for his hand, twining her fingers through his. "I was so scared when Webb reported that you'd run alone into the gunfire at Scrully's place." A strangled breath caught in her throat. "God, Aric. If you had died tonight too—"

"I didn't." He pulled her close, into the circle of his arm. Her freshly washed hair was sweet and silky soft against his lips as he kissed the top of her head. "I'm right here, baby."

She nestled against him, her fingers stroking over his

clean T-shirt at the places where his torso had taken multiple enemy rounds, including more than one UV bullet. The wounds were healed now, but the entry points were still raised and tender. "Does it hurt when I touch you?"

"Only in the best way." He lifted her chin and gazed down into her soft eyes. "Touch me anytime you like. You're never going to hear me complain."

He brushed his lips over hers, groaning when the brief kiss shot through him like pure flame. He tore away from her sweet mouth with more restraint than he realized he possessed. But only barely. Everything Breed in him yearned to take Kaya . . . to claim her as his regardless of the separate paths their lives were on.

Maybe she sensed the thinness of his control. God knew it was hard for her to miss the sudden surge of his fangs behind his lip, or the simmering glow of his irises as he stared at her, doing his damnedest to bite back the word that leapt to his tongue every time he looked at her.

Mine.

She drew back from him, retreating a few inches closer to her corner of the sofa. "I'm sorry if I'm to blame for some of your wounds tonight. You told me to stay put, but I couldn't just sit and wait for the danger to pass."

"I wish to hell you were better at following instructions," he said, offering her a wry smile. "But you were a help to me in there, Kaya. You've got great warrior instincts and skill."

She lifted her shoulder in a mild shrug. "I've had good training. And it helps to have a good partner."

"Yes, it does." Aric held her meaningful gaze. "I don't think I could hope for anyone better."

Something flickered in her dark eyes, shadows that seemed to dim the tender regard she held him in before shuttering her gaze to him completely. She got up from the sofa and poured a glass of wine, taking a drink of it as she strode in front of the fireplace.

"Maybe we're not that good together." It was an abrupt redirect, steering their conversation away from the awareness he knew she felt as strongly as he did. "We finally identified Mercier's Opus contact, but in the end it was all for nothing. The Order's come back less one of our best members and we're no closer to stopping Opus Nostrum than we were before you and I met."

Aric rose and moved over to where she stood, her arms crossed in front of her, fingers grasped around her wineglass as if it was the only thing holding her together.

"We did suffer losses today. But so did Opus. They've got one less member of their inner circle now too. And we've got substantial intel collected from Scrully's estate and computers. We've also taken a van full of UV weapons away from Opus's arsenal."

Without the time or preparations to detonate the recovered cache of arms and munitions, the crates were currently stowed in the bowels of the command center, a fact that was making more than a few of the Breed warriors a bit twitchy.

"They knew we were coming, Aric. The timing of Scrully's killing and the Order's arrival couldn't have been coincidence, right? Opus's assassins didn't just get lucky when they brought a van filled with UV weapons to that estate to kill Scrully. They were waiting for us. They knew we were coming and they knew when."

He stilled, somewhat taken aback to hear her say the very thing that the Order's commanders had been discussing ever since they'd returned tonight. Rafe had made no secret of his suspicions over the past few days either, pressing the very likely possibility that the Order had a leak with loyalties to Opus somewhere in their intel chain. Or somewhere closer than that.

Even Aric had to admit he had doubts—too many of them centered on the beautiful woman standing in front of him now.

She spoke so earnestly, so convincingly, she was either innocent or one hell of a cold-hearted liar.

And he had to be some kind of fool for how eagerly he grasped for the former while pretending he could ignore the latter. Staring into Kaya's soulful eyes made him want to ignore a lot of the things his logical mind was telling him.

That his life and all of the goals he had for his future as a warrior with no chains to hold him down were still the things he wanted most.

That his duty to the Order came before the woman he couldn't resist.

That he couldn't possibly be in love with her after only a handful of days.

He stared into her sincere gaze, wishing he had her power to read a mind with his touch. "You're right about what happened tonight. Opus had to be tipped-off by someone. After what happened with Angus Mackie the other night as well, the Order is all but certain we have a mole somewhere."

She blanched a bit, then glanced down into her glass. "I hope that's not true."

"So do I, Kaya."

He could smell her anxiety as he took the wine from her hand and set it on the mantel. She was afraid now.

He saw it in the heavy drum of her pulse, which ticked in a faster tempo at the base of her throat. Instead of feeling suspicion, even anger, at the sight of that frantic, throbbing vein, what he felt the most was hunger.

A need so primal and sexual it rocked him to his core.

She looked up again, into his eyes. He didn't have to wonder if they were glowing with the ferocity of his desire; Kaya's face said it all. He couldn't pretend he didn't want her, or that the truth of his feelings toward her didn't go far deeper than that.

He caressed her cheek, a low curse hissing out of him. "When I realized you were in that house with me tonight, I was so fucking furious at you. I knew the instant you'd been shot by that bastard on the stairs. I heard your scream, Kaya. Then I smelled your blood." He shook his head, his flawless memory providing a replay that tore at him all over again. "I wanted to kill every last one of those fucks who tried to hurt you. But that's not all I wanted."

He let his hand drift along the side of her neck, smoothing his thumb over the artery that beat so strongly below her ear. Kaya sucked in her breath, her gaze widening. When her lips parted on that shocked gasp, Aric took her face in his hands and kissed her.

It was a fierce claiming, his tongue invading without permission or mercy. Possessive and heated, he ravished her mouth with all the passion and raw hunger that had been riding him ever since he first set eyes on her.

She kissed him back with equal intensity, until a small moan bubbled up from her throat. She broke away from him, panting. "Aric."

She took a step back, his brave Kaya who had

charged headlong into a building filled with enemy gunmen only hours ago, now trembled after his kiss.

"Are you afraid of me?" He waited in dread for her answer.

"No." She shook her head as if to reaffirm it. "I'm afraid of myself . . . of what I might agree to if I let you stay in this room with me any longer."

Her confession shouldn't have given him as much pleasure as it did. Bolstered by it, he moved closer, denying her retreat. He touched her face again, running the backs of his knuckles along her cheek then down the velvety column of her neck.

"Are you afraid you'll let me do this?" he asked, continuing his slow caress down the length of her toned arm before moving onto her breasts.

She gave him a weak nod, a sigh shuddering out of her as he kneaded the perfect mounds until her nipples rose as tight as pebbles beneath the thin fabric of her shirt.

He lifted the hem and brought both hands under, freeing the clasp of her bra. When her breasts were uncovered and filling his palms, he bent and suckled each of them, the points of his fangs lightly grazing her tender skin.

"What about this, Kaya?" he murmured, tugging one nipple between his teeth and flicking the tip of it with his tongue. She dropped her head back and moaned in pleasure, going a little boneless in his embrace.

"Or this?" he asked, reaching into her panties to stroke her sex as he brought his mouth back up to hers. "Ah, Christ."

She was drenched and soft, so fucking hot. He groaned, his blood already on fire and racing through his veins. She moved against his palm, encouraging him to delve deeper into the wet cleft that felt like liquid silk on his fingertips. He penetrated her with one finger, then two, swallowing her jagged cry with his kiss. His heart hammered in his chest and every pulse point, his cock surging with the need to be inside her.

Releasing her on an impatient snarl, he peeled away her clothing so he could feast his gaze and mouth and hands on every strong, beautiful inch of her body.

"I need to touch you too," she murmured tugging his shirt up and raking her short nails over his bared skin.

They undressed him together. Kaya's hands traced his *glyphs* while her mouth dropped tender kisses on the raised, reddened skin of the many healed gunshot wounds that covered him.

He wasn't prepared for the moment she sank down in front of him and took his engorged erection into her hands. Her touch drew a choked moan from him as she worked his length with her fingers and palms, before lowering her mouth over the broad tip of his cock.

"Fuck." He couldn't keep his hips from moving in time with the wet strokes of her tongue. Fisting his hands in her dark hair, he pumped and grinded, uttering her name through clenched teeth and fangs.

Too soon, he felt his control unraveling. His need for release was too savage for her mouth. He needed to be inside her. Needed to see if the raw yearning he felt for her now could be slaked with a hard fuck and a blistering release.

"On the bed," he growled, pulling her off him and lifting her into his arms. He didn't have time to walk with her there. Desire owned him now.

This female owned him, and there was a part of him

that knew no other would satisfy him again.

He placed her on the mattress, then climbed on top of her, spreading her legs wide as he settled his big body between her thighs then drove in deep. She cried out with the first hard thrusts. Aric couldn't stop, not when she was clutching at his shoulders, her legs wrapped around him, opening herself to him completely and encouraging him to push them both to the limits.

And so he did.

Claiming her mouth in a fierce kiss, he rocked into her without mercy, filling her tight sheath with every hard inch of his cock. Her soft gasps and pleasured cries spurred him on. His arousal was a possessive thing, hungered and wild.

Her delicate muscles gripped him as he bucked in an increasingly savage tempo. He felt the jolting ripples of her body against his shaft. Roared when he felt her go tense beneath him, her orgasm seizing her. He pumped harder, until her scream ripped loose and she shattered with the force of her release.

Aric wasn't far behind her. He couldn't slow the thundering onslaught of his climax. It exploded out of him, a knot of pure heat blazing a scalding path through every fiber of his being before erupting in a fevered stream inside the haven of Kaya's body.

For several moments, he kept thrusting, convulsions racking him as the waves of pleasure and staggering release finally ebbed. But he was still hungry for her. Still in need of the woman who clung to him, her long legs still wrapped around him, holding him inside her.

"What have you done to me, Kaya?"

Braced on his elbows above her, Aric slowed his rhythm to let her catch her breath. Her heart was racing.

He could feel the power of it vibrating against him, tempting the other hunger he refused to indulge.

Yet that didn't keep his amber-soaked gaze from drifting to the pulse point that pounded just beneath his mouth. Her carotid hammered, a beat he heard in his ears and temples. One that echoed in the hard throb of his own veins.

He kissed her once more, lost to the feel of her all over again.

Had he really thought he could screw this woman out of his system? It would take a lifetime of trying, and even then he felt certain he was destined to fail. He still wanted her.

He loved her.

Even if she had secrets. Even if there was a part of her he might never be able to reach.

His fangs filled his mouth, gums aching as the sharp points surged in anticipation of their own reward.

In the back of his mind, a selfish part of him whispered that all it would take was one small sip of Kaya's blood and he would know all of her.

The bond would connect him to her deepest emotions, including whatever it was that put those impenetrable shadows in her eyes.

One taste and he would feel her in his veins forever.

Hell, he was halfway there already, even without shackling her to him by blood.

Besides, how crazy would he have to be to activate an eternal link to her when he wasn't even sure he trusted her?

The reminder chased through his conscience like a black wind. Aric swept it aside, pushing all thoughts of blood and betrayal from his mind in favor of the one thing they did have that he could trust. Pleasure.

On a low growl, he pulled out and flipped Kaya onto her stomach. Then he lifted her onto her knees and thrust back into her sweet, wet heat again.

CHAPTER 24

Kaya's body felt the delicious reverberations of Aric's lovemaking all through the solemn ritual the Order observed to celebrate the birth of Nikolai and Renata's child the next morning.

She sat beside him in the command center's small candlelit sanctuary, swamped with emotion as she watched the new parents present their son to the audience of their closest friends and comrades. Yet to call the Breed males and their mates anything other than family was to diminish what they all had become to one another over the years. The Order's members were kin in ways Kaya had not fully appreciated until this moment.

Inside a circle of eight tall white candles at the front of the gathering, Nikolai and Renata stood with Rio and Dylan, all of them garbed in long white tunics. With Mira holding her tiny brother nearby, the two couples had woven eight strips of snowy white silk into a cradle they held suspended between them for the infant who would be cherished and protected by all four of them—parents and chosen godparents—for as long as any of them lived.

"Who brings this child before us today?" Lucan asked, officiating the ritual.

"We do," Nikolai and Renata answered as one. "He is our son, Dmitri Jack."

It was the first time the baby's name had been announced. Kaya couldn't help smiling at his middle name, no doubt given in tribute for the old man who'd been so kind to her when she needed shelter, but also, as Aric had informed her, kind to Renata and Niko years before her.

Lucan nodded to Mira and she brought the naked baby to Renata, transferring him carefully to his mother's arms. Renata held Dmitri up for all gathered to see.

"This babe is ours," she and Niko said, reciting words Mira had once described to Kaya. Hearing them spoken in this setting, in this moment, was more powerful than she could have imagined. "With our love we have brought him into this world. With our blood and lives we sustain him, and keep him safe from harm. He is our joy and our promise, the perfect expression of our eternal bond, and we are honored to present him to you, our kin."

As one, Kaya included, the assembly answered with the traditional reply: "You honor us well."

Now, the baby was laid in the center of the white silk cradle, and next came the vow by Dmitri's godparents. Lucan pivoted to Rio and Dylan. "Who pledges to protect this child with blood and bone and final breath should duty call upon it?"

The couple answered solemnly, "We do."

And with that promise spoken, Rio sank his fangs into first his wrist, then Dylan's. Together, the pair held their open wounds over the squirming baby, their blood spilling in droplets onto his bare skin to symbolize their vow to give their lives in order to keep him safe.

Kaya watched through vision blurred with welling tears and a throat thick with happiness for the four friends and the tiny child whose life would be immeasurably blessed by their love and protection. Little Dmitri would want for nothing, Kaya was certain. How she wished she could feel even a fraction of that confidence when it came to her sister and her unborn child.

Aric caught the tear that slid down her cheek. His solemn gaze was tender on her, even though this touch was the first he'd given her since leaving her bed in the early hours of the morning. As the ceremony concluded, they rose with everyone else seated in the pews.

It was humbling to be among the witnesses of the tradition-steeped ceremony. An honor to be welcomed as one of these people, even though there was a part of her that knew she was the outsider. An interloper who would never fully belong until she had brought all of her secrets out of the shadows of her past and into the light.

Including the secret she felt certain Aric already suspected, or was close to figuring out.

She had almost told him last night. But then he mentioned the likelihood that the Order was being betrayed by a mole who had not only warned Big Mack to evacuate, but alerted Opus to the fact the Order would be moving in on Lars Scrully last night. If she told him she'd been concealing the fact that she had gone to Angus Mackie's bar the very day of the Order's raid, why would Aric or anyone else ever believe that she had nothing to do with giving Opus the intel they needed to come to Scrully's place armed with UV weapons?

All Kaya knew was that the pit she had begun digging for herself by withholding her shame about her past and the people who raised her was coming home to roost in ways she never imagined in her worst nightmares.

And in the center of all her regrets for those actions was Aric.

She owed him the truth.

The vague distance she felt from him today only fortified her resolve. He had to know why she was so terrified of her feelings for him.

Particularly after last night, when she'd been all but certain he had been just a hairbreadth from sinking his fangs into her carotid. One bite and he would know all of her secrets and shame. One sip from her vein and he would be bound to her forever.

It wasn't fear she felt at that idea. It was a fierce longing. But she could never allow it to happen while she was betraying him with her silence.

"Kaya, would you like to meet my baby brother?" Mira beamed like a proud mama herself.

Looping her arm through Kaya's, she excitedly tugged her forward without waiting for her reply. Aric loomed beside her, flanked by Kellan and Rafe.

"Why didn't you bring Siobhan?" Mira asked, frowning. "I hope she didn't feel unwelcome."

"No." Rafe shook his head. "She was awake most of the night again. Sometimes the nightmares of her roommate's killing are too much. She was so exhausted this morning, I told her to stay in bed and rest."

Mira gave him a sympathetic nod. "We're all exhausted today, I think. Losing Bal on top of all the other setbacks we've had lately . . . well, at least we have Dmitri to celebrate. God knows we needed something positive to carry us through."

Renata smiled as the group of them approached the Order elders standing at the front of the sanctuary. She was radiant in her white ceremonial attire. Nikolai seemed even taller today, and unabashedly proud. The cool Russian Breed male kept his muscled arm circled around Renata's shoulders, his icy blue gaze shining with a joy Kaya had rarely seen in him.

"It was a beautiful ceremony," Kaya told the commander and his mate. "Dmitri Jack is a lovely name. He would be delighted, I'm sure."

With a small nod, Renata glanced down at the dozing baby in her arms. "I hope so."

"Is Dmitri a family name?"

"My brother," Niko answered. "He died a very long time ago, but I will never forget him."

Renata turned a tender gaze on her man. "Love has no expiration date. Dmitri will be in your heart forever."

He nodded. "I want my son to grow up knowing he was named for two great men, and that he now has the responsibility to live a life that honors them both."

"I'm sure he will," Aric said. "Dmitri's got some of the best parents he could hope for. Not to mention excellent backup."

Rio chuckled at the praise. "The bar is set fairly high by a lot of others in this room, but Dylan and I will do our best not to disappoint."

The Spaniard's red-haired Breedmate flashed a gorgeous smile as she leaned her cheek against his thick biceps. "What he means is, we intend to spoil this child as thoroughly as Niko and Renata will allow us to."

Kaya laughed along with everyone as the conversation continued, but it was hard to focus on anything other than Aric, who seemed to regard her in an almost brooding silence.

"What about your godparents?" she asked him, searching for a way to bring him out of the sullen mood that had been clinging to him since they'd made love last night. "You and Carys must have someone watching over you too."

He glanced at his parents and gave a short nod. "My sister and I have the good fortune of calling Tess and Dante our godparents."

The other couple smiled warmly at him. Then Dante smirked. "Growing up, you and Carys probably should've had a pair and a spare considering how wild and headstrong you both were."

"Were?" Chase quipped drolly. "I've been cursed with children who proved to me time and again that they were as hard-headed as I am. They still do, more often than not."

"And we wouldn't have either of you any other way," Tavia added, reaching out to squeeze the hands of both Aric and Carys, who had now joined the gathering along with her hulking mate, Rune.

Kaya looked over at Rafe. "I suppose your godparents are no mystery, seeing what close friends you and Aric are. Chase and Tavia, right?"

"No," he replied, exchanging a look with his parents. Dante and Tess seemed a bit uncomfortable now too.

"My godparents are Gideon and Savannah. And I'm damned lucky they are. They've been my rock more times than I can count."

Aric's quiet had deepened as well. A sudden awkwardness fell over the group. Kaya glanced at Chase and saw a regret in his blue gaze that made her wish for the floor to open up and swallow her. "I'm sorry if I said something wrong. I didn't mean to pry."

"You didn't. And you aren't," Chase said. "What no one here wants to say is that I was supposed to be godparent to Rafe, but I lost the privilege. Deservedly so. I had some . . . issues many years ago. I thought I could hide a big problem from my brethren and it cost me their trust. If I hadn't found a reason to turn it all around, I wouldn't be standing here today."

"Probably none of us would be," Dante said soberly, nothing but respect and affection for his fellow comrade and friend.

"What happened?" Kaya blurted before she could curb her question. "I mean, if you don't mind me asking, that is."

Aric was the one who answered. "He had to come clean about the thing that was destroying him and everything he cared about."

"That's right," his father confirmed. "I had a problem that was bigger than I could handle on my own. For me, it was blood addiction. But the solution is the same for anything that seems impossible to repair. The only way past a problem is through it." He turned an adoring glance on Tavia. "So much the better if you have the right person to help you to the other side."

He lifted his mate's face and kissed her in front of everyone, neither of them ashamed of their devotion—

or the palpable heat of their bond.

As for Kaya, she couldn't help but see the parallel between her own troubles and Sterling Chase's near forfeit of his place among the Order and the family he'd made there. And when she thought of family, it was impossible not to think of her twin.

As children, she and Leah had never known this kind of kinship and security with the people who bore them and raised them.

Nor this kind of love.

As much as she owed the truth to Aric and Mira and all the other people gathered in the sanctuary along with her, she couldn't turn her back on her sister.

Although Leah claimed not to want her help, Kaya had to give her another chance at a better life.

"Speaking of problems and finding our way through them," Dante said, his black brows knit over whiskey-colored eyes that narrowed on his warrior son. "How's Siobhan holding up? With everything that's happened since you and Aric picked her up, it's easy to forget the trauma she survived."

Rafe nodded. "She's doing her best to put the attack behind her, but it's not easy. Witnessing her roommate's brutal murder and being beaten unconscious by the Opus thugs who broke in that night has taken a toll. Siobhan's sensitive. She's . . . delicate. She's also the most captivating woman I've ever known."

Aric shot a wry smirk at his friend. "You never could resist a pretty damsel in distress."

"You trying to tell me I've got a type?" Rafe volleyed back, grinning. "Hard to recall even looking at anyone else now that I've met Siobhan."

His father grunted, clearly surprised by the news.

"Anyone with eyes can see how much you care for her. But I've gotta say, I never thought you'd find a woman to live up to your impossible standards. Did you, Tess?"

She gave the faintest shake of her blonde head, eyes the same arresting aquamarine color as Rafe's studying her son in a curious silence.

Kaya felt a stare holding on her too.

"Don't think I've forgotten about that private conversation you asked about," Nikolai told her. "Anytime you want to talk, my door is open for you."

She had to swallow past the knot of guilt that sat in her throat as she offered the commander a nod and murmured thanks. She felt the weight of Aric's silence beside her. With dread and regret crushing down on her, it was all she could do not to bolt from the room and scream out in self-directed anger and frustration.

She had to put her past to bed and either leave her sister behind for good or find some way to bring her into the light.

All she knew was she couldn't bear another day of holding the truth inside.

CHAPTER 25

Aric sat in the war room with Rafe, the Order elders, and all the rest of the Breed males on site at the command center, trying like hell to pay attention while they reviewed the events of the past few days and the resulting intel that Gideon had sent from D.C.

It wasn't that he had no interest. He was as determined as anyone to chase every trail that might lead the Order to Opus Nostrum—or to the leak that had somehow opened up in the Order's otherwise airtight pipeline of allies and informants.

And deep down, in spite of the instincts that had been gnawing at him relentlessly the past couple of days, he was hoping like hell that none of those trails led to Kaya.

After the ceremony celebrating Dmitri, Kaya had gone up to the mansion with the other women to enjoy the small feast they had prepared. Aric had been looking for the chance to get Kaya alone for a few minutes after the ceremony, but she seemed more than eager to get away from him once the sanctuary had cleared out.

So instead of chipping away at the wall of unanswered questions and increasingly troubling suspicions that stood between them, he was cooling his heels across the table from Lucan and his father on the verge of crawling out of his own skin.

Finally, he couldn't take it.

Offering a lame excuse, he ducked out of the meeting and beelined for the mansion and the sounds of women's laughter and conversation in the kitchen. He had let Kaya stonewall and evade him long enough.

He loved her, and if telling her that wasn't enough to loosen the knots in her tongue, then he needed to know now.

If she wasn't going to be totally honest with him— open to him in every way—then he needed to hear her say the words to his face. Then maybe he could get back to the business of living his life without her.

And if it turned out that she actually loved him, then by God he needed to hear that too.

He stalked through the kitchen entry like he was heading to war. "Kaya."

All the conversation ceased. Seven beautiful female faces swiveled in his direction, not one of them hers.

He frowned. "Where's Kaya?"

"Probably in her quarters," his mother replied.

Mira nodded. "She said she was tired and wanted to rest for a while."

Carys arched a brow at him, grinning. "You shouldn't be surprised to hear that, considering you spent most of last night in her room."

Ordinarily, he might take his twin sister's bait and come back with a smartass comment of his own. Not now. He was too tense for his own peace of mind and Kaya's absence pricked his suspicions more than he wanted to acknowledge. "How long?"

"What is it, Aric?" Tavia asked.

"When did she leave?"

The women exchanged uncertain looks. "About twenty minutes ago," one of them said.

He didn't know who, and didn't offer any acknowledgment. His feet were already moving beneath him, heading at almost a run toward the corridor that would take him to her private living suite in the residence.

He rapped on her door. "Kaya?" When no answer came, he knocked again. Then tried the knob and found it locked. "Damn it." He didn't like the idea of intruding on her without permission, but he didn't like the feeling he was getting about her absence even more. Exhaling a curse, he freed the lock with his mind and opened the door. "Kaya? Are you here?"

Utter silence. Her quarters were empty.

She was gone.

"Fuck. Damn you, Kaya."

He knew by the cold understanding in his veins that he wasn't going to find her anywhere in the command center. She had left base without telling anyone. That knowledge settled over him like a shroud.

In an instant, he was on the sunlit pavement outside the command center, flashing there with all the Breed velocity he possessed. He didn't know where she might have gone. Or, rather, he didn't want to think that he knew.

It took him only minutes to cross the city into Dorval.

To his relief, the ramshackle house down at the river that had been Angus Mackie's most recent address was still vacant. All the rats had fled that ship the night of the Order's raid and had evidently not returned.

Aric sped to the bar and found much the same situation. Empty building. No sign of the gang leader with the black scarab tattoo or any of his faithful followers. He came out of the tavern and raked a hand over his head, his heart rate finally decelerating now that all of his hunches seemed to have been wrong.

And thank fuck for that.

Some of the fury and dread that drove him down to this shitty neck of the woods began to ebb. At least it did until he glanced down the street and a glimpse of long dark hair and endless legs poured into dark denim caught his eye.

Kaya came out of a grimy auto garage with a grease-covered skinhead she appeared to know. No mistaking the piece of human garbage for anything other than one of Angus's ilk. Kaya's hand was locked on the man's forearm as she spoke to him. She took some cash out of her pocket and gave it to him. Then she got into a piece of shit sedan parked at the curb and drove off.

Aric could hardly control his rage.

He wanted to wring answers out of the human with his bare hands, but Kaya was the only one who could tell him what he really needed to know.

His body vibrated with menace as he gathered the shadows around himself and followed her up the street. The instant she stopped at a traffic light, he tore open the passenger door and dropped into the seat beside her.

"I call shotgun."

Her head swiveled toward him on a choked gasp. "Aric! What are you—"

"What am I doing here?" he finished for her, fury stripping his voice to its barest growl. "That's exactly what I came here to ask you, Kaya. What the hell are you doing down here alone on Big Mack's turf?"

Her brown eyes were bleak. "It's not what you think."

"Really?" He scoffed. "That's good. That's one huge goddamned fucking relief, Kaya. Because what I think is that you just crept away from base in broad daylight to meet up with one of the Order's enemies. What I think is that the heat is getting a little too intense back and the command center and maybe our mole's decided it's time to run back to whatever hidey-hole she crawled out of in the first place."

She looked away from him and shook her head, misery in the sound that escaped her lips. "I'm not a mole, Aric."

"Unfortunately, it's going to take a hell of a lot more than that to convince me now."

"I'm not a mole," she said, finally meeting his hard stare again.

"But you are on your way to see Big Mack now."

"Yes."

"Are you the reason he knew the Order was coming for him the other night?"

She swallowed hard, then lowered her head. "Yes. I'm sure I must be."

"What do you mean by that?"

"That day when I went for a run, I ended up going to Mackie's bar."

Aric let his curse go. It was sharp and rage-filled, lashing out with such force Kaya flinched on the other side of the vehicle. He realized only now how badly he'd been hoping for her denial, despite the strength of his suspicions. Instead, what she was telling him was even worse.

"I didn't go there looking to break the Order's trust. I went there because I needed to see someone."

"Someone who runs with Big Mack?" His voice sounded wooden, but whether it was from anger or shock, he wasn't sure. He refused to allow that it might be due to the sudden strangulation of his heart as he struggled to process the fact that the woman he loved was about to tell him she was in league with the Order's enemies. "No one who associates with those murdering cowards is worth your time. If I had my way, I'd cut a bloody track through the heart of every last one of them."

He saw her slight flinch as he said it. There was shame in the expression she turned on him. And regret. "Aric, I was born and raised with people like him. My mother was one of them, hate-filled and nasty. That was my world too. It was the only world I knew for a very long time."

"You're not like that," he pointed out.

"No, but I'm tied to that world. As much as I despise it, there's a part of me that might always be tied to that world."

Aric recalled everything she told him the night they made love on Summit Hill. She'd divulged that her childhood had been brutal, hate-filled. But now he was certain there was a missing piece to the puzzle of Kaya's past.

"This person you went to see at Mackie's bar. It's someone important to you?"

"Yes." She slowly shook her head. "I hadn't seen her in a long time. Not since we were sixteen."

Sixteen. The age Kaya had been when her mother was murdered and she was forced to kill in retaliation and self-defense before fleeing for her life into the city.

"After I saw those murders at that Darkhaven, I knew Big Mack's people were responsible. What I didn't know was if my sister had been aware of it too. It was a question I needed her to answer before I decided to shut her out of my heart and my life for good."

"Your sister," Aric murmured. "Both of you sixteen when your mother was killed."

Kaya nodded. "My identical twin. Her name is Leah. Or, rather, it was her name. Now they call her Raven."

"You have an identical twin who's been running with Big Mack and his cronies all these years?" Aric felt like he'd just taken a punch to the side of his head. "Ah, Christ. The security guard at the Rousseau estate. The one who turned out to have ties to Mackie. The one who claimed he knew you . . ."

She stared at him, miserable. "He thought I was her. He cornered me and then everything happened so fast."

"This secret of yours was the reason our mission went south that day."

"I know. I wanted to say something, Aric, but I was scared." She reached out to him, her palm coming to rest lightly on his cheek. "Aric, I love you."

The words lashed him now. "You lied to me."

"No."

"You lied by saying nothing," he bit off harshly. "You've been lying to us all."

"Aric, I wanted to tell you. I planned to tell you just as soon as I saw Leah one more time—"

"Stop." He drew back, his eyes hot with burning amber sparks. She was saying everything he wanted to hear, but there was still one large question looming. One there would be no coming back from, depending on her answer. "Tell me what you know about the ambush that waited for us at Lars Scrully's place."

"I don't know anything about that."

"How did you leak our plans to Opus? Or did you only have to leak them to Angus Mackie and he took care of the rest?"

"I didn't do any of that. I would never betray the Order to Opus Nostrum. Not to anyone. I would never betray you either." She shook her head. "Aric, you have to believe me."

"No, Kaya. I don't. Not anymore."

Her brow pinched as if she were in pain. Maybe she was. And maybe she was still lying, pretending to be wounded and laughing on the inside for how easily she could fool him, the male of a species she'd been schooled to view as something less than human. Monsters to be hated and destroyed.

Behind them, an angry pickup truck driver laid on his horn as the light changed. Aric impatiently waved the other vehicle around, baring his fangs at the belligerent scowl of the man as he passed them. The truck swerved and jolted before the driver stomped on the gas and fled in terror.

When Kaya glanced at him, he was glad for the savagery of his transformed face. Let her see him—really see him. Let her know what she was professing she loved.

"Where is he?" he demanded. "Angus Mackie. You need to tell me where to find him. I know you know, Kaya. If that skinhead back at the garage didn't willingly tell you, your hand on his arm was enough to siphon the truth from his so-called mind."

She looked worse than terrified. "Aric, you can't come with me."

"Come with you?" His chuckle was cold with malice. "I'm dropping you back at the command center, then I'm going after Mackie alone. When I'm finished, Big Mack and all of his followers will be nothing but bad memories and a lot of bleeding flesh and bones."

Her face blanched. "Aric, you don't understand. You can't do any of that."

"Give me one good reason why I shouldn't."

"Because my sister is with him. Aric, she's pregnant."

CHAPTER 26

A ric took the wheel, and Kaya directed him to the
place Mackie's friend at the garage had surrendered
to her unwillingly through his thoughts. The abandoned
house sat on a weed-choked empty lot near the city
dump.

"A fitting refuge for excrement like Big Mack," Aric
muttered as they parked the vehicle behind a rusted old
water tower and prepared to execute the rough plan
they'd discussed on the way. "You may not see me, but
I promise I'll be close."

She nodded, reassured by his presence even if the
conflict between them felt as wide as a cavern.

As soon as they were out of the car, Aric dissolved
into shadows.

Kaya walked to the front porch of the sagging one-
story eyesore and knocked on the door. A tall, scrawny
man answered several moments later. Stringy hair

covered his mottled skull, and beneath the scraggly brows that climbed high on his forehead at the sight of her, his bleary eyes blinked rapidly in confusion.

"What the fuck?" He blinked, then rubbed his eyes and blinked again. "You ain't Raven."

"No, I'm not." Kaya smiled pleasantly, her hand resting at the small of her back where the pistol she'd brought with her from the command center was tucked into the waistband of her jeans. "Step aside. I'm here to talk to my sister."

No sense pretending, she and Aric had decided. They were going to take Leah out of there and they were prepared to do so with guns blazing.

The aged junkie at the door gave a vigorous shake of his head. "Big Mack won't like this. Raven ain't takin' visitors right now."

"I say she is." Aric's deep voice and bared fangs as he emerged out of the shadows near the open door sent the man scrambling back into the house.

Mackie's poor excuse for a guard frantically reached for the gun holstered at his hip. Mistake. Aric shot him dead in an instant.

He glanced over at Kaya, his eyes ablaze with battle rage. "Ready, partner?"

She nodded. "Let's go get her."

At the same moment, the house erupted in chaos following the sound of gunfire. Two men charged from the back. Kaya took out one with a bullet to the head. Aric got the other. Indistinct shouts joined the panicked sounds of half a dozen men caught unaware by the invasion.

"Leah!" Kaya shouted. She didn't know where to look for her, only that the man at the garage knew

Mackie had her sister with him at his hideout following the failed raid. She could be anywhere. Kaya only hoped her twin wouldn't be coming at them as an enemy. "Leah, where are you?"

A blast of bullets from a semiautomatic ripped into the bowed wood paneling near Kaya's head as she and Aric pushed farther inside the small house. They ducked out of range but only barely. Splinters rained down into Kaya's hair.

"Leah!" Aric called now, his low bellow vibrating the floorboards beneath Kaya's feet.

Then she heard it.

The smallest cry coming from somewhere down the far end of the hall. Female. It was Leah. And she sounded to be in pain.

Aric shot a big man who barreled out of a bedroom ahead of them. The body sprawled across the floor, blocking their clean path. The woman's cry came again, more distinct now.

They hurried toward a closed bathroom door at the end of the narrow passage. Aric kicked it in with his boot. The thin door shattered off its hinges. And there, huddled in the filth of the avocado-tiled prison was Kaya's twin.

"Oh, my God. Leah."

She was handcuffed to the sink pipes like an animal, a gag tied around her mouth. Her clothing was torn and dirty. Bruises rode her left cheekbone. A scab covered an ugly split in her swollen lip.

Kaya's heart lurched at the sight of her sister's abuse. She hurried to her side along with Aric, who made quick work of the cuffs with a mental command that broke the locks open while Kaya unfastened the tight knots of the gag.

Leah's sob as the punishing restraints fell away shredded all of the misgivings she'd ever had for her estranged sibling.

"I'm going to look for Mackie," Aric said.

"Be careful." It was Leah's voice that spoke the words that were also on Kaya's tongue. Leah glanced at both of them, remorse in her dark brown eyes. "Angus has weapons hidden everywhere."

Aric nodded curtly, then vanished.

~ ~ ~

As furious as he had been for the fact that Kaya hadn't trusted him enough to share the truth about her sister and her past with him, Aric's rage had gone nuclear at the sight of her pregnant twin shackled like a dog inside Mackie's newest hideout.

It was too easy to see Kaya in the pretty, battered face that stared up at them so helplessly and broken. Too easy to think of Kaya being subjected to the punishing hands and lecherous cravings of men like Angus Mackie and his ilk.

For that, every man in this place would die.

Aric moved through the house as a stealth assassin, keeping to the shadows except to fill each of Mackie's men with lead. And now he had only to find the king of the rats.

Aric swept through the place, leaving no corner unturned.

And then he spotted the bastard.

Unshaven, dressed in only a pair of saggy yellowed cotton briefs, his hairy belly drooped in front of him and jiggling as he ran, the purportedly fearsome Big Mack made a hurried dash for the basement door. It banged behind him, followed by the hasty thudding of Mackie's bare feet on old wooden steps.

Aric snarled and leapt across the distance. He was just about to throw the door open with his mind when a shotgun blast exploded the panel in front of him. He dodged the spray and of wood and shrapnel in time to avoid the worst of it, then he dove through the opening and body slammed Mackie to the bottom of the stairs.

The fat coward screamed as Aric seized hold of him by the throat. His fangs felt as immense as daggers in his mouth, his eyes lighting up Mackie's face like an amber spotlight. "Not so brave now, are you?"

"What the fuck!" His eyes went wide, full of shock and terror. "Daywalker?"

"That's right," Aric snarled. "Your worst nightmare."

Not far from where he had Mackie pinned, crates that looked disturbingly similar to the ones the Order had recovered from the van at Scrully's estate were lined up on the concrete floor of the basement. Easily a dozen of them.

He growled a curse and tightened his chokehold on the gang leader. "Now, before I eviscerate you, you're going to tell me where you got this UV. I'm guessing from that black bug you've got tattooed on your right tit that your buddy Fineas Riordan hooked you up before the Order wasted him."

"I'm not telling you shit." Mackie gritted his teeth, struggling against Aric's unyielding hold. "You'll have to kill me. If I squeal, Opus will make sure I'm dead."

Behind him on the stairs, Aric heard Kaya's soft

footsteps. "The house is clear."

Aric nodded tightly, dragging Mackie up off the floor by his throat. "You and Leah all right?" he asked, looking at her because he needed to see for himself.

Kaya had come to the bottom step. Leah stood behind her halfway down, looking like a ghost version of her vibrant sister. "We're okay."

"Good. As soon as this sack of pus tells me what I want to know, we can be out of here."

"Fuck. You." Mackie sputtered.

Kaya walked up next to Aric. "There's another way to get the information we need."

She touched the human's flailing arm and asked him the same questions Aric had. But now Mackie's mind was open, his thoughts spilling loose at just a suggestion from Kaya. "Riordan supplied the ultraviolet weapons and rounds. Mackie has had contact from Opus, but never in person. He doesn't know any of the members."

"In other words, he's useless," Aric said, hardly disappointed to have the license to end the bastard. But there was still one very important question that he suspected Mackie could answer. "Where is Opus getting all of their intel on Order movements?"

Kaya sucked in a breath. "They have someone on the inside. Mackie knows it."

"Who?" Aric demanded, squeezing his throat nearly to the point of crushing it.

The human attempted a chuckle. "I love seeing you bloodsuckers chase your tails. Almost as much as I like seeing you smoked in a pile of ash under my boots."

Aric roared his fury. "Tell us, goddamn you."

"There *is* a mole," Kaya confirmed, her voice wooden. "They've got someone embedded. Someone who's feeding them high-value intel on a regular basis now. Data files too."

"What the fuck?" Aric scowled, beyond enraged. "Who is it? Say the name or say goodbye to your larynx."

"Some Irish bitch," Mackie finally relented. "Iona something."

Aric reeled back. He caught Kaya's confused gaze too. "If you're talking about Reginald Crowe's mistress, Iona Lynch, she's dead. I saw her savaged body with my own eyes last week."

"Yeah?" Mackie taunted despite the strangling hold on him. "Then she must be sending messages from hell because she's the one who got a warning passed on to me that the Order was after my ass a few nights ago."

"What?" Kaya swiveled a questioning look at her sister. "I thought you warned him after I came to see you."

Leah shook her head. "This son of a bitch has been holding me against my will for six months, threatening to kill me and my baby if I try to leave. I would never tell him anything."

Aric's blood ran ice cold. When he glanced at Kaya, her face showed the same astonished dread that was currently coiled around him.

"Oh, my God," Kaya murmured. "Rafe."

CHAPTER 27

A t the insistence of their mates the Order's meeting in the war room had broken up half an hour ago, sending the Breed elders up to the mansion to join the women. Mira's comrades had invited Rafe to the weapons room for some sparring and the usual bullshitting and ball-busting that was a staple of warrior life in any of the Order's command centers, but he had declined the offer.

He had other diversions in mind.

Namely, Siobhan.

He'd been surprised to discover she wasn't in her guest room in the main residence. Curious to find she hadn't even stopped by to see Renata or fawn over the baby, which she'd seemed to be so excited for whenever he spoke about the pending arrival of the Order's newest family member.

As Rafe strode back down to the command center,

the only place she could possibly have gone, he felt a niggling pang that he was tempted to call suspicion. He might have, if his faith in Siobhan wasn't so complete. Had she gotten lost down in the maze of corridors that threaded through the labyrinthine nerve center of the warriors' domain? She knew the area was restricted to Order members, but she was an inquisitive woman and maybe she had simply woken from her long nap and gone looking to find him.

The idea comforted him, sweeping away the colder sense he had that he was missing something. That he was blind to something right in front of his face.

That his obsession with Siobhan was making him weak in ways he didn't quite comprehend.

"Ridiculous," he muttered as he trekked through yet another twisting passageway and found no sign of her.

He pivoted to go back, then he noticed that the elevator that connected the mansion's living quarters and command center was stuck on the lower level of the compound. There was nothing in the subterranean bowels of this place but basement storage.

The elevator never sat down there for this long.

Rafe pressed the call button, but nothing happened.

On a frown, he glanced to the stairwell. He took the steps in stealth silence, uncertain why he felt the need to approach whatever waited for him down there with the caution of a soldier. He froze in place as his gaze lit on the propped open elevator door and the crates of ultraviolet munitions that packed the car.

Siobhan was inside. She had something in her hand, wiring it to the crates.

Rafe's warrior instincts scraped him with confusion. Suspicion. A dread so deep it staggered him.

He saw the scene for what it was: Siobhan with a detonation device in hand, a remote lying next to her.

Fury flared in him, burning past the weaker feelings of disbelief and apprehension.

"Siobhan. What the fuck are you doing?"

She wheeled around, her hand flying to her breast. "Rafe."

Surprise filled her pretty face, along with an emotion he was tempted to call displeasure. But then she smiled and tilted her head, those hazel eyes of hers reaching out to him—into him—and making him wonder if he was wrong to feel the doubt the clawed at him.

"You startled me," she said, her voice sweet and shy, utterly innocent.

He wanted to rail at her, but the words dried up on his tongue. "I've been looking for you. I just searched the whole damned place trying to find you."

"Did I worry you?" she asked gently. "I'm sorry if I did."

He stood there, bewildered and enraged, yet his anger seemed elusive when she was holding him in her adoring gaze. Her tender smile did something to him. Burned all of his negative feelings and suspicions away, as if he were seeing her through a distorted lens, one that could not maintain focus on logic, but only the beautiful woman he adored.

He tried to shake loose of the odd sensation, but it clung tenaciously. "What's going on here, Siobhan? What are you doing down here by yourself?"

She drifted toward him, her lips still curved in a warm smile, her eyes still locked on his. God, she was so lovely. So petite and delicate looking. How could he entertain the idea that she was anything but the sensitive innocent that had so captivated his heart?

His eyes saw an angel, even though his blood was still hammering as though he were facing a demon.

"I got lost trying to find you after I woke up a few minutes ago," she said, telling him the precise thing he wanted to hear.

He relaxed as she said it, his heart desperate to believe her. She came closer, until there was hardly scant inches between them. The more she held him in her steady, earnest gaze, the less he could keep hold of a single doubt.

Yet when he glanced over her petite shoulder to the crates of UV now wired for detonation, his vision wobbled. It felt as if he were looking through oil-smeared glass. And the warrior in him could not ignore the danger licking at his conscience.

"What were you doing with that shit?" he pressed in the moment his logic managed to penetrate the haze of his affection for her. "Why were you messing with it?"

"I found the crates in the elevator," she rushed to explain. "Someone must be trying to move them out of the command center."

She tried to lead him away now, her hand looped around his arm. Rafe's feet refused to budge. He shook his head, pushing against the thick mud that seemed to entrench his sense of reason.

"No, Siobhan. You put those inside this car. The wires on the crates, the detonator box. You did all of this?" The accusation sounded like a question, one his mind still couldn't seem to fully grasp.

She reached up to touch his cheek but he drew away—barely. It was hard to resist her. It was as if this female held him under a spell.

"Holy hell."

Just like that, he saw through it. Only for the briefest second, but it was enough.

Rafe set her away from him on a snarl. "What have you done to me?"

With effort, he shook off the strange veil that seemed to cover him, obscuring his vision—his true sight. The power of his mind was struggling against whatever power she held over him, giving him little glimpses of sanity.

And the incredible depth of her deception.

"What the fuck have you been doing to me, Siobhan?"

"Me?" She tilted her head, her gaze reaching for his, working to draw him back under. "I haven't done anything, Rafe."

"Yes. You have. You've been lying to me. You've . . . Jesus, how are you doing this? You're mesmerizing me somehow, trying to make me believe you. Trying to make me love you."

Her expression fell into a pretty pout. "That hurts me, Rafe. How can you doubt me? I love you—"

"No!" He shook himself, tasting her lie like bitter acid. Poison she'd been feeding him for days. Christ, ever since that night he and Aric rescued her after the attack she'd barely survived.

He took hold of her delicate shoulders. "I can feel you in my head now, Siobhan. You're trying to weave some kind of spell."

"No," she murmured softly. "No, Rafe, that's not true."

"It is, damn it." He could feel her attempting it again. The surge of tender feelings she coaxed inside him, her false love pushing at his mind, at his heart. He growled, denying her access. Now that he could see the allure for what it was—a trick—it was losing most of its power. "Tell me what the fuck you've done to me, Siobhan!"

He shook her violently, dangerously close to wanting to kill her with his bare hands.

Her face turned sour, twisted. Then she laughed, an empty, awful sound. "Finally, you've pierced my thrall. Took you long enough."

Anger lashed him. Humiliation too. "This is your Breedmate talent? Seduction? Enthralling a man into thinking he loves you, blinding him to the fact that you're really a hideous gorgon underneath your pretty face and innocent words. This has all been a game to you, Siobhan? One big fucking lie."

A sadistic sneer pulled her lips flat. "You saw what you wanted to see. That is the power of my ability. And you can stop calling me that name. I'm beyond tired of hearing it."

Rafe frowned at this new revelation. "If you're not Siobhan O'Shea, then who are you? Tell me everything, you deceptive bitch."

Then it hit him. "Ah, fuck. Iona Lynch didn't die in that flat outside Dublin. Siobhan O'Shea did."

"I knew the Order had me in their crosshairs after they killed Reginald Crowe. It was only a matter of time before they closed in on me. I was preparing to leave when you and Aric Chase showed up at the flat I shared with Siobhan. I had already killed her to ensure her silence, but you arrived too soon. I had no hope of getting away fast enough, so I decided to hide in plain sight."

"You're sick," Rafe seethed.

"No," she said, unfazed. "I'm a soldier, just like you. And I'm very good at what I do."

He grunted, despising her now. "Why not break loose as soon as we got you to London? You had ample opportunity. The Order treated you with nothing but trust and kindness. You could've bolted to freedom anytime you wanted."

"I thought about it," she admitted, no emotion in her voice at all. "I expected to be deposited somewhere in that city and then disappear. Instead, the Order informed me they intended to bring me to their headquarters in Washington, D.C. So, I decided to use that unexpected advantage to finish the work Opus Nostrum failed at before. Killing the Order's leader, Lucan Thorne."

Rafe's curse was airless with his shock. "You never would've gotten close enough to him to try."

"Maybe not. The last thing I wanted was this detour away from my goal. But then imagine my surprise when I learned that Lucan and nearly all of the Order would be coming here instead."

"You're the mole." Rafe nearly spat the words. "I was so sure it would be Kaya, but it was you leaking intel to Opus." He glanced once more to the crates of wired ultraviolet ammunition and his veins iced over. "Now you're planning to kill us all."

She smiled. "You've all made it so easy. How can I resist when you've brought me the very weapon I need to take out most of the Order in one fell swoop?"

Pretty, evil eyes looked up at him sweetly. "But now you have to die first."

Pain seared him, a sudden sharp jolt to his gut. He didn't realize she held a weapon concealed somewhere on her person. Perhaps whatever power she'd been wielding over him when he found her here a few minutes ago had obscured the threat from his notice.

She stabbed him again, driving the blade into the center of his chest. Directly into his heart.

His fangs erupted from his gums on the roar that ripped out of his throat. She darted back, out of his reach as he sagged to his knees, astonished by the accuracy of her strike.

Blood poured through his fingers, too much of it and the wound far too grievous. His ability to mend wounds with his hands only worked on others. As for his Breed capacity to self-heal, he hadn't taken a blood Host for nearly a week, starving for the Breedmate who had denied him her vein only to smile as she now stood before him and took his life.

His vision fading, Rafe collapsed to the floor, a growing pool of blood gathering all around him.

Iona Lynch watched him suffer for a moment, then she turned and went back to her work.

CHAPTER 28

Aric reached the command center so fast it was as though his feet had wings. Kaya had insisted she and Leah would be fine making their way back in the car, leaving him only one crushing concern. The life of his best friend and comrade.

Siobhan O'Shea—or, rather, Iona Lynch—was only a diminutive female but the depth of her treachery knew no bounds. And Rafe was more than halfway mad in love with her, which Aric feared might prove to be an obstacle all of its own.

Rafe needed to be warned of the woman's deception, but to his marrow, Aric dreaded it might already be too late.

He thought back to the excuses Iona had made for missing the ceremony earlier today. Excuses that had left Reginald Crowe's bitch alone for hours while everyone in the command center was preoccupied with the ritual and celebration that followed. And the fact that there was a sizable cache of ultraviolet arms and ammunition at her disposal didn't exactly ease any of the bone-deep dread that strangled Aric with every rapid beat of his heart.

He decided to check that hunch first, speeding directly to the lowest floor of the command center where the evidence from Scrully's estate was stored. The scent of spilled blood was a punch to his system. The sight of his immense, practically immortal friend lying unmoving in the center of that dark, sticky lake was even more of a shock.

Crouched inside the open car of the stalled elevator was Iona Lynch. She held an electronic device in her hand, working frantically in front of several crates of UV now wired to blow.

"You fucking bitch."

His seething growl brought her strawberry-blonde head up with a start. She squeaked at the sight of his transformed face and growing fangs.

Aric grabbed her in savage hands and threw her against the wall. She hit with a hard thump, bones cracking. Stunned, momentarily rendered immobile, she dropped in a petite heap on the floor.

While she was disabled, Aric went to Rafe's side. He'd been stabbed in the abdomen and in the chest—a direct blow to his heart, from the catastrophic look of it. And the blood. So much fucking blood.

"I didn't mean to do it." Iona's voice sounded small and tear-choked behind him. "Rafe gave me no choice, Aric."

He glanced behind him, not because he cared what the duplicitous slut had to say but because he didn't want to end up with a blade in his back.

"He was crazy, Aric. I think he intended to use this UV to kill himself and all the other Breed males under this roof."

As she spoke in that quiet, desperate voice, Iona's hazel eyes seemed huge in her pretty face. She was a beauty, even he had to admit that. And she was looking at him with a kind of helpless desperation—a trembling innocence—that would have been hard for any man to resist.

Except for him.

"You can drop the damsel in distress act. It's not going to work on me."

Her mouth twisted. "No. Your friend was much easier to read. I only had to show him what he wanted to see and he fell right into my hands. And between my legs."

Aric cursed, hating that his animus for this heartless witch had to take him away from trying to help his wounded friend. Iona's gaze widened as he stood up and faced her fully.

"I've never been with a daywalker," she murmured, turning from coy waif to sultry siren in an instant. "It's a pity. I'll bet you and I would burn up the sheets, warrior."

Aric snorted. "Even if my heart didn't already belong to Kaya, I'd never dirty my hands on Reginald Crowe's leavings."

She laughed at that. "You think he was my lover? Reginald Crowe was my father."

Aric sneered. "In that case, the Order's going to have a good time wringing you dry for information on Opus Nostrum and the Atlantean queen he served."

"No," she said, shaking her head. "I don't think so."

Without another word or warning, she hit the timer device in her hand and threw it into the elevator before closing the doors and sending the packed car upward to the mansion.

Then she brought her knife up to her throat and sliced it all the way across.

"No!" Aric cursed as the Order's best source of Opus intel dropped to the floor.

But even worse than that loss—exponentially worse—was the ultraviolet bomb now making its way into the heart of the command center.

He put all of his concentration into halting the car with his mind. Then he stalled the timer on Iona Lynch's detonator. He would deal with the rest of that problem later.

Suddenly, Aric was no longer alone in the room. All of the Breed males in the place had been alerted to the overwhelming scent of so much spilled blood. Dante went directly to his fallen son on a roar that shook the concrete walls. His bellow was followed by Tess's anguished cry. She fell to her son's side, her healing hands covering the blood-soaked area of his pierced heart.

"He's alive," she gasped. "Oh, thank God. Rafe's still alive."

Aric did his best to explain what he'd walked in on, and the reason he'd known the Breedmate lying dead nearby was the betrayer the Order had been looking for.

The Order elders crowded in around him, a hundred questions issued at the same time while Tess and Dante and several of the other Breedmates moved in to carry Rafe away for treatment of his wounds.

Kaya now raced down to the room as well. Aric had never seen a more welcome sight. She went to his side on a soft exhalation, wrapping herself around him in front of everyone in the room. He held her close, never intending to let her go.

CHAPTER 29

K aya stood within the circle of Aric's strong arms, the warm water of the shower having washed away all of the blood and grime and stress of the day's ordeals.

They had just made love beneath the soothing spray, an unrushed mating they'd both seemed to need with equal desperation. They held each other close, neither of them seeming to be able to stand more than an inch of separation after all of the loss and anguish that surrounded them.

But there was hope too.

Rafe was recovering in the infirmary. Aric had reached him in the nick of time, and now Tess was doing everything in her power to ensure her son's healing was complete. His body would bear no scars from today, nor would his punctured heart. His flesh and organs were restored, but no one seemed confident that the angry, vengeful male who had awoken from the betrayal he suffered would ever be the same on the inside.

"I still can't believe how thoroughly Iona Lynch deceived us all," Kaya murmured as she and Aric caressed each other with slick, soapy hands. "None of us suspected a thing."

Aric grunted. "Only Tess had an inkling that something wasn't right."

"She did?"

He nodded. "More or less, at any rate. A few weeks ago, when Mira and Kellan needed Tess's healing help, she accidentally gazed into Mira's eyes."

Kaya drew back, looking up at him in surprise. "Do you mean Tess saw a vision?"

Without the lavender contact lenses Mira wore, her eyes were mirrors that reflected the future to anyone who stared into her naked gaze. Aric acknowledged with a sober expression.

"What did Tess see?"

"Rafe and his blood-bonded mate. Tess saw him happy with a family of his own, and the woman he was with was not Siobhan O'Shea. Or Iona Lynch, as the case may be."

"Then who?"

Aric shook his head. "No one Tess has seen before. She says she was surprised to see Rafe so smitten with someone who didn't fulfill the prediction, but she never dreamed the meek little waif could be a danger to her son or anyone else."

Kaya considered for a moment. "No wonder she seemed oddly quiet at the ceremony when Rafe was talking about how captivated he was with Siobhan. Er, Iona. Let's just call her Reginald Crowe's daughter."

Aric exhaled a sharp breath. "I still can't believe that

part of her secret. All this time the Order assumed Crowe was spending so much time in Ireland with a mistress. I guess nothing should surprise us anymore." His embrace tightened around her, strong muscles flexing as he drew her against his hard, wet body. "You have been the only good surprise to come out of all this."

She warmed at his praise, and at the evident sincerity of his affection for her. She couldn't hold back her small moan of pleasure as he moved his hips against her, his arousal thick and enticing where it jutted between her thighs. "I can't imagine not being with you, Aric. When I think about how close I came to losing you because of the things I was too afraid to say, all the things I was ashamed to admit to you . . . I'm just so relieved that you and the rest of the Order have forgiven me."

"You didn't do anything wrong, Kaya. Not until you stayed silent instead of trusting me and the other people who love you."

She glanced up at him in hopeful silence. "What did you just say?"

"That I love you, Kaya Laurent." He stroked her cheek, his eyes smoldering and full of something far deeper than desire. "I love you with everything I am. If memory serves—and we both know it does—you also said you love me."

"Yes." A smile broke over her to hear him say the words that had been living inside her from the beginning. "Yes, Aric, I do love you. I've been trying to convince myself that it's impossible that I fell in love with you practically from the time we met, but it's true. I love you."

He grinned. "You've had me under your spell from our first meeting too."

"My spell?" She frowned and smacked his muscled chest. "Promise never to joke about that again."

He smirked and bent his head to kiss her. "Okay, I promise. But I am going to say this. I don't want to know what it feels like to live a day, or a night, without you at my side. This detour was only supposed to be temporary. I never dreamed I'd find forever here."

She swallowed, realizing just now that there was still one obstacle that they would have to navigate around. "But the Order is going back to D.C. as soon as Rafe is fully recovered. Won't you be going with them?"

He nodded. "Yes. For a short while. Then I'll be going wherever the Order needs me the most. The threat from Opus looms larger than ever before, now that both UV and Red Dragon are in play."

Kaya knew what he said was true. Using the data they'd collected from Lars Scrully's computers, Gideon had found a link between Stephan Mercier's lucrative deal with the Opus member and the manufacture and proliferation of the Breed-targeted narcotic. And Mercier wasn't the only one who'd been tapped to launder money and play the mule for Opus Nostrum. There were others in the chain, and now the Order needed to be ready to go after the organization with every advantage and weapon they had.

"I've been assigned to a new team," Aric said. "I start effective immediately."

Kaya didn't dare hope that team would be hers, here in Montreal. She stroked her hands over his back and tight ass, wanting to memorize every inch of him in case this was the last time she would see him for a while. "Is that why Lucan pulled you aside after everything that happened today? To give you this new assignment?"

"Yes." His gaze held hers, pride and purpose in his green eyes. "I've been tasked with heading up a new division of the Order. A Special Ops team comprised of daywalkers and other specially skilled warriors."

"Aric, that's amazing news." She couldn't pretend it wasn't. Not even if this new role would undoubtedly send him away from both D.C. and Montreal. "I'm thrilled for you."

"I hoped you would be," he said, lifting her chin for his kiss. "I also hoped I might be able to convince you to be part of the group. My first team member and best partner. You did say you always wanted to see the world. So, do it with me."

"What?" Elation soared through her, but her joy had a slender tether too. Everything inside her leapt at the thought of being his partner, his comrade. His lover. "But what about Leah? We've just reunited. She needs support, especially now that she's got a baby on the way."

Kaya had been torn between relief and sorrow when Leah told her the sad circumstances of how she'd become a prisoner to Angus Mackie's threats. She'd fallen in love with a man inside the group, a kind man. When she became pregnant, they plotted their escape, only to be stopped by Big Mack. Leah's lover was murdered in front of her and Mackie threatened to do the same to her and her unborn child if she ever attempted to leave the gang.

"The Order won't leave your sister on her own," Aric assured her. "Renata and Niko are already making arrangements for her at Anna's Place. The shelter is in need of a manager, and Leah needs a safe home for her and her baby."

Kaya closed her eyes, swamped with gratitude not only for Aric's love and kindness, but for the rest of the Order as well.

"I don't know what to say."

"Say yes, Kaya." He held her face in his palms, his eyes glittering with amber sparks. The sharp points of his fangs gleamed as he spoke, sending a coil of dark need spiraling through her. "Say you're mine."

"I am, Aric." She stared up into his glowing eyes, overwhelmed with the power of everything she felt for this incredible man. This Breed male she loved more than anything she ever knew. "I am yours."

"I won't settle for anything less than forever," he murmured thickly, his fangs growing even longer, sharper, with each earnest word.

He stroked the side of her neck where her pulse throbbed. His touch made her veins ache for something more. As if he knew what she needed, he lowered his head and suckled the tender flesh above her carotid. The slightest graze of his elongated canines nearly made her come on the spot.

"Tell me this is what you want, Kaya."

"It is," she gasped. "Aric, I want this more than my next breath. I want you. Forever."

He uttered her name, and then she felt the stunning pleasure of his bite. He drank from her, hard, possessive tugs that made everything female in her erupt with heated desire. And love. So much love she wept with the power of it.

Aric's possessive growl filled her ears, echoing in the veins he now owned. Veins that would connect them for the rest of their days.

"You're mine," he growled, pausing to lick her

punctures and seal them closed. "You have my body and my heart, Kaya. You have my love forever. Now, will you have my bond?"

"Yes, Aric." She'd never wanted anything more. "Oh, God. Yes."

He brought his wrist up to his mouth and bit down on his own flesh, opening his veins for her. She had never tasted anything so wondrous, so erotically powerful as the first sip of his blood. The roar of it filled her senses as their bond came to life within her, within both of them.

"Mine," Aric growled, spreading her legs to receive him as he fed her from his open vein. "You're mine forever now, Kaya."

She moaned, incapable of words as he filled her body and nourished her heart and soul with the power of his blood and his bond. And when he brought them both to shattering climax a few minutes later, he came shouting her name like a promise and a prayer.

"Forever," she murmured, holding his fiery gaze.

She couldn't wait for their future to begin.

~ * ~

Watch for the next book in the bestselling
Midnight Breed Series from Lara Adrian!

Break the Day

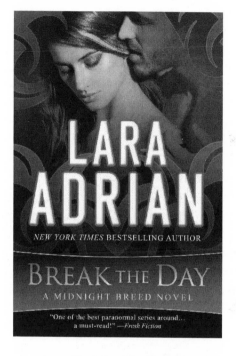

Available Fall 2018

eBook * Paperback * Unabridged audiobook

**For more information on the series and upcoming
releases, visit:**

www.LaraAdrian.com

Discover the Midnight Breed
with a FREE eBook

Get the series prequel novella
A Touch of Midnight
FREE in eBook at most major retailers

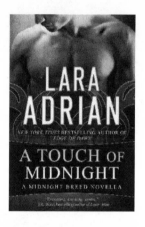

After you enjoy your free read, look for Book 1

The Hunters are coming!

Presenting an all-new Midnight Breed spinoff series
you won't want to miss…

The Hunter Legacy Series

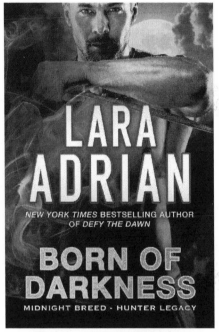

Born of Darkness
Coming Spring 2018

Thrilling standalone vampire romances from Lara Adrian
set in the Midnight Breed story universe.

For information on this series and more, visit:

www.LaraAdrian.com

Never miss a new book from Lara Adrian!

Sign up for the email newsletter at
www.LaraAdrian.com

Or type this URL into your web browser:
http://bit.ly/LaraAdrianNews

Be the first to get notified of Lara's new releases,
plus be eligible for special subscribers-only exclusive
content and giveaways that you won't find
anywhere else.

Bonus!
When you confirm your subscription, you'll get an
email with instructions for requesting free bookmarks
and other fun goodies, while supplies last.

Sign up today!

Turn the page for an excerpt from this recent release in the Midnight Breed vampire romance series

Midnight Unbound

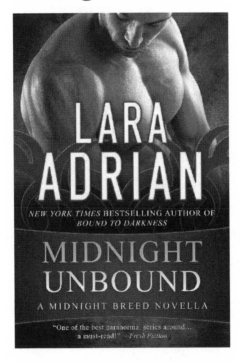

Available now in ebook, trade paperback and unabridged audiobook

For more information on the series and upcoming releases, visit:

www.LaraAdrian.com

A lethal Breed warrior is called upon by his brethren in the Order to bodyguard a beautiful young widow he's craved from afar in this new novella in the "steamy and intense" (Publishers Weekly) Midnight Breed vampire romance series from New York Times and #1 international bestselling author Lara Adrian.

As a former Hunter bred to be a killing machine in the hell of Dragos's lab, Scythe is a dangerous loner whose heart has been steeled by decades of torment and violence. He has no room in his world for love or desire--especially when it comes in the form of a vulnerable, yet courageous, Breedmate in need of protection. Scythe has loved--and lost--once before, and paid a hefty price for the weakness of his emotions. He's not about to put himself in those chains again, no matter how deeply he hungers for lovely Chiara.

For Chiara Genova, a widow and mother with a young Breed son, the last thing she needs is to put her fate and that of her child in the hands of a lethal male like Scythe. But when she's targeted by a hidden enemy, the obsidian-eyed assassin is her best hope for survival . . . even at the risk of her heart.

~ ~ ~

"It was such an AMAZING feeling to be diving back into the dangerous and sensual world of the Midnight Breed... If you are looking for a fast-paced, paranormal romantic suspense, full of passion and heart, look no further than MIDNIGHT UNBOUND."
—Shayna Renee's Spicy Reads

Chapter 1

Scythe had been in the dance club for nearly an hour and he still hadn't decided which of the herd of intoxicated, gyrating humans would be the one to slake his thirst tonight. Music blared all around him, the beat throbbing and pulsing, compounding the headache that had been building in his temples for days.

His stomach ached, too, sharp with the reminder that it had been almost a week since he'd fed. Too long for most of his kind. For him—a Breed male whose Gen One blood put him at the very top of the food chain— a week without nourishment was not only dangerous for his own wellbeing, but for that of everyone near him as well.

From within the cloak of shadows that clung around the end of the bar, he watched the throng of young men and women illuminated by colored strobe lights that flashed and spun over the dance floor as the DJ rolled seamlessly from the track of one sugary pop hit to another.

This tourist dive in Bari, a seaside resort town located at the top of Italy's boot heel, wasn't his usual hunting ground. He preferred the larger cities where blood Hosts could be hired for their services and dismissed immediately afterward, but his need to feed was too urgent for a long trek to Naples.

And besides, that journey would take him past the vineyard region of Potenza—an area he made a habit of avoiding for the past few weeks for reasons he refused to consider, even now.

Hell, especially now, when blood thirst wrenched his gut and his fangs pulsed with the urge to sink into warm, tender flesh.

A snarl slid off his tongue as he let his gaze drift over the crowd again. Against his will, he locked on to a petite brunette swaying to the music on the far side of the packed club. She had her back to him, silky dark brown hair cascading over her shoulders, her small body poured into skinny jeans and cropped top that bared a wedge of pale skin at her midsection. She laughed at something her companions said, and the shrill giggle scraped over Scythe's heightened sense of hearing.

He glanced away, instantly disinterested, but the sight of her had called to mind another waifish female— one he'd been trying his damnedest to forget.

He knew he'd never find Chiara Genova in a place like this, yet there was a twisted part of him that ran with the idea, teasing him with a fantasy he had no right to entertain. Sweet, lovely Chiara, naked in his arms. Her mouth fevered on his, hungered. Her slender throat bared for his bite—

"Fuck."

The growl erupted out of him, harsh with fury. It drew the attention of a tall blonde who had parked her skinny ass on the barstool next to him fifteen minutes ago and had been trying, unsuccessfully, to make him notice her.

Now she leaned toward him, reeking of too much wine and perfume as she licked her lips and offered him a friendly grin. "You don't look like you're having much fun tonight."

He grunted and glanced her way, taking stock of her in an instant.

Human. Probably closer to forty than the short leather skirt and lacy bustier she wore seemed to suggest. And definitely not a local. Her accent was pure American. Midwest, if he had to guess.

"Wanna hear a confession?" She didn't wait for him to answer, not that he planned to. "I'm not having much fun tonight, either." She heaved a sigh and traced one red-lacquered fingernail around the rim of her empty glass. "You thirsty, big guy? Why don't you let me buy you a drink—"

"I don't drink."

Her smile widened and she shrugged, undeterred. "Okay, then let's dance."

She slid off her stool and grabbed for his hand.

When she didn't find it—when her fingers brushed against the blunt stump where his right hand used to be, a long time ago—she recoiled.

"Oh, my God. I, um... Shit." Then her intoxicated gaze softened with pity. "You poor thing! What happened to you? Are you a combat vet or something?"

"Or something." Irritation made his deep voice crackle with menace, but she was too drunk to notice.

She stepped in close and his predator's senses lit up, his nostrils tingling at the trace coppery scent of human red cells rushing beneath her skin. The rawness in his stomach spread to his veins, which now began to throb with the rising intensity of his blood thirst.

His body felt heavy and slow. The stump at the end of his wrist ached with phantom pain. His normally razor-sharp vision was blurred and unfocused.

Usually, in some dark, bizarre way, he relished the sensation of physical discomfort. It reminded him that as dead inside as he might feel—as disconnected as he had been ruthlessly trained to be as a Hunter in the hell of Dragos's laboratory—there were some things that could still penetrate the numbness. Make him feel like he was among the living.

This particular kind of pain, though, bordered on unbearable, and it was all he could do not to grab the woman and take her vein right there in the middle of the club.

"Come on. Let's get out of here."

"Sure!" She practically leaped at him. "I thought you'd never ask."

He steered her away from the bar and out the club's exit without another word. Although the Breed had been outed to their human neighbors for more than twenty years, there were few among Scythe's kind—even a stone-cold killer like him—who made a habit of feeding in public places.

His companion wobbled a bit as they stepped out into the crisp night air. "Where do you wanna go? I'm staying at a hotel just up the street. It's a shithole, but we can go there if you want to hang out for a while."

"No. My vehicle will do."

Desire lit her features as she stared up at him. "Impatient, are you?" She giggled, smacking her palm against his chest. "Don't worry, I like it."

She trailed after him across the small parking lot to his gleaming black SUV.

In some dim corner of his conscience, he felt sorry for a woman who valued herself so little that she would traipse off with a stranger who offered her nothing in return for the use of her body.

Or, in this case, her blood.

Scythe had been born nothing better than a slave. Had nearly died one. The concept of taking from someone simply because he had the physical prowess to do it pricked him with self-loathing. The least he could do was make sure that when he took he left something behind as well. The woman would be weak with an unexplainable satisfaction once he was finished with her. Since he was feeling an uncustomary twinge of pity for her, she'd also walk away with a purse fat enough to rent a room for a month in the best hotel in Bari.

"This way," he muttered, his voice nothing more than a rasp.

She took his proffered arm and grinned, but it wasn't the coy smile that had his blood heating. It was the pulse fluttering wildly in her neck beneath that creamy flesh that had his fangs elongating. They punched through his gums and he went lightheaded with the need to feed, denied for too long.

They got into his vehicle and he wasted no time. Pivoting in the seat, he reached for her with his left hand, his fingers curling around her forearm. She uttered a small, confused noise as he drew her toward him and brought her wrist to his mouth.

Her confusion faded away the second he sank his fangs into her delicate flesh.

"Oh, my God," she gasped, her cheeks flushing as her whole body listed forward.

She speared the fingers of her free hand into his long black hair, and he had to resist the urge to jerk away as blood filled his mouth. He didn't like to be touched. All he wanted to do was fill the gaping hole in his gut until the next time he was forced to feed.

She moaned, her breath coming in quick pants as he drank. He took his fill, drawing on her wrist until he could feel the energy coursing through his body, replenishing his strength, fortifying his cells.

When he was done, he closed the tiny bite marks on her skin with a dispassionate swipe of his tongue as she twitched against him breathlessly.

"Good Lord, what is this magic and where do I sign up for more?" she murmured, her chest still heaving.

He leaned back against the cushioned leather, feeling the calm begin to move over him as his body absorbed the temporary nourishment. When the woman started to shift toward him with drugged need in her eyes, Scythe reached out and placed his palm against her forehead.

The trance took hold of her immediately. He erased her memory of his bite and the desire it stirred in her. When she slumped back against her seat, he dug into the pocket of his black jeans for his money and peeled off several large bills. He tossed them in her lap, then opened the passenger door with a silent, mental command.

"Go," he instructed her through her trance. "Take the money and go back to your hotel. Stay away from this club. Find something better to do with your time."

She obeyed at once. Stuffing the bills into her purse, she climbed out of the SUV and headed across the parking lot.

Scythe tipped his head back against the seat and released a heavy sigh as his fangs began to recede. Already, the human's blood was smoothing the edge from his whole-body pain. The malaise that had been worsening for the past twenty-four hours was finally gone and this feeding would hold him for another week if he was lucky.

He started up his vehicle, eager to be back on the road to his lair in Matera. He hadn't even pulled out of the lot when his cell phone chirped from inside his coat pocket. He yanked it out with a frown and scowled down at the screen. Only three people had his number and he wanted to hear from exactly none of them right now.

The restricted call message glowed up at him and he grimaced.

Shit. No need to guess who it might be.

And as much as he might want to shut out the rest of the world, Scythe would never refuse the call of one of his former Hunter brethren.

On a curse, he jabbed the answer button. "Yeah."

"We need to talk." Trygg's voice was always a shade away from a growl, but right now the Breed warrior's tone held a note of urgency too. Scythe had heard that same note in his half-brother's voice the last time he called from the Order's command center in Rome, and he could only imagine what it meant now.

"So, talk," he prompted, certain he didn't want the answer. "What's going on?"

"The Order's got a problem that could use your specialized skills, brother."

"Fuck." Scythe's breath rushed out of him on a groan. "Where have I heard that before?"

Six weeks ago, he'd allowed Trygg to drag him into the Order's troubles and Scythe was still trying to put the whole thing behind him. As a former assassin, he didn't exactly play well with others. He damned sure wasn't interested in getting tangled up in Order business again.

But there were only a handful of people in the world who knew exactly what Scythe had endured in the hell of Dragos's Hunter program, and Trygg was one of them. They had suffered it together for years as boys, and had dealt with the aftermath as men.

Even if they and the dozens of other escaped Hunters didn't share half their DNA, their experience in the labs couldn't make for truer brothers than that. If Trygg needed something, Scythe would be there. Hell, he'd give up his other hand for any one of his Hunter brethren if they asked it of him.

Scythe's preternatural ability to sniff out trouble told him that Trygg was about to ask for something far more painful than that.

"Tell me what you need," he muttered, steeling himself for the request.

"You remember Chiara Genova?"

Scythe had to bite back a harsh laugh.

Did he remember her? Fuck, yeah, he remembered. The beautiful, widowed Breedmate with the soulful, sad eyes and broken angel's face had been the star of too many of his overheated dreams since the night he first saw her. Even now, the mere mention of her name fired a longing in his blood that he had no right to feel.

He remembered her three-year-old son Pietro, too. The kid's laugh had made Scythe's temples throb with memories he'd thought he left dead and buried behind him more than a decade ago.

"Are she and the boy all right?" There was dread in his throat as he asked it, but his flat tone gave none of it away.

"Yes. For now." Trygg paused. "She's in danger. It's serious as hell this time."

Scythe's grip on his phone tightened. The woman had been through enough troubles already, starting with the unfit Breed male she'd taken as her mate several years ago. Chiara's bastard of a mate, Sal, had turned out to be a gambler and a first-class asshole.

Unable to pay his debts, he'd wound up on the bad side of a criminal kingpin named Vito Massioni. To square up when Massioni came to collect, Sal traded his own sister, Arabella, in exchange for his life. If not for the Order in Rome—more specifically, one of their warriors, Ettore "Savage" Selvaggio—Bella might still be imprisoned as Massioni's personal pet.

As for Chiara, she was essentially made a captive of Massioni's as well. Sal's treachery hadn't saved him in the end. After his death, Chiara and her son lived at the family vineyard under the constant threat of Massioni's danger.

Six weeks ago, it had all come to a head. The Order had moved in on Massioni, taking out him and his operation... or so they'd thought. Massioni had survived the explosion that obliterated his mansion and all of his lieutenants, and he was out for blood.

Chiara and her son had ended up in the crosshairs along with Bella and Savage, putting all of them on the run. Trygg sent them to Scythe for shelter, knowing damned well that Scythe wasn't in the habit of playing protector to anyone. Least of all a woman and child.

And he still wasn't in that habit now.

Nevertheless, the question rolled off his tongue too easily. "Tell me what happened."

"According to Bella, Chiara's had the sensation she was being watched for the past week or so. Stalked from afar. Last night, things took a turn for the worst. A Breed male broke into the villa. If she hadn't heard him outside her window and had time to prepare, she'd likely have been raped, murdered, or both."

"Motherfu—" Scythe bit off the curse and took a steadying breath. His rage was on full boil, but he rallied his thoughts around gathering facts. "Did the son of a bitch touch her? How did she manage to get away?"

"Sal kept a sword hidden beneath the bed in case Massioni ever sent some muscle there to work him over for the money he owed. After he died, Chiara left the weapon in place. By some miracle of adrenaline or determination, she was able to fight the bastard off, but barely."

Holy hell. As he thought of the tiny slip of a woman trying to fight off a healthy Breed male he shook his head slowly in disbelief. The fact that she survived was beyond lucky or even miraculous, but Trygg was right. The odds of her doing it again were slim to none.

Which was, apparently, where Scythe and his specific set of skills came in. Not that it would take a request from Trygg or the Order to convince him to hunt down Chiara's attacker and make the Breed male pay in blood and anguish.

The very idea of her cowering as some animal attempted to harm her made Scythe's whole body quake with fiery rage.

"So, the Order needs me to find this bastard and tear his head off, then?"

"Just killing him isn't going to get to the root of the problem. We don't think this attack is random. The Order needs you to protect Chiara and Pietro while we work to figure out who's after her and why."

Scythe could not hold back the snarl that built in his throat. "You know I don't do bodyguard duty. Damn it, you know why too."

"Yeah," Trygg said. "And I'm still asking you to do it. You're the only one we can trust with this, brother. The Order's got all hands on deck with Opus Nostrum, Rogue outbreaks, and ninety-nine other problems at the moment. We need you."

Scythe groaned. "You ask too fucking much this time."

Protecting the woman would cost him. He knew that from both instinct and experience. For almost a score, he'd kept his feedings down to once a week. His body's other needs were kept on an even tighter leash.

He'd only spent a few hours with Chiara Genova six weeks ago, yet it was long enough to know that being under the same roof with her was going to test both his patience and his self-discipline.

But the kid? That was a no-go. There were things he just couldn't do, not even for his brother.

He mulled over Trygg's request in miserable silence.

"What's it gonna be, Scythe?"

The refusal sat on the tip of his tongue, but damned if he could spit it out. "If I do this, we do it my way. I don't answer to the Order or to anyone else. Agreed?"

"Sure, you got it. Just get your ass to Rome as soon as you can so we can go over your plan and coordinate efforts."

"What about her?" Scythe demanded. "Does Chiara know you've contacted me to help her?"

The stretch of silence on the other end of the line told him all he needed to know and he grimaced.

"Savage and Bella are bringing Chiara and Pietro in as we speak," Trygg said. "They should all be here within the hour."

Scythe cursed again, more vividly this time. "I'm on my way."

He ended the call, then threw the SUV into gear and gunned it out to the street.

MIDNIGHT UNBOUND

is available now at all major retailers in eBook, trade paperback, and unabridged audiobook.

Although this extended novella can be read as a standalone story within the series, it also connects the Midnight Breed Series with the exciting new Hunter Legacy spinoff launching Spring 2018!

Thirsty for more Midnight Breed?

Read the complete series!

. . . and more to come!

If you enjoy sizzling contemporary romance, don't miss this hot series from Lara Adrian!

For 100 Days

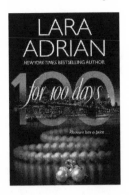

The 100 Series: Book 1

"I wish I could give this more than 5 stars! Lara Adrian not only dips her toe into this genre with flare, she will take it over . . . I have found my new addiction, this series." --The Sub Club Books

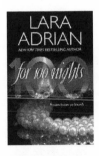 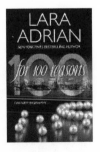

All available now in ebook, trade paperback and unabridged audiobook.

More romance and adventure from Lara Adrian!

Phoenix Code Series
(Paranormal Romantic Suspense)

"A fast-paced thrill ride." –Fresh Fiction

Masters of Seduction Series
(Paranormal Romance)

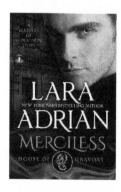 

"Thrilling, action-packed and super sexy." –Literal Addiction

Award-winning medieval romances from Lara Adrian!

Dragon Chalice Series
(Paranormal Medieval Romance)

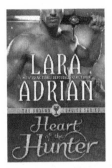  

"Brilliant . . . bewitching medieval paranormal series." –Booklist

Warrior Trilogy
(Medieval Romance)

"The romance is pure gold." –All About Romance

ABOUT THE AUTHOR

LARA ADRIAN is a New York Times and #1 international best-selling author, with nearly 4 million books in print and digital worldwide and translations licensed to more than 20 countries. Her books regularly appear in the top spots of all the major bestseller lists including the New York Times, USA Today, Publishers Weekly, Amazon.com, Barnes & Noble, etc. Reviewers have called Lara's books "addictively readable" (Chicago Tribune), "extraordinary" (Fresh Fiction), and "one of the consistently best" (Romance Novel News).

Writing as **TINA ST. JOHN**, her historical romances have won numerous awards including the National Readers Choice; Romantic Times Magazine Reviewer's Choice; Booksellers Best; and many others. She was twice named a Finalist in Romance Writers of America's RITA Awards, for Best Historical Romance (White Lion's Lady) and Best Paranormal Romance (Heart of the Hunter). More recently, the German translation of Heart of the Hunter debuted on Der Spiegel bestseller list.

Visit the author's website and sign up for new release announcements at www.LaraAdrian.com.

Find Lara on Facebook at
www.facebook.com/LaraAdrianBooks

Connect with Lara online at:

www.LaraAdrian.com

www.facebook.com/LaraAdrianBooks

www.goodreads.com/lara_adrian

www.twitter.com/lara_adrian

www.instagram.com/laraadrianbooks

www.pinterest.com/LaraAdrian

Made in the USA
Columbia, SC
25 January 2018